ABOUT THE AUTHOR

Susan Grossey graduated from Cambridge University in 1987 and since then has made her living from crime. She spent twenty-five years advising financial institutions and others on money laundering – how to spot criminal money, and what to do about it – and has written many non-fiction books on the subject.

Her first work of fiction was the inaugural book in the Sam Plank series, *Fatal Forgery*, set in London in the 1820s and narrated by magistrates' constable Sam Plank. This was followed in the series by *The Man in the Canary Waistcoat*, *Worm in the Blossom*, *Portraits of Pretence*, *Faith, Hope and Trickery*, *Heir Apparent*, and *Notes of Change* which was the seventh (and final) book in the Sam Plank series.

Sizar is the second book in Susan's new series, the Cambridge Hardiman Mysteries. The first in the series was *Ostler* and there will be three more books in this series, again set in the 1820s, but this time with Gregory Hardiman, a university constable in Cambridge, at the heart of them.

BY THE SAME AUTHOR

<u>The Sam Plank Mysteries</u>

Fatal Forgery
The Man in the Canary Waistcoat
Worm in the Blossom
Portraits of Pretence
Faith, Hope and Trickery
Heir Apparent
Notes of Change

Portraits of Pretence was given the "Book of the Year 2017" award by influential book review website Discovering Diamonds. And *Faith, Hope and Trickery* was shortlisted for the Selfies Award 2019.

<u>The Cambridge Hardiman Mysteries</u>

Ostler

Ostler was shortlisted for the Selfies Book Award 2024.

Non-fiction books

The Solo Squid: How to Run a Happy One-Person Business

Susan in the City: The Cambridge News Years

SIZAR

Susan Grossey

Susan Grossey Publisher

Copyright © 2024 by Susan Grossey

All rights reserved.

No part of this publication may be reproduced, distributed or transmitted in any form or by any means, including photocopying, recording, or other electronic or mechanical methods, without the prior written consent of the author, except in the case of brief quotations embodied in critical reviews and certain other non-commercial uses permitted by copyright law. Thank you for respecting the hard work of this author.

This novel is a work of fiction. The events and characters in it, while based on real historical events and characters, are the work of the author's imagination.

Author contact details:

susangrosseyauthor@gmail.com

www.susangrossey.com

Sign up for my free monthly e-newsletter and receive your FREE complete e-book of *Fatal Forgery* (the first book in the Sam Plank Mysteries series)

www.susangrossey.com/insider-updates

Sizar / Susan Grossey -- 1st edition

ISBN 978-1-915491-02-2

For my fellow crime-reading addicts at the Crime Crackers book group in Cambridge

In thanks for their enthusiasm and encouragement, cunningly disguised as frequent repetition of the question "When's the next Gregory book coming out?"

> And when we bid adieu to youth,
> Slaves to the specious world's control.
> We sigh a long farewell to truth;
> That world corrupts the noblest soul.
>
> *An extract from "To A Youthful Friend"*
> *by Lord Byron (1808)*

Author's note

Any period of history has its own vocabulary, both standard and slang. The Regency was no different, and to capture the spirit of the time I have used words and phrases that may not be familiar to the modern reader. Moreover, Gregory is a Norfolk boy and sometimes uses words and phrases from his childhood. At the end of this book there is a glossary of these terms and their brief definitions. This glossary also contains an overview of the currency used at the time, and its equivalent modern spending power.

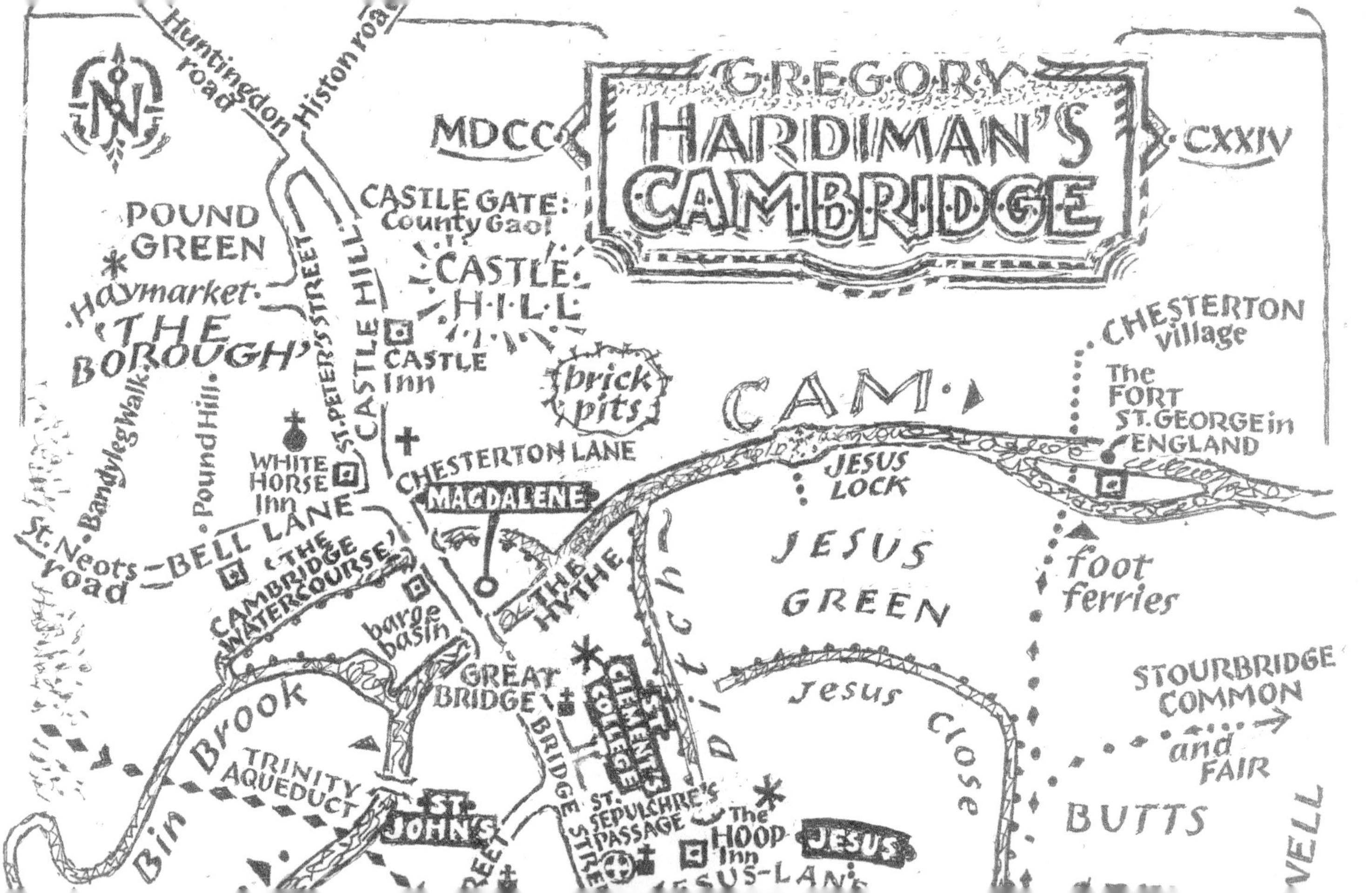

GREGORY
HARDIMAN'S
CAMBRIDGE
MDCC
CXXIV
N
Huntingdon road
Histon road
POUND GREEN
Haymarket
'THE BOROUGH'
Bandylegwalk
Pound Hill
St. Neots road
BELL LANE
ST. PETER'S STREET
CASTLE HILL
CASTLE GATE: County Gaol
CASTLE HILL
CASTLE Inn
WHITE HORSE Inn
brick pits
CHESTERTON LANE
MAGDALENE
'THE CAMBRIDGE WATERCOURSE'
barge basin
THE HYTHE
GREAT BRIDGE
BRIDGE
CAM
JESUS LOCK
JESUS GREEN
Ditch
CHESTERTON village
The FORT ST. GEORGE in ENGLAND
foot ferries
Jesus Close
ST. CLEMENT'S COLLEGE
ST. SEPULCHRE'S PASSAGE
The HOOP Inn
JESUS
STOURBRIDGE COMMON and FAIR
BUTTS
Bin Brook
TRINITY AQUEDUCT
ST. JOHN'S

WEST FIELD
HOSTEL LANE
TRINITY HALL
SENATE HOUSE
The Schools
KING'S
RIVER
Nicholson, bookseller
MKT. ST
MARKET HILL
CONDUIT
PETTY CURY
The EAGLE
Fisher's Bank
BENE'T STREET
Botanic Gdn.
BLACK BULL Inn
TRUMPINGTON
SILVER STREET
MILL PIT
KING'S and BISHOP'S MILLS
Sheeps Green
NEWNHAM MILL
Coe Fen
river
upper
Parson's Brook
LTL. ST MARY'S LANE
STREET
PETER HOUSE
River pot/PEM Brook
The
the
HOSPITAL
the
marsh
leys.
DOWNING PLACE
Spinning House
Town Gaol
ST. ANDREW'S STREET
King
CHRIST'S PIECES
PARKER'S PIECE
CAUSEWAY
Newmarket road
(new TOWN GAOL)
LENSFIELD ROAD
London road
Hobson's Brook
NEW TOWN, 'NEW ZEALAND'
Hadstock road
old orchards
SCALE
1/2 mile
J.H.
24

Chapter One

CAROUSING

I opened my pocket diary and counted again: only three days until the end of term. And not a day too soon. If I had ever thought that being a university constable would be easy, two terms in the job had opened my eyes. The intention, according to the Vice-Chancellor, was to assemble a body of a dozen constables so that no man would be on duty more than two days a week. But even the Vice-Chancellor of this great university cannot conjure suitable recruits out of thin air, and since October last we had battled on as a band of only eight, patrolling the whole town every evening, often working three or even four shifts a week.

There was a knock at my door. I opened it, and my landlady Mrs Jacobs held out a plate covered with a cloth. She shook her head as she handed it to me.

"I don't hold with sending a man out into the night with only a cold meal inside him, Mr Hardiman," she said. I shrugged and smiled; we had some version of this conversation every evening that I was on duty.

"It's good of you to offer, Mrs Jacobs," I said, "but you know that I need to be light on my feet. Some of these undergraduates take a bit of chasing, and a full belly would hold me back." I put the plate on my small table and lifted the cloth.

"Mutton pie," she said. She sniffed and crossed her arms. "Fresh made – not like whatever warmed up offering you had for your midday meal at the Hoop today."

On days when I was working in the evening, I took care to have a hot midday meal at the Hoop Inn where I worked as ostler. This day I had had some very tasty sole but I knew better than to mention it to Mrs Jacobs; she was only a middling cook and I usually ate better at the Hoop, but telling her that would serve no purpose.

"It looks delicious, Mrs Jacobs," I said. "I'll bring the plate down on my way out."

"Hardiman." One of my fellow constables that evening held out his hand and I shook it. George Swanney worked at a drapers' shop on Market Hill, where his prospects had improved significantly since he had started courting the owner's rather plain daughter. He was a neat, well-dressed man, as you would expect, but what was less obvious was his speed. From a standing start, there were few who could better Swanney in a sprint. I'm different: I'm not quick off the mark, but once I settle into my stride I can keep going for miles.

"Where's the other two?" I asked as I checked my reflection in the small looking glass on the wall and straightened my hat. Swanney shrugged and shook his head.

The door of the Proctors' Court opened and in came Nicholas Temple, the Senior Proctor.

"Good evening, gentlemen," he said. "Just the two of you?"

"So far, yes, sir," I replied.

He looked from me to Swanney and back again. "You're a pair, aren't you?" he asked. "A sprinter," he pointed at Swanney, "and a distance man?"

"I believe so, yes, sir," I said.

"In that case, take your truncheons and we shall head out," said Temple. "I shall speak to Mr Venn about the importance of being on duty at six o'clock sharp." As the words left his mouth, we heard the bell of Great St Mary's mark the hour, and the Junior Proctor Henry Venn barrelled into the room, followed by two constables.

"Good evening, Mr Venn," said Temple, looking pointedly at the clock on the wall. "My constables and I are already on duty. We will head southwards. When you and your men manage to gather and equip yourselves, you will head northwards. We shall see you back here at ten o'clock sharp." He swept from the room and Swanney and I followed him. The constable holding the door open for us – a good-natured waterman called Gilbert – gave me a swift wink and whispered "Good luck" from the side of his mouth.

If any period during a Cambridge term can be said to be quiet, it is the weeks of Lent. And with the end of term almost upon us, most undergraduates were engaged in finishing their work, packing their trunks and keeping out of trouble. You'd think I would like a peaceful patrol, but in all honesty it is easier to stay vigilant when there is activity. I remember soldiers saying the same: the still, silent nights in camp were the most unnerving and exhausting. And with the Senior Proctor being a stickler for dignity, Swanney and I could not even amuse each other with light conversation. Mr Temple would walk for about fifty yards then stop, hold up his hand and indicate that we should all three listen carefully. When I had first accompanied him, I had dared to ask what it was we were listening for. "Carousing, sir," he had replied, rolling the r as though sampling its taste. "Carousing and impropriety." When we reached the door of an inn or public house, he would throw the door open, stride in and bellow, "Ten o'clock, gentlemen – pay mind to ten o'clock!" No surprise, then, that he had acquired the nickname Ten o'clock Temple.

When church bells told us that it was a quarter to ten, we turned our step back towards the Schools. Around us, undergraduates hurried back to their colleges, their billowing black gowns making them look like bats returning to the roost. After the notice of 10 October last concerning academical dress (you see how a constable is required to be aware of these things), we now rarely saw a university man without his gown and cap. Unless of course they were being pursued by a constable, at which point they would fling off their gown in order to run the faster – and by doing so they simply added to the tally of offences reported to their college.

Once we had reached the Senate House, the Senior Proctor halted. Swanney and I took up our positions on either side of him, and we all three faced Great St Mary's. We heard rapid footsteps and the Junior Proctor and his two constables arrived and lined up alongside us. We waited for perhaps a minute, and the church bells tolled the hour.

"A quiet night, gentlemen," said Temple. "The University is safe. You may complete your patrol." We trudged down Senate House Passage and into Trinity Lane. Swanney, as the first in line, rapped on the door with his truncheon and the watchman let us in. We four constables filed into the Proctors' Court and returned our truncheons to the hooks. On a small high table near the door was a ledger, and we each signed our name in it. The proctors followed us in, checked that we had returned our weapons, and then signed the ledger in their turn. The Junior Proctor made to leave, but Temple was having none of it.

"A word, if I may, Mr Venn, about punctuality," he said.

I slipped from the room, nodding farewell to the other three constables and then to the watchman, and walked out once more into the flickering gloom of Trinity Lane. With the undergraduates safely behind locked gates and honest townsfolk tucked up in bed, I was uneasy when I spied a shadowy figure in the gateway of Gonville and Caius. I walked closer to the wall of the Senate House, thinking to protect at least one flank.

"Mr Hardiman," whispered the figure as I drew level with him.

I stopped and peered at him. "Good heavens, Mr Chapman," I said, perhaps a little crossly. "What is the porter of St Clement's doing, skulking about at this time of night?"

Chapman stepped out into the passage. "Skulking is a bit strong," he objected. "I was waiting, is all. Mrs Jacobs said you were on patrol tonight."

"You went to my lodgings?" I asked. "What is so urgent, Mr Chapman, that it couldn't wait until the morning?"

He shook his head and looked serious. "It's not something to discuss in the street, Mr Hardiman," he said, looking about him. "But Mr Vaughan is waiting for you in college."

Five minutes later Chapman was pushing open the gate to St Clement's College and I followed him into the silent court. Here and there we could see the dim flickering of a candle at a window as an undergraduate prepared for bed, but most rooms were already in darkness. I had expected to go to the Master's rooms, but the porter led me instead to the opposite corner of the court and up the cold stone stairs to the first floor. There were four identical wooden doors on the landing and Chapman knocked quietly on one of them before pushing the door open a little.

"Mr Vaughan, sir," he whispered. "I have Mr Hardiman for you."

He stood back and indicated that I should go into the room. I looked at him but he shook his head. I walked into the room and the porter pulled the door closed behind me.

Standing in front of me was Francis Vaughan, the Master of St Clement's. As polite as ever, he held out his hand to shake mine, but as I held it I could feel that it was cold and with a slight tremor.

"Mr Hardiman," he said quietly. "You will forgive me for summoning you at this late hour, but in the past you have been a good friend to the college and, well, to be frank, I was not sure where else to turn."

As he said this, he stood to one side so that I could look into the room. On the desk was a burning Argand lamp which cast a good light about the room, but when I saw what was on the floor, I rather wished it darker. As I walked towards the body, something caught my eye in the shadows created by the lamplight: a length of fabric hanging from the ceiling.

"A bed-sheet," said Vaughan from behind me. "The porter and a kitchen boy cut him down."

I knelt beside the body. Without my having to ask, the Master walked over to the desk and moved the lamp further forward so that I could see more clearly.

"Have you called the coroner?" I asked.

"Not yet," said Vaughan. "We only found him about an hour ago. No point disturbing the coroner's sleep – there's nothing to be done for the lad now."

I could see that for myself as I knelt down beside the body. The dead man was young, dressed for relaxation in his room: dark breeches with stockings and slippers, and a loose white shirt undone at the neck. His face was swollen and purpled, but thankfully his eyes were closed. The young soldier I had found in the stables in Salamanca had stared at me with lifeless eyes, seeing for eternity the horrors that had driven him there. I swallowed hard and pushed the picture from my mind.

"Edward Fleming," said the Master. "A fellow commoner, but no empty bottle."

I sat back on my heels and looked up at Vaughan. "You will have to explain all of that, sir," I said.

"Of course," said Vaughan. "Foolish and ill-mannered of me to expect everyone to know our university jargon. Fellow commoners are from families of means and consequently pay their own way. If minded, they can take their ordinary degree after only six terms in residence." He must have caught an expression on my face. "I know, I know. But at least it keeps them away from the temptations of London for a while, and perhaps some of our better qualities rub off on them during those six terms."

I raised a cynical eyebrow. "Empty bottle?" I asked.

"That's what the other gownsmen call them – I suppose because of their empty heads," he replied.

"But not Mr Fleming?" I asked.

Vaughan shook his head. "Some fellow commoners have brains as well as money, and choose to stay on in order to take their examination and gain an honours degree. Mr Fleming was one such. We had high hopes for him."

I turned back to the young man's body. There was a livid mark across his throat, and the blood had pooled in his hands, leaving them red and swollen.

"Will the coroner mind if we put him on the bed, do you think?" asked the Master.

I pushed myself to my feet. "I doubt it," I replied. "As long as we leave the..." I gestured to the bed-sheet. "So that he can see where it happened."

I lifted the body under the arms while Vaughan took the legs. Fleming was quite a weight and we staggered a little as we carried the young man to his bed. I stood back and watched the Master pull a blanket up over the body, arranging it neatly.

"There," he said softly. He sighed deeply. "What a terrible waste of a young life." He leaned forward and for one moment I thought he might kiss the corpse's face, but he contented himself with patting the shoulder. "I shall have to write to his mother." His shoulders slumped. "A terrible letter to write – but a worse one to receive." He heaved another sigh then turned to me. "Will you join me in a glass of port, Mr Hardiman? I feel very much in need of something warming."

It was chilling down in the Master's rooms. His footman, Wells, had doubtless banked the fire before retiring, but it was now nearly midnight and the embers were barely glowing. Vaughan went to his sideboard and poured us two generous measures of port. He handed me mine and then raised his.

"Edward Fleming," he said simply.

"Edward Fleming," I echoed.

We both sipped our drinks, and the Master indicated that we should sit in the armchairs by the fireplace. We both stared into the grate.

"Do you have any idea what drove him to it?" I asked after a few minutes. "To self-murder?"

"I have been asking myself the same question," said Vaughan. "Fleming has – had – been here at St Clement's for five terms, and he seemed settled and happy. And a gifted mathematician." He shook his head sadly.

"A mathematician?" I asked. "Like you?"

"The same discipline, yes," agreed the Master, "but I think he would quickly have surpassed me. He had a natural way with numbers – a sympathy with them, perhaps. It is rare."

"I envy him," I said. "I can manage adding and subtracting, and a bit more if I have to, but numbers have no shape to them for me. Not like words. Words attract me – they become my friends."

"Do you still keep your vocabulary book, Mr Hardiman?" asked Vaughan.

I patted the pocket of my coat. "Indeed I do," I said.

"You are lucky to have a curious mind," he observed. "Most men do not, and it makes them too easily contented. Greed can also drive a man on, but curiosity is a more admirable force."

"People are certainly going to be curious about Mr Fleming," I said.

"About how he died, you mean?"

"That," I agreed, "and about why he died."

"I would rather not have any... gossip about it," said Vaughan. "There is no need to alarm the other gownsmen. And St Clement's certainly cannot afford to scare away potential applicants." He looked at me and then drained his glass. "I have to be realistic, Mr Hardiman. And to that end, I have a favour to ask you."

Chapter Two

BOOKS

The church bell had just tolled the quarter hour when I pushed open the heavy wooden door of St Clement's. The porter was waiting for me.

"Good morning, Mr Chapman," I said.

"Mr Hardiman." He dipped his head in response. "The Master says I'm to take you to Mr Fleming's room." He turned and led the way around the court. "The coroner and his men came first thing. They had a look around the room and took the body." He stopped at the foot of the staircase and shuddered. "There's a job I wouldn't fancy, poking around dead folk." He stood to one side. "You know where you're going, Mr Hardiman. I'll leave you to it, if you don't mind. I've things to see to, back at the lodge."

"You go on, Mr Chapman," I said. "I'll let you know if I need anything."

I climbed the stone stairs to the first floor and tapped lightly on the door to Mr Fleming's room – habit, I suppose. I pushed open the door and shivered: someone, probably the coroner, had opened the window wide and the cool March air was blowing in. I pulled the window shut and stood with my back to it, looking around the room. The bedding had been straightened and the lamp extinguished, but otherwise the room was as I remembered it from the night before, down to the strip of fabric hanging from the rafter.

There was a small fireplace with a single sagging armchair in front of it. On the floor next to the chair was a pile of about five books, slips of paper jutting from them. There were more books, some open, on the desk near the window. In the middle of the room, near the hanging fabric, was a plain chair – I guessed that Mr Fleming had stood on this to reach the rafter and then kicked it away. The chair was upright, and I thought back to the previous evening – had the Master replaced it, or had I? On hooks on the wall were a few items of clothing, including an academic gown.

I turned and looked again at the room. There was nothing to suggest that Mr Fleming had been putting his affairs in order, but then a young man overcome with despair is not the same as a square toes making his peace with the end of his natural term. I stooped to pick up the pile of books from the floor beside the armchair. One was a Bible which looked if not exactly unread, then certainly little read. It was inscribed: *To dearest Edward from your loving Mother and Father*. The other four books were mathematical volumes, busy with slips of paper and pencil markings in the margins. The books on the desk were likewise mathematical, and an open notebook alongside them showed some recent calculations, although I could make little sense of what I saw. I tried the drawer under the desk and it slid open. Inside was a jumble of pens and papers and, beneath them, a larger notebook with green covers. I took it out and opened it at a random page. More numbers. But this time they looked more familiar. I remembered the banking ledgers that George Fisher had shown me when I was asking about college finances; with its columns and check-marks, this notebook looked like them. I closed the desk drawer and took two of the mathematical books and the large green ledger to show to Mr Vaughan.

Once his footman had poured us some of his excellent coffee and I had been persuaded to take not one but two slices of fruit loaf, Francis Vaughan started to examine the books I had brought from Fleming's room.

"Ah yes, well, I could have guessed he would be interested in this," said the Master, nodding, picking up the first of them. "Peacock's application of differential and integral calculus."

"Of course," I said. "Who could fail to be interested?"

Vaughan looked up at me, one eyebrow raised. "My late wife used to say the same thing," he observed lightly. "Calculus is not quite as absorbing as algebra – my own area of expertise, as you know – but it is still worthy of study." I reached into my coat pocket for my little vocabulary book and a pencil.

"Calculus," I said to myself slowly as I wrote it down, then I looked back up at the Master.

He smiled at me and explained. "Calculus is used to calculate things that are moving or changing, such as the orbit of the planets." He picked up the second book. "I remember using this one myself. *Wood's Elements of Algebra.*" He opened the book to one of the paper slips. "Yes, you see: he's been reading the appendix that they need for the examination, on the application of algebra to geometry. Equations for curves and the like." He closed that book and took hold of the large green ledger, opening it at a random page. "His own notebook, I see... ah, no, not a notebook. An account book." He looked up at me. "Did you read this?"

"I tried," I said. "It reminded me of a banking ledger – monies in, payments out and so on. But I couldn't make sense of anything except the numbers." I leaned forward and pointed at the page. "The rest seems to be in a secret code."

"Are you a gambling man, Mr Hardiman?" asked Vaughan.

I shook my head. "There was never any spare money when I was a boy," I said, "and when I was in the army I saw too many good men ruin themselves and their families when their pay was tempted out of their pockets by some wager or other."

"Indeed," said the Master. "I think I told you once that I enjoy a wager myself, now and again."

I put up a hand in apology. "I didn't mean to sound such a prig," I said. "I have no objection to others enjoying themselves – it's just not for me."

"Each man chooses his own vices," said Vaughan with a smile. "I asked about gambling because I think these might be records of wagers – odds, winnings, losses and so on."

He handed the ledger to me and I looked again. I turned a page, and then another.

"But there are hundreds of wagers here," I said, "if that's indeed what they are. Hundreds." I turned over several more pages.

"I suspect that Mr Fleming may have been something of an organiser," said the Master. "Taking wagers from other undergraduates, laying them against other wagers, keeping records of it all."

"Robbing Peter to pay Paul, you mean?" I asked.

Vaughan shrugged. "If he were good at it, there would be no need to rob anyone – he would accept only those wagers that he felt he could honour."

"But if it went wrong," I suggested, "it might explain why he felt unable to continue."

The Master heaved a sigh. "What a terrible waste," he said again.

Chapter Three

INTENTIONS

"What's that, then?" asked Mrs Jacobs, peering over my shoulder. She had been cleaning the hallway when I arrived home – not by chance, I suspected – and had invited me into the kitchen to keep her company while she prepared the meal. William Bird liked to tease me that she had her eye on me as a future Mr Jacobs, but I knew what the innkeeper did not: that there was not a man yet born who could match her peerless late husband, and that her ceaseless reminiscences about him had seen off most of her friends. In short, the poor woman was lonely, and I had not the heart to turn down her invitation to sit in the kitchen.

"It is my pocket diary, Mrs Jacobs," I said, closing it to show her the cover. "I was given it by Mr Giles, who thought it might be of use now that I have various duties in different places."

The landlady returned to the stove and lifted the lid on a pot, sniffing as she did so.

"Mr Giles – your bookseller friend at Nicholson's," she said.

"That's the one," I agreed.

She returned the lid to the pot and sat down.

"May I see it?" she asked, wiping her hands on her apron.

I pushed the little book across the table to her and she picked it up and inspected it. "Very pretty," she said, looking at the spine with its gold lettering and the colours at the page edges. She opened it carefully at the page marked by the narrow silk ribbon. "So there is a page for each week, with each day headed, and you write your business for the day under the heading." She looked up at me and I nodded. I knew she prided herself on being able to read; her late husband had been a coal merchant and had taught her to read and write so that she could help him with his ledgers. Sometimes when she saw me writing in my vocabulary book she would ask me to teach her a new word. "You need more to occupy you, Mr Hardiman," she said, turning forwards and then backwards a week or two. "A man's day should be full of endeavour." She closed the book and handed it back to me, then stood and reached up to the shelf for the plates.

She was right. Setting down my day in the diary had shown it starkly. The Hoop, despite William Bird's grand ambitions, had not yet managed to attract more regular coaches to call. Between them, the *Defiance* and the *Fakenham Day* took up no more than three hours of my time in the middle of the day. And stabling and feeding the horses of anyone staying at the inn overnight was not enough to fill the remaining daylight hours. Three or fours evenings a week I was on duty as a constable, of course, but only from six o'clock until ten. I needed something more to fill my time – and my purse. My daughter had already turned fifteen and with little to recommend her by way of family – a dead mother and a foreign father – she would need a good dowry to find a decent husband. Fifteen years old, and we had never met. Her mother had been only a year older than that when I had first seen her. In those days I was much more pleasant looking – if not handsome, then certainly not ugly. I put a hand to my face and felt the long, raised, uneven line of my scar. Lucia had been so beautiful, with her thick dark hair, her deep brown eyes and her long eyelashes, which she gave me plenty of opportunity to admire when she looked modestly down from my gaze. I hoped my daughter had the same eyes.

My thoughts were pulled back from Spain by a loud knocking on the street door. Mrs Jacobs turned to me, ladle in hand, and I went to see who was visiting at dinner time. Standing on the step, a book tucked under his arm and rubbing his hands together to warm them in the evening chill, was George Chapman. I beckoned him into the hallway. The kitchen door opened and Mrs Jacobs looked out.

"It's the porter from St Clement's," I said. "Mr Chapman. And this is my landlady, Mrs Jacobs."

The two nodded at each other and Chapman shuffled the book he was carrying into one hand and took off his hat with the other. "I hope you have not come to summon Mr Hardiman to college," said Mrs Jacobs. "We are about to sit down to our dinner."

"It smells good," said Chapman. I looked at him but he seemed to be telling the truth. "Very good."

Mrs Jacobs smiled. "If you've not had your own dinner, Mr Chapman," she said, "you are very welcome to take a plate with us. Unless Mrs Chapman is waiting for you."

"My mother is no longer with us," said the porter, "and I have never had the good fortune to marry."

There was a long moment of silence, during which I felt very much in the way.

"In that case, Mr Chapman," said my landlady at last, "Mr Hardiman and I would be delighted to have you join us."

After cleaning his plate and accepting a second helping and cleaning it again, Chapman finally sat back in his seat.

"That was very flavoursome, Mrs Jacobs," he said. "Very flavoursome indeed."

In my opinion the rabbit stew had been no more than passable, but if we all liked the same things the world would be a very dull place. In any event, his praise made my landlady beam.

"It's a pleasure to cook for a man who knows good food," she said. "Mr Hardiman here, I sometimes think I could serve him a boiled boot for his supper and he wouldn't notice."

I wisely held back from the obvious response and simply smiled.

Chapman chuckled. "Well, I have my midday meal at college most days, Mrs Jacobs, made by a professional cook, and your rabbit stew is the best I've had for a long time."

They smiled at each other, and once again I felt in the way. It was years since I had done it myself, but I could certainly recognise flirting in others.

I stood up. "Well, if you'll both excuse me..." I started.

This seemed to bring Chapman back to his senses. "Ah, no, wait a moment, Mr Hardiman," he said. "I wanted to show you something." He reached down to the side of his chair, where he had propped the book he had brought with him. "But perhaps..." He glanced at Mrs Jacobs.

"Ah," she said. "College business. Shall I make a pot of coffee for you to take up to Mr Hardiman's room?"

"Well," I said once we were settled by my fireplace, a cup of coffee poured for each of us. "I don't think Mrs Jacobs has ever offered to make me a pot of coffee to bring up here before, so all that fudge about her rabbit stew has worked wonders."

Chapman looked puzzled. "Fudge?" he repeated. "But I was being honest. That was a very tasty stew. You're a lucky man, with food like that waiting for you every night." He paused and glanced at me. "And a woman like that." He looked at me again and then stared into the fire.

"If you're asking whether I have any... intentions towards my landlady," I said, "I can assure you that I do not." Chapman said nothing but nodded once, decisively. "Now, what's that book you've been carrying around?" I asked.

The porter put down his cup and picked up the book. He laid it in his lap and put a protective hand on it. "Mr Fleming's bedmaker found it this morning, when she was tidying his room. Under the mattress. She didn't know what it was, but with it being hidden and all, well, she thought it might be something that Mr Fleming would not want his family to see. She brought it to me to ask my advice. And I thought it might help you."

He handed the book to me. I could see straight away that it was a personal journal, a place for Edward Fleming to write down his thoughts. I looked at the porter. "Have you read it?" I asked.

"A few pages," he said, "as best I could. His hand is shocking. And some of it, well... He was an unhappy young man."

I opened the journal to a random page. The porter was right: Fleming's writing was difficult to read. His mathematical notebooks and the ledger had been tidy enough but this was different. The letters were poorly formed – some large and looping, others small and cramped, with ink spatters and crossings out adding to the jumble. I turned the wick on the lamp to throw more light onto the page.

"I must stop," I read aloud. "I must find the..." I angled the page and peered at it, "the strength to master myself. Lead us not into temptation. Lead us not into temptation." I turned the page. "I must turn my face from it before it is too late. Lead us not into temptation." I looked up at Chapman.

"He writes that a lot," said the porter. "Like I said, very unhappy. What do you think he was doing, then? Drinking? Women?"

I pictured the ledger I had given to the Master. "Perhaps," I replied. "But I found another book in his room that suggests he was something of a gambler."

"Mr Fleming?" said Chapman, surprised. "But Mr Fleming had no spare funds for wagers." It was my turn to be surprised and the porter gave a wry smile. "Porters eventually hear everything in college, Mr Hardiman," he said. "Surely you know that by now. And I happen to know that Mr Fleming needed his degree so that he could support his widowed mother and his four sisters. The father died last year, leaving a packet of debts and very little else. If Mr Fleming did fall into gambling, well, it was out of desperation and not for idle fun, I can tell you that. Poor man: what a terrible end to the term for us all."

Chapter Four
SWELLS

Once I had seen the *Fakenham Day* off to Swaffham, I knocked on the door of William Bird's room. When there was no reply, I pushed open the door, thinking to leave a note, and was surprised to see the innkeeper slumped onto his desk, his head resting on his forearms, fast asleep. I bent down to peer into his face, fearing that he had been taken ill. He opened his eyes suddenly, making us both jump.

"Are you unwell, William?" I asked.

He stretched his arms above his head, rolling his neck. "No: just worn out," he said. "Young master George is part owl, Hannah says – he prefers to be awake at night. And his teeth are coming in, which makes him bad-tempered along with it."

"Poor little chap," I said. And there I reached the limit of my observations about babies, having never had much to do with them myself.

"And poor big chap," said William, yawning widely and pointing to himself. "I sometimes envy you your bachelor life, Gregory."

"But only sometimes," I said.

William grinned. He sat more upright. "So, Mr Hardiman, what can I do for you?" He indicated the chair opposite him and I sat down.

"I wanted to ask you about gambling," I said.

"Gambling?" said the innkeeper. "Surely you are not thinking of wagering your pay?" Some months ago I had taken him into my confidence, and he had agreed that each week he would keep back ten shillings from my wages and put them into the safe for me. I reasoned that what I didn't have I wouldn't miss, and no more would I be tempted to spend it.

I shook my head. "No, not me. I saw enough of men being brought low in the army when the gambling fever took hold of them. Wager on anything, they would: which donkey would snap its teeth at a fly first, who would get the largest potato with their midday meal." I shook my head at the memory. "No harm for the officers, with money to spare, but for the others, with family at home relying on their pay... Men coming to blows over the outcome of a wager, and men stealing from each other."

"And not just in the army," added the innkeeper. "You see enough of it here in Cambridge."

"Do you?" I asked. "That's what I wanted to know about. Where do you see it? Not here at the Hoop, surely?"

William shook his head decisively. "Absolutely not," he said. "I've had offers, of course – even a couple of threats."

"Threats?" I repeated.

He shrugged. "Sharps looking for somewhere to ply their trade. Suggesting that they run a gambling room here, pay me a cut of their takings. But I'm not interested in running that sort of establishment. I want the Hoop to be respectable place, a family hotel. I'm thinking of having that painted on the wall outside." He jerked his head to indicate the front wall of the inn, on Bridge Street. "Hoop Inn and Family Hotel." He smiled. "Sounds grand, doesn't it?"

"Very fine," I agreed. "But I am sure not all innkeepers are as high-minded as you are."

"Indeed not," said William, raising an eyebrow.

"Like who?" I asked. "Where would a man go to lay a wager in Cambridge?"

William leaned back in his chair and put his arms behind his head. "Well, now," he said. "I suppose it's not unlike the army. There are places for ordinary working men, like you and me. And there are places for swells."

"Let's say the swells," I said. "Where would they go?"

"London, if they can," he replied.

"London?" I repeated. "For a wager?"

"Not in person," clarified William. "They send their instructions with friends who are going to their clubs in town, or with a trusted coachman. Tip him a few shillings and he'll take your wager right to the table in St James's for you and bring you your winnings."

"How can you be sure he's laying the bet, and not just pocketing your stake?" I asked.

"You can't," admitted the innkeeper, "but next time you're in town you can check with the club that the bet was laid and any winnings paid out, and word soon gets around who you can trust and who you can't. A trusted coachman makes more from his commission than he would from filching a few stakes."

I made a note of what he had said and then looked up at him again. "And if you want to gamble here in Cambridge, where do you go?" I asked. "If you're a swell, I mean."

"Nowhere officially," he replied. "The University takes a dim view of gambling. You remember the proclamation last year, about horse-racing." I nodded. "But, as the Bible teaches us, forbidden fruit tastes all the sweeter."

I laughed. "I hadn't taken you for a man of God, William," I said.

"I'm not," he said, rolling his eyes, "but my wife's mother has been staying with us and she insists on reading the Bible to us after our evening meal."

"For the husband is the head of the wife, even as Christ is the head of the Church," I said, smiling.

"Now who's the man of God," retorted William. "And only a single man would believe that." He sighed. "But to go back to your question: in private, is the answer. Swells gamble in Cambridge mostly in private. Groups of them bet amongst themselves. On horses, or these long-distance walking races."

"Pedestrianism," I suggested.

"That's it," said the innkeeper. "And boxing. But the horses are the most popular. You should get yourself to Newmarket – you'll find out all about it there."

Chapter Five
Newmarket

Charlie Grantham yawned widely, rolled his shoulders and gave a shake on the reins to encourage the horse, who took no notice at all and continued plodding at his steady rate.

"And how is Mrs Grantham?" I asked. It was Charlie's interest in Agnes, who had been working with me at the Sun Inn, that had brought us together twelve months ago. Young love had progressed as it will, and the two had been married for a six month, with – as Agnes had told me with a broad grin a few days ago – a baby well on the way.

Charlie looked across at me and shook his head, but he was smiling. "Agnes has plans," he said. "Grand plans. First we're to have the baby, then I'm to find another employer."

"Are things still no better with the young Mr Barker, then?" I asked. "I thought after that business with the over-charging last year – a stern word from the Vice-Chancellor and all that?"

Charlie shrugged. "As far as I can tell, Mr Hardiman, they are sticking to the straight and narrow with their college customers. But without that extra coming in, business is even tighter. That's why days like this are important. But I'm still uneasy, if I'm honest." He sighed. "But a job's a job, and I've others to think of now. Agnes says we're to move out of my mother's place and get our own rooms, then we're to have another baby – and then, well, I leave that to her." He looked out over the horse. "We're very happy, though."

"That's good to hear," I said. And it was. I looked around me. We were now well clear of Cambridge and Teversham and were heading along the road towards Quy. After that would come Bottisham, and eventually Newmarket. From time to time we would hear a halloo behind us and a man on horseback would trot past, waving a greeting. I had hoped for a warm spring day but it was not to be. I had woken to rain and walked through it to the yard of Barker and Eaden, where I had met Charlie in the dawn light at half past six. The rain seemed to have passed, but the wind was picking up ever more fiercely, making the horse uneasy and he was tossing his head, making the harness jingle.

"If you want to shut your eyes for a while," I said to Charlie, "I can take the reins."

Charlie shook his head. "I'm awake now, but perhaps on the way home. If I manage to sell that lot," he jerked his head to indicate the crates on the cart behind us, "I'll be dog-tired."

"Does Mr Barker send you to all the meetings at Newmarket?" I asked.

"Not all of them, no," replied Charlie. "He studies the form, you might say."

I was surprised. "The horses, you mean? Looking for winners to bet on?"

Charlie laughed. "No: Mr Barker is more interested in the people. He looks in the London papers to see who is expected to attend. Yesterday, for instance, was the first day, and the Duke of York was there, along with plenty of other toffs."

"So why not go yesterday?" I asked. "Surely they would welcome a bottle or two of Mr Barker's finest wine."

"No," Charlie shook his head. "The fashionables travel with their own supplies, and because the Duke is in attendance, everyone on the Heath is watching out for strangers. Much better for us to go on the second day: still plenty of thirsty toffs about, but the Duke has gone home and everyone is more relaxed. And Major and I can sit quietly on Cambridge Hill, overlooking the courses and providing essential refreshment."

With perfect timing, the horse lifted his tail and deposited a pile of dung onto the road.

"He's not much of a royalist, our Major," said Charlie.

―――

As Charlie had said, his spot on Cambridge Hill was an excellent vantage point. From it he indicated for me the various courses – the Beacon, which leads into the famous Rowley Mile, and the Round.

"And that's where people will start to gather," he said, pointing. "That's the weighing house, for the jockeys. And there, and there, and there," he swung his arm, "those are the betting posts." At each I could already see a small knot of people, men on horseback and on foot, presumably checking the day's races and deciding how much to wager. Charlie jumped down to the ground. "Not as many as I had hoped, but I daresay the weather is keeping some of them indoors. Mind you, this dusty wind will make the ones who are here more thirsty, which is all to the good." He untied the cords holding the cover in place, and folded it back so that the writing on the side of his cart could clearly be seen: "Barker & Eaden, Cambridge: Fine Wines". Next he took a peg and mallet from the cart, released Major from the traces, and walked him a little way to a fresh patch of grass before driving the peg into the ground and securing Major to it by a long strap. The horse dropped his head to the grass and starting tearing at it.

"That won't keep him going all the way home," I observed. "It's all water."

"I've a bag of feed in the cart for him," said Charlie. "He can have that an hour or so before we set off. Talking of which..." He reached into his coat pocket and pulled out a folded newspaper. "It says here that there are two main races today. The Breakfast Stakes starts at half past noon, and the Oakland Stakes will be at about three o'clock, so I reckon we'll be packing up at about five." He looked up at me and tapped the side of his nose. "Gives the winners time to drink to celebrate and the losers time to drink to forget. With a bit of luck, we'll be back in Cambridge by nine o'clock – Major will have had a good rest and his dinner, and if I do my job right, the cart will be empty."

Once I had walked down the hill I stood at the railings alongside the course for a few minutes to admire the beautiful horses walking and cantering past to stretch their legs. The conditions were not good, with strong winds and clouds of dust unsettling the animals. I have always thought that the finest horse in the world is the Suffolk Sorrel, with its kindly nature and sturdy build, and its glorious red coat. As a boy in Norfolk, I had often leaned with my cheek against the sturdy shoulder of Penny, the gentlest of my father's three plough-horses, taking comfort from her warmth and her silence and her solidity. Compared to Penny, these animals were creatures from another world, with their long legs and their nervous high-stepping, side-stepping movements and their snickering and whinnying.

"There!" a man called behind me, making me jump and earning him a sharp look from the jockey nearest the railing. "That's the one. That's The Dragon. That's where my money's going."

I turned to look at him. Sitting on a well-kept black horse was a young man of about eighteen, dressed in a fine dark coat and with boots polished to a shine. His eyes widened slightly at the sight of the scar on my face and he quickly looked away. Surrounding him, on slightly less glossy animals and wearing slightly less grand clothes, were four other young men.

"Wasn't it worth getting up early to see this, gentlemen?" he said loudly to them. "I tell you, the Vice-Chancellor is a fool; a day away from his dry books, blowing away the cobwebs out here – well, it would do him the power of good!" He took in the whole of Newmarket with a sweep of his arm. "To The Dragon – God speed, my fine fellow!"

The jockey on the horse I took to be The Dragon turned his back and that of his animal smartly to the self-appointed foreman of the jury and cantered away. For his part, the group's spokesman hauled his horse around roughly and led his group in the direction of one of the betting posts. I followed. When they reached the post, they all dismounted. One of their number held the horses while the others reached into their saddlebags. Each of them brought out a linen bag, and from each linen bag was extracted a fair pile of banknotes. Their leader approached the man at the betting post and spoke to him. They seemed to be disagreeing, and then reached a point that both could accept; they shook hands, and the Cambridge man beckoned to his friends. One by one they handed their banknotes to the man at the betting post, and he gave each a receipt. He carefully locked the money into the strongbox at his feet, and the group mounted their horses and rode away.

I walked up to the man as he was writing figures into a small notebook; when he saw me, he quickly closed it and shoved it into his pocket. He smiled at me, but it was not a genuine smile.

"Fancy your luck, do you, sir?" he asked. "A small wager to add some spice to the spectacle?"

"Those men you just dealt with," I said.

The smile fell from his face. "And what's that to do with you?" he asked. "I've a licence for this – you can ask anyone."

I held up my hands. "I do not doubt it for a moment," I said. "Only a fool would take illegal wagers out here in the open. And I can see that you're no fool." I indicated his strongbox with my foot.

"Well, then," he said. "What business is it of yours?"

"Those young gentlemen," I said, "are undergraduates at the university in Cambridge. And last year the Vice-Chancellor of that university – the man in charge of the whole place – proclaimed that any undergraduate found to be betting on, or even watching, horse-racing would be in serious trouble." The man looked uneasy but said nothing. "And I should imagine that the Vice-Chancellor would be severely displeased with anyone found to be helping gownsmen to break that proclamation." I paused a moment to let that information take root and then looked over my shoulder and back at the man as though taking him into my confidence. I dropped my voice so that he had to lean towards me. "But if I were able to tell the Vice-Chancellor how helpful you had been, how concerned you were to keep undergraduates on the path of righteousness..."

"I don't want any trouble," he said.

"No more do I," I agreed. "In fact, helping me is the best way to avoid trouble, because as sure as anything, doing business with those men will bring it."

"What do you need to know?" he asked.

―――

"Did you enjoy the racing?" asked Charlie as he steered the cart out onto the Cambridge road, raising a hand in farewell to the man at the toll gate.

"I enjoyed admiring the horses," I replied. In truth, I had been unsettled by the thundering hooves and the jostling of the animals at high speed as their jockeys whipped them to the finish. I could see the alarm in the horses' eyes and the slick of sweat on their haunches, and my instinct had been to comfort and calm them. "And you," I asked, "did you have a successful day?"

Charlie smiled broadly at me. "Less than a crate of full bottles to take back to Cambridge," he said. "They drank me dry, Mr Hardiman."

"That should please Mr Barker," I said.

"And Agnes," added Charlie. "I'm promised a bonus." He yawned widely. "But I have earned it, that's the truth. Up at dawn, loading the cart, standing by it all day, dealing with, well, you saw some of them. I don't mind the mellow ones, nor yet the maudlin ones, but some of them go too far. And then it's fists flying and the rest." He shook his head. "But as a constable you've seen plenty of that, I'm sure." He yawned again.

"I'll tell you what, Charlie," I said. "Hand me the reins. You settle yourself in the back and get some kip. Major and I will get along just fine."

And so we did, walking steadily back to Cambridge, into the setting sun.

Chapter Six

PRIVY

"Watch your step," said George Chapman grimly as he held the door open for me. "There's blood on the stones and you don't want to fall over in there, I'm telling you."

No matter how much I protested, since my appointment as a university constable the porter of St Clement's had decided that I was the person to call if there was any crime on college premises. I had explained several times that my duties related only to patrols in the evenings, and then only to making sure that undergraduates were back under lock and key before curfew, and indeed that I had equal responsibility to all the colleges and not just to St Clement's, but it made no difference.

—ℓℓ—

This morning I had been shaving when a loud banging at the street door had summoned Mrs Jacobs from the yard. She had called up the stairs to tell me that a lad was waiting with a message from St Clement's, and when she heard that I was needed urgently by the Master she had all but wiped the soap from my face for me before thrusting my coat into my hands and pushing me out into the street.

To his credit, the lad kept the shock from his eyes as he looked at me, and gave a wide grin. "He said I'd know you," he said as he turned to go. "Mr Chapman – he said I'd know you."

Hopping impatiently from one foot to the other and leading me down Jesus Lane towards town, the lad had told me breathlessly that the Master had been in his nightgown, that the porter had looked "proper shook up", and that he was due a tanner for his trouble. I put a hand into my coat pocket and felt for the right coin. I also felt a barley twist that I had bought the day before and I gave both to the lad. His eyes shone.

"You can scarper now," I said. "I know my way to St Clement's."

"If you need me again, sir," he said, walking backwards ahead of me, "Mr Chapman knows where to find me. Joe Lassiter, that's me. I'm fast!" He jogged on the spot, arms pumping to indicate his great speed, and almost fell over.

I put out a hand to catch him. "Have a care, Joe," I said. "You'll take a tumble and then your ma will be vexed."

"I don't have a ma," he said conversationally, falling into step beside me as we turned into Bridge Street. Nor a pa. It's just me and Sally – she's my little sister. She's like you." He put a hand to his face and made a circle to take in the whole of it. "Hare lip, they call it. That's why I weren't scared of you," he added with a note of pride. He danced in front of me again and turned to look at me. "But that's not a hare lip, is it? Was you hit in the face? Fell off a horse?"

I smiled at his open curiosity. Most people take a quick look and then their eyes slide off my face and they pretend not to have noticed anything amiss.

"I was cut by a sabre – a type of sword. In Spain, during the wars," I explained.

Joe stopped dead and I almost barrelled into him. "You was a soldier?" he asked. "Fighting Boney?" He assumed a fighting stance, imaginary sword at the ready.

I shook my head. "I was looking after the horses of a soldier. I was in the wrong place at the wrong time – nothing brave about it at all."

Joe's arm dropped and he took another look at my face. "Still, it looks brave," he decided.

I put my hand into my pocket again and found another sixpence. I gave it to him. "For that sister of yours," I said. "Buy her a dolly or a ribbon or whatever it is that little girls like."

"A posy of flowers," he said decisively. "She loves flowers, does Sally. And strawberries." He scampered off in the direction of the market, raising his arm in farewell.

George Chapman was right: I did not want to fall over in the privy. The stone floor was slick with dark liquid, and whatever it was, I did not want to touch it. My eyes adjusted to the gloom. There were two stalls, each with a wooden door. The majority of the liquid seemed to be coming from the further stall. I pushed open the door, and sitting on the bench, slumped into the corner, his chin to his chest, was the body of a young man. Dark, spreading patches stained the front of his clothes.

"Name's Joshua Pears. Stabbed, I reckon," said Chapman behind me.

"Who found him?" I asked.

"One of the bedders," he replied. "She knocked on the door, as always, to check no-one was in here. No reply, so she came in with her bucket and mop, and found him. I heard the scream."

"Her scream, or a man's?" I asked, turning to look at Chapman – and to stop looking at the poor broken body.

"Oh, hers," said the porter with certainty. "I reckon he's been dead a while. Looks very pale to me." He peered past me.

"Before the bedder this morning," I asked, "when did the last person come in here? Before him, I mean."

Chapman shrugged. "Any of the gownsmen could have come in during the night. They all have pots, of course, but some prefer to come here." He stopped to think. "One of the bedders would have come in last thing to clean – about eight o'clock last night."

"Does anyone else know about this?" I asked.

Chapman shrugged. "I should think so, by now – we've had to turn away a few men looking to use the facilities. I gave the bedder a tot to steady her, and a half-crown to silence her, and sent her home."

Francis Vaughan had aged visibly in the weeks since I had last seen him. His face was grey, his shoulders were rounded, and his voice cracked as he greeted me.

"Mr Hardiman," he said, holding out his hand to shake mine, "I begin to think that we are cursed here at St Clement's." He attempted a smile but failed.

"You are a man of mathematics and logic, sir," I said, taking the seat that he indicated. "You cannot believe in such things."

"At times like this," said the Master wearily, sitting in the chair next to mine, "a man can start to believe all sorts of things." He sighed mightily and put his head in his hands.

I took out my notebook and looked at what I had jotted down after leaving the privy. "The porter told me the dead man is a gownsman called Joshua Pears. My own eyes told me that he was stabbed, and quite recently."

Vaughan looked up. "Overnight, you mean?"

I nodded. "A bedder went into the privy at about eight o'clock last night to clean it. So the murder," I saw the Master shudder when I said the word, "the murder took place between then and now."

"Which means that whoever did it came into the college, or was already here," said Vaughan.

"I asked Mr Chapman about that," I confirmed. "He says that there were no visitors to the college yesterday evening – everyone who was here last night was a member of the college."

We were both silent. Eventually the Master spoke. "Two gownsmen dead in two months, Mr Hardiman," he said. "We will have to report this... this murder to the magistrates. If we cannot find an explanation in a timely manner, they will send in the town constables to tramp through our courts and upset our undergraduates. The Vice-Chancellor will question whether I am a fit person to be in charge of St Clement's. If parents fear they cannot send their sons to me to be educated and returned safely to them..." His voice rose with emotion.

"Mr Vaughan," I said sternly, "you did not loop the sheet around Mr Fleming's neck," the Master flinched, "and you did not wield the knife that killed Mr Pears. It is a great sadness when a young life is ended, and we all mourn that, but you are not to blame."

"Then who is to blame?" asked the Master, thumping the arm of his chair. "Mr Fleming was self-murder, of course..." He stopped. Vaughan was a clever and observant man, and I should have remembered this. "Did you shake your head, Mr Hardiman?" he asked.

I leaned forward and clasped my hands. "I was uneasy from the start," I began. "About the finding of self-murder."

Vaughan jumped to his feet. "Uneasy?" he repeated. "Uneasy? Mr Hardiman, you take your duties too far." I bowed my head and he continued. "You are a university constable. You are not a coroner nor yet a surgeon. And yet you presume, you presume…" He walked around his room, breathing heavily, before returning to his chair and slumping into it. He was silent for a long moment before saying in a low voice, "Tell me."

"Thank you, sir," I said. "As I say, I was uneasy… troubled about Mr Fleming. His ledger and his journal suggested that he was in debt thanks to his habit of gambling."

The Master nodded. "I have them still," he confessed. "When we returned Mr Fleming's belongings to his family, I thought it would distress them further to read of his unhappiness, his torment." He looked quickly at me. "The Vice-Chancellor would see that as proof that I was seeking to conceal my own culpability. That I did not want Fleming's family to know how gravely I had failed him."

"In your shoes," I assured him, "I would have done the same." A thought occurred to me. "If you did not tell his mother about the gambling, what reason did you give her for Mr Fleming's actions?"

"I told her that Fleming was such a conscientious student that he overworked himself, that the expectations he had of his own academic greatness were too burdensome," said the Master. "It was partly true: I am convinced that, had he lived, he would have proved a great mathematician."

"Have you looked again at the ledger?" I asked.

"Since you gave it to me that day?" asked Vaughan. I nodded. "No," he said. "I locked it away in my cupboard – there." He pointed.

"Could we have another look at it?" I asked.

The Master frowned slightly but stood and walked over to the cupboard. He took a key from his waistcoat pocket and opened the lock, then reached behind a pile of books for the green ledger. He held it quietly for a moment, then brought it over to me. I put it on the low table between our chairs.

"Please sit down, sir," I said. "I rather fear that we missed something when we last looked at it."

The Master sat and I opened the ledger. As before, I stared at the close-written columns of figures.

"When we found this on the day that Fleming died," I said, "we were looking for a reason for him to kill himself. We realised that he was gambling – more than that, that he was taking wagers from others – and assumed that he was in debt. That he was losing money and owing money. But what if we read it wrong? What if he was not losing money, but making money?" I pointed at the columns. "Could these be read the other way round?"

Vaughan leaned forward and pulled the ledger towards him so that he could see it more clearly. He read one page closely in silence, then turned the page and read another, and another. He looked up at me. "I am still uncertain as to the meaning of the words," he said. "References to other gamblers, perhaps, or horses, or pugilists – who knows? But if we look only at the figures, then, yes, they could be showing winnings rather than losses. And if that is the case, then Mr Fleming was doing very well, especially just before he died. Financially, at least. His journal, on the other hand..."

I nodded. "Yes, he sounded tormented. We assumed that it was about the losses, but what if it was guilt about his illegal activity, guilt about his inability to stop gambling?"

"If that is the case," said Vaughan, sitting back in his chair, "why did he kill himself on that day? Why could he no longer bear it?"

"You said that you have the journal as well," I said.

Vaughan went back to his cupboard and retrieved the journal. He handed it to me and I turned to the last page. The entry for Sunday 12 March was neater than some of the others but written in the same vein: *Lead us not into temptation, forgive us our sins.* But the entry for 13 March, written the day before we discovered Fleming's body, was very different. *18 March. Pedestrianism: Huntingdon to Shoreditch. 60 miles. 11 hours. 200 sovs. Close book 6 o'c 17 March.* I pointed at it. "This surely shows that he was thinking of the future and not planning to end his life." A thought came to me, and I paged back through the journal.

"Have you found something?" asked the Master.

"Perhaps," I said. "These entries about temptation and forgiveness. I thought they were all the way through, but there is a pattern to them. Look," I turned the ledger so that Vaughan could see it. "They are all written on a Sunday. So Mr Fleming went to church, was overcome by guilt, vowed to mend his ways – and went back to his normal behaviour on Monday." I looked again at the journal. "Oh, apart from this one. It's the usual stuff about temptation and forgiveness, but written on a Monday, 30th January."

Vaughan stood and walked over to his desk and picked up a small book. I could see that it was very similar to my own pocket diary. He turned a few pages and then looked up at me. "That was the feast day of King Charles the Martyr – it is marked with a sermon in Great St Mary's in the morning and a speech in the Senate House in the afternoon. If Mr Fleming attended the sermon..."

"It would have the same effect as going to church on Sunday," I concluded.

The Master came and sat down beside me again. "If we assume, therefore," he said, "that Mr Fleming was riddled with guilt only after attending church, and was able to throw off that burden and continue with life as normal on all other days, and if our new reading of the ledger reveals that far from drowning in debt he was actually doing rather well, then his two motives for taking his own life have disappeared."

I nodded. "And if it was not self-murder," I said, "that leaves us with only two possible explanations for his death. An accident –

and the manner of his death makes this unlikely. Or death at the hands of another."

"And with this second violent death, you are now wondering whether there is a connection," said Vaughan flatly.

"What more can you tell me about Mr Pears?" I asked.

―――ele―――

I rubbed my hand across my eyes, then leaned back in my chair and stretched my arms above my head. I had been sad to miss my book club meeting that evening, but with so much to think about I had not dared distract myself in case I forgot something important. My notebook was open on the table in front of me; in it I had written everything the Master of St Clement's had been able to tell me about Joshua Pears.

Like Mr Fleming, Mr Pears had been a fellow commoner. His father was a Manchester cotton merchant, well able to afford the £5 quarterly fees – and no doubt happy to pay for the respectability and special advancement that came with a university degree. But unlike Mr Fleming, Mr Pears had been academically weak and lazy. His parents had plans for him – their third son – to go into the church, but Mr Pears had shown little aptitude for a life of God-fearing service. He was not a reprobate, the Master was keen to stress: just a young man who liked to spend freely and enjoy the freedom of being away from the paternal gaze. My thoughts had turned immediately to gambling: had Mr Pears shared that interest with Mr Fleming? And might their involvement in it have led them both to a violent and early grave?

Chapter Seven
LATIN

Again I found myself looking around a room at St Clement's, trying to find anything that would explain the sudden death of the man who had lived there. Unlike Mr Fleming, Mr Pears did not seem to care much about his studies: there were no piles of books, no ledgers or journals. And again unlike Mr Fleming, it seemed that Mr Pears had been of a tidy turn of mind. On the desk in front of the window, instead of academic items, Mr Pears had ranged his hairbrushes, pomade pot and mirror. A fine porcelain bowl sat on the dressing table, with a razor, leather strap and shaving brush lined up to the left of it, and a bone toothbrush and ceramic pot of tooth powder to the right. A linen cloth embroidered with the initials JP was draped neatly over the bowl.

Against the wall was a most impressive large wardrobe. Hanging from pegs in one section were three, no, four dark coats. Folded neatly on the shelves were shirts – perhaps eight or ten of them. I opened the locker that should have contained dirty linen, and to my surprise found a half-dozen empty wine bottles.

To one side of the wardrobe was a small framed sampler that seemed out of keeping with the rest of the masculine room. I walked over and peered at it. Stitched in the centre was a simple house flanked by trees, then various birds and flowers around them, and finally "To my beloved brother" picked out in letters across the top and "Margaret Pears August 1824" along the bottom of the piece. I thought of Mr Vaughan struggling to find the words to break the worst of all news to another family.

I walked over to the bed, which had been neatly made, a pair of red slippers on the floor to the side. I opened the drawer of the bedside table. There was a pile of snowy handkerchiefs, and on top of it a neatly-wrapped slim parcel of brown paper. I lifted it out and unfolded it, and found myself looking at a skin condom. It was so unexpected that I gave a bark of laughter.

"And who might you be?" said a loud voice.

I turned to see a young man standing in the doorway. He was wearing an outfit that could easily have been taken from Mr Pears' own wardrobe: a plain black coat and trousers, white shirt and high stock, a fine black hat in his hand and highly polished boots on his feet. He held himself extremely upright, his head tilted back so that he could look down his nose at me. At exactly the same moment, we realised that we had seen each other before, on Newmarket Heath.

"You," he said.

I carefully folded the brown paper back around the condom and replaced it in the drawer and closed it.

"My name is Hardiman," I said.

"And what is your business here?" asked the visitor. He glanced around. "Joshua will be most displeased to hear that you have been ransacking his private rooms."

"I am here with the permission of the Master," I said.

"And just why is the Master giving permission for a stranger to go through a man's private possessions?" he asked. "Where is Joshua – Mr Pears?" He looked less confident now.

"Perhaps you had better sit down, Mr…" I said, indicating a chair.

"Lawrence," he said, making no move to come into the room. "What have they done to him? What has happened?"

"I am sorry to tell you that Mr Pears is dead," I said.

Lawrence's hand shot out and he grasped the door jamb but said nothing.

"Please, Mr Lawrence," I said. "You have had a shock. Take a seat."

But Lawrence turned on his heel and disappeared. I heard him running down the steps and across the court. I closed the door of Pears' room behind me and went after him.

George Chapman was standing outside the porters' lodge. "So you told him, then," he said. "He looked a bit green."

"Do you know him?" I asked. "Lawrence, he said his name was."

Chapman shrugged. "I recognise him – used to call on Mr Pears quite regularly. Pals, I suppose."

"But not a St Clement's man?" I asked.

The porter shook his head. "I can find him if you need him," he offered. "Ask around among the porters – someone will own to him."

"Perhaps," I said. "Thank you, George." I made to leave the college but Chapman put a hand on my arm.

"If you've a moment, Gregory," he said. "I've something to show you. It might be nothing, but on the other hand, well." He went into his lodge and came back out a moment later with a clean cloth folded around something. He handed it to me and I unwrapped it. Inside was a piece of paper, torn from a notebook, and with dried brown stains on it. I looked up at Chapman. "It's blood," he said. "We found it in the privy after they took the body away yesterday. I thought it might have been in his pocket, or dropped by whoever did it to him. Can't make head nor tail of it myself."

"It's Latin," I said. "And that's as much as I know."

Chapter Eight
OMNES

Once the final horse had been taken from the Hoop's stables and I had cleaned out the stalls, I took my coat from the hook and put my head around the door of the kitchen. Standing with his back to me, bent over the sink and whistling quietly to himself through the gaps in his teeth, was Poor Jamie.

"Jamie," I called loudly. I knew that going over to him and putting a hand on his shoulder would startle him.

He turned and smiled. "Mr Hardiman," he said.

"I'm going on an errand, Jamie," I said, "and I wanted to leave a message with you."

Jamie took his hands from the sink and dried them carefully on the light brown apron he was wearing, which he then straightened and smoothed down. He was very proud of his apron; he had never had one when he worked at the Sun, and when I had persuaded William Bird to bring Jamie with us to the Hoop I had also suggested that an apron might make him feel like a proper kitchen worker. Poor Jamie was certainly no scholar, but he was not nearly as pudding-headed as people thought. For I was teaching Jamie to read. From the moment he saw me writing in my notebook he decided that he too would learn to understand the black marks on the page. At first I thought he would tire of the effort, but his mother warned me that Jamie was a stubborn soul who liked routine and so it had proved. If I was in the yard during the quietest time of the day – just after the midday meal – Jamie would appear, a reading primer in his hand, and we would find ourselves a peaceful spot for what he proudly called his lessons. We had moved on from the very simple stories for little children; Jamie had not fancied the fairy tales I suggested but showed a great interest in adventure and danger. He particularly liked tales of voyages on the high seas, which he found both thrilling and frightening. When I told him that I had been across the world to Australia, his eyes grew as large and round as saucers. And now he was asking me to teach him to write as well.

"I have my paper," he said, digging into the pocket of his apron. "And my pencil." He pulled out a much-folded and rather grubby piece of paper that I had torn from my notebook for him, and a stub of pencil that he had found on the floor of the inn's parlour and had begged to be allowed to keep. "I'll write it down so I don't forget," he said grandly. He put the paper on the kitchen counter, licked the end of his pencil and looked at me.

"Tell Mr Bird," I said slowly, tilting my head so that I could see what he was writing. "That's it: B I, no, I, R D. Good. Tell Mr Bird that I will be back by eleven o'clock – just put eleven in numbers, that's 1 and another 1. In time for the *Defiance*. That's a hard word, that one. Just put the first bit – D E F. He will know what you mean."

"Like that?" asked Jamie, holding the paper out to me.

"That's just right," I said. "Very clear. Now you read it back to me."

Jamie took the paper in both of his hands, holding it steady, and read slowly. "Mr Bird. You will be back by eleven for the Def." He looked up at me. "That's the *Defiance*, coming from London."

"Good lad," I said. "When you've finished the pots, you go and find Mr Bird and read that to him. Saves me a job, that does – worth your weight, you are, Jamie. And now for your wages: one barley twist."

I took the bag of sweeties from my coat pocket and held it out to him. He peered into it, taking his time to choose the largest one, then popped it into his mouth and smiled delightedly, like the child he really was.

Geoffrey Giles was busy with a group of three gownsmen when I pushed open the door of the bookshop. He glanced over and smiled at me; I lifted a hand in acknowledgement and then started to look through the small piles of books on the counter. They were a mixture of new stock and returned library volumes waiting to be put on the shelves, and I picked up a couple that caught my eye. I was not a subscriber to Nicholson's library, as I could borrow two volumes a week from my book club, but when I was in funds I would sometimes buy a book to add to my small collection.

"Mr Hardiman," said a voice, and I looked up to see that Giles had come across to the counter. "You are tempted?" he asked, indicating the books.

"Always," I replied. "But I have more pressing calls on my money today, I am afraid."

The bookseller gave a gentle smile but said nothing; he never pestered me to tell him anything I did not want to discuss.

"I wondered if I could ask for your guidance," I said. "I have found this." I looked over my shoulder at the three gownsmen but they were not at all interested in me, instead laughing at some shared joke as one held open the door for his companions and they left the shop. I took from my pocket the scrap of paper that Chapman had given me and put it on the counter, flattening it as best I could before turning it so that Giles could read it.

"Is that...?" he asked, pointing at the brown stains.

"Blood," I confirmed flatly. "But the words – do you recognise them? Do you know what they mean?"

The bookseller looked at the note and narrowed his eyes as he considered it. "No – not exactly. And yes. I mean to say: I can translate it for you, but I am not sure where it is from. It seems familiar, but I just can't think."

"No matter," I said. "The translation will be very useful." I took my notebook and pencil from my pocket.

"Well, it's not too difficult," said Giles. "*In unum omnes contulerunt.* You'll know most of it already." He smiled encouragingly. "*Unum?*"

"One?" I suggested.

"Exactly," he replied. "And *omnes?*"

"Everything – all," I said.

"There – I told you that you knew most of it," said the bookseller. "The verb is more obscure, I'll grant you. *Contulerunt* – from the irregular verb *conferre*, to bring together. They were all brought together in one. That's not terribly elegant; perhaps, they all contributed to one. Something of that sort."

I wrote down everything he said. "But you do not know where it is from, or maybe it is not from anywhere – just an original note," I said.

Giles shook his head. "No: it has the flavour of a motto about it. It is tickling me here." He tapped on the back of his head. "If you will permit me, I can note it down and ask a friend of mine who knows much more than I do about these things."

"I would be very grateful," I said. "But you will not tell him who is asking, or about the blood, will you?"

"I shall tell him that it is a riddle I am trying to solve," said Giles, looking up as the door opened and an elderly man with the unmistakable air of a professor walked in. "He will believe that: I am always asking him obscure questions about riddles and puzzles."

Chapter Nine

Mother

I was not surprised to receive a note from Vaughan asking me, in his usual neat hand and polite manner, to call on him at my earliest convenience. But I was surprised, when I reached his rooms at St Clement's, to find a woman there with him. The Master stood when I entered and the woman turned to look at me. She was not a beauty but there was a dignity to her, a determination in the set of her shoulders. Her eyes were dark and her face pale, and I suspected that more delicate colours suited her better than the harsh black she now wore.

"Mr Hardiman," said Vaughan, holding out his hand for me to shake, and then pulling me towards the woman. "Mrs Fleming, this is Mr Hardiman."

Mrs Fleming inclined her head at me and I bowed to her. "Please accept my condolences, Mrs Fleming," I said. "I did not know your son, but Mr Vaughan tells me that he was a fine student and a great loss to the college."

The Master had brought a chair over from the table and sat on it, indicating that I should take the armchair opposite Mrs Fleming.

"And Mr Vaughan tells me that you helped him when he found my poor boy," she said once I was seated, closing her eyes for a moment and swallowing hard. Her hands were clasped in her lap and I saw the knuckles whiten. "And that you have seen Eddie's – Edward's – papers. Which show that he was gambling." She looked at me sharply. "Mr Vaughan also said that you are a constable."

"A university constable, yes," I agreed.

"Spying for the Vice-Chancellor, I daresay, looking to shift the blame for my son's death," she said.

I was taken aback and looked at the Master for help.

"Mrs Fleming," he said calmly, "it is simply a coincidence that Mr Hardiman is a constable – I mention it only to demonstrate that he has some authority to be here today. The Vice-Chancellor is of course aware of Edward's death, and is saddened by it. But there is no question of anyone spying on his behalf."

Mrs Fleming listened, looking from the Master to me and back again.

Vaughan continued. "When we found the ledger in Edward's room, and then his journal, we were concerned to learn that he had been gambling. And especially that he had been gambling on racehorses, which was explicitly forbidden by the University last year. But I have been Master of St Clement's for many years, and I have known hundreds of young men, and discovering that they are doing what is forbidden does not even surprise me, let alone shock me."

"Young men will be young men, Mrs Fleming," I chimed in.

"But if it is not to have Edward's behaviour made... public in some way," she said, "why is Mr Hardiman involved?"

"When we looked at Mr Fleming's journal," I explained, "Mr Vaughan and I were alarmed to read how unhappy he had been."

Vaughan leaned forwards. "I am – was – a father myself, madam," he said, "and I do not like to think of a young person being so tor..." he caught himself and tried again, "so miserable. I expect our undergraduates to be busy with their studies, overwhelmed sometimes, and for them to blame me and the Fellows and the tutors – all of this is normal. But I do not expect a young man to be so miserable that he wants to die, at least not without me noticing it."

"And nor did I notice it," said Mrs Fleming, shaking her head sadly. "Since his father died, I have relied too heavily on Edward, told him too much of my own grief, my own difficulties." She looked quickly at me. "My late husband left me with some debt, Mr Hardiman." She took a sharp breath, held it for a moment and then decided. "Edward's father was a gambler. He taught Edward to gamble when he was only a boy – small wagers on insignificant things, but the excitement was there, the thrill. I tried to object, but he said that Edward had to learn to be a man and not hide behind my skirts." She spoke fiercely. "I thank God every day that Edward is – was – our only son. There was no question of teaching our daughters to gamble." She sighed. "When I married I brought a considerable fortune with me, although my mother was not happy at the match – I married for love, you see. But I was determined and my mother was recently widowed and had not the strength to refuse." She smiled sadly. "And my love blinded me to my husband's faults. I am certainly not the first woman to say that. By the time Jeremy died, there was nothing left: no love, and certainly no fortune. I could not face admitting to my mother that she had been right, and so I confided in Edward. He had always been a sensitive child and I suppose he took his responsibility greatly to heart."

"He certainly tried to resist the temptation to gamble," I said. "That much is clear from his journal."

Mrs Fleming nodded. "I can imagine that he would," she said. "Edward held himself to a high standard." A tear slipped from her eye and she quickly brushed it away. "It seems impossible that he would do this. He knew how much we loved him and needed him, his sisters and I. He was so angry at his father for leaving us in difficulty. And then to kill himself – it makes no sense, Mr Hardiman. It makes no sense at all."

Chapter Ten

Hobnail

George Chapman's information was, as usual, correct. I had been sitting in a dark corner of the parlour of the Angel in Market Street for only ten minutes before Richard Lawrence came in. I am not a great believer in coincidences, and it seemed significant to me that I had run into this gownsman both in Newmarket and in Pears' room at St Clement's.

Just as in Newmarket, Lawrence was surrounded by four or five others who jumped around him like puppies eager for attention. He sat down and watched with detachment while two of the puppies jostled to be the first to catch the innkeeper's eye and order drinks for the table. I waited until the pot boy had brought their tankards and the group had settled before getting to my feet and approaching the table.

"Mr Lawrence," I said. He looked at me and I knew that he recognised me.

"Yes?" he said.

"My name is Hardiman," I said, "and I would be grateful for a moment of your time."

"Well, as you can plainly see, Hardiman," he said, indicating his companions, "I am otherwise occupied. Another time." He picked up his drink.

I held up the green ledger that I had borrowed from Francis Vaughan. "And as you can plainly see, Mr Lawrence," I said, "we have important things to discuss."

Lawrence put down his drink. "Leave us," he said, and the four abandoned their tankards without a word of objection and walked out of the parlour. Without waiting for an invitation, I sat down.

"Where did you get that?" he asked rudely. So I knew I had rattled him.

"Mr Fleming's ledger, you mean?" I asked.

"I daresay you filched it from his room," he said. "You're the wily fellow I caught sneaking around in Pears' room."

"As I explained at the time," I said mildly, "I was there with the permission of the Master."

"And at Newmarket," he said. He leaned forward and all but snarled at me. "I think it's time you told me what interest an ugly hobnail like you can have in me and my friends."

"Hobnail!" I repeated, and laughed.

Lawrence flushed, like the young bully he was. I could see him clenching his fists under the table.

I leaned forward. "Mr Lawrence," I said, low and menacing. "You would do well to remember that you are still a cub, while I am an ex-soldier and a university constable. You may have more book learning than me, but I know enough to understand this particular book." I tapped the cover of the green ledger. "And what it tells me is that Mr Fleming was gambling. Breaking the laws of the University. Putting his soul in danger. And when he could not face his guilt any longer, he strung himself up, Mr Lawrence." I saw him flinch. "Have you ever seen a hanged man, Mr Lawrence? Not just in a sketch in the broadsheets, but in real life?" He shook his head. "I thought not. It's a stinking, pitiful, ugly business, Mr Lawrence. And if finding out why Mr Fleming was driven to self-murder gives a moment of peace to his poor mother, then by God you will sit here and tell me what I want to know." I put the ledger on the table, opened it and pointed at one of the entries. "Let's start here."

"So for all his swagger," said Francis Vaughan, draining his glass, "Richard Lawrence is little more than an errand boy." He stood and walked over to the sideboard, and refilled his glass from the decanter. He held it up but I shook my head.

"I'm on patrol this evening," I said. "It wouldn't do to be thick-headed."

I had called in to see the Master of St Clement's on my way home, knowing that he would be curious to hear what I had found out about the ledger and its contents.

He came and sat beside me again. "I can hardly believe it," he said, shaking his head. "One of our tutors. Which one?"

"Why not a tutor?" I asked, ignoring his question for now. "Any man can be tempted."

"Of course," agreed the Master, "but tutors are well-paid and well-regarded. Their positions here at the University are coveted. It is a great deal to risk."

"I am surprised to hear that they are well-paid," I said. "I thought it was the fellows who are most prized by the University."

Vaughan shook his head. "Fellows have security, certainly: once a man is appointed, he may well hold his position for life, with few duties required of him. But his stipend will be modest, with most benefits coming in the form of college accommodation, and time and space to conduct his own academic studies. You've met some of the fellows here..." He jerked his head to indicate the college about him, and did not finish his sentence.

I nodded. "So the tutors are different?" I asked.

"Oh yes," said the Master, sipping his drink. "The tutors are the teachers of the University – the schoolmasters, if you will. And, like schoolmasters, they are responsible for instructing their pupils and for taking care of them – and they are paid for their efforts. Generously paid, and a canny tutor can turn his position to further advantage."

"In what way?" I asked.

"Well, as the tutor is *in loco parentis* for his pupils, he manages their money," explained the Master. "Their tutorial fees are paid into his bank account – which is where the generous remuneration comes from." He saw me reach into my pocket for my vocabulary book and pencil. "Remuneration," he said again, slowly. "R E M U – then as it sounds. From the Latin *remunerare*, to pay." He waited as I wrote. When I had finished, he continued. "A nobleman will pay ten pounds a quarter to his tutor, for example, and a fellow commoner five pounds."

I raised my eyebrows. "How many pupils does a tutor have?" I asked.

"We have three here at St Clement's", replied the Master, "with the undergraduates shared between them." He paused and frowned at me. "I sense you are unwilling to tell me which man you mean, Mr Hardiman."

"Not unwilling, no, but certainly reluctant," I replied. "As you say, it is a great deal for a man to risk, and sharing an unproven suspicion would be wrong of me."

Vaughan shrugged. "Perhaps," he allowed.

"With three tutors here at St Clement's," I continued, "that means they have more than ten pupils each."

The Master nodded. "Most tutors hire an assistant tutor to take on some of the teaching for them."

I thought for a moment. "You said something about taking further advantage," I prompted him.

Vaughan did not answer immediately.

"I am looking for reasons to put your man in the clear," I said.

He sighed. "I have never asked a tutor about this, but Masters suspect that it happens," he said. "Most of our students are minors, and as such they cannot set up their own accounts with tradesmen and shops. Instead, their tutor accepts their bills for necessities – from grocers, tailors, hosiers, hatters, booksellers and the like – and lets their parents know how much is to be paid." He paused. "And the tutors have worked out that if they are sent money promptly by the parents but do not settle the tradesmen's accounts for some time, they can make interest on the money while it sits in their own account."

"You can't expect a clever man not to use his brain for his own benefit," I pointed out.

"Indeed," agreed the Master with a smile. "Although the other side of the coin is that the tutor takes the risk if the parents do not pay promptly, or if his pupil runs up debts and then leaves town. A wise tutor will watch for signs of extravagance and have a word before it gets out of hand." He drained his glass. "And now, Mr Hardiman, I must insist that you tell me the name of the tutor."

The Master was right; he had asked me to find out what I could, and it was not my place to hide things from him.

"The man involved is Joseph Brown," I said. "It seems that he has been encouraging Mr Lawrence and other undergraduates to place wagers on horse races in Newmarket. And he has been helping them to understand the mathematics to improve their chances of winning."

"You must be mistaken," said Vaughan, shaking his head. "Another man, perhaps – but not Mr Brown."

"Because he would not risk dismissal from his post?" I asked.

"Because he would not risk his eternal soul," replied the Master. He looked into his empty glass and thought for a moment. "I am about to tell you something, Mr Hardiman, in the strictest confidence. I trust you will respect that confidence."

"I am no whiddler, I can assure you, sir," I said.

"No more I thought you were," said Vaughan with a small smile. "But there are those in the University who would use knowledge of this as a stick to beat me. Joseph Brown is one of the ablest mathematicians in Cambridge, a fine tutor – and a Quaker."

Chapter Eleven

CABALLING

I was just pulling open the door of the Bull Hotel when I heard someone calling my name. I turned to see Geoffrey Giles walking towards me along Trumpington Street, his hand raised in greeting.

"Mr Hardiman," he said once we had met. "And how are you, this fine evening? You were missed at our meeting last week," he continued without allowing me time to answer, as he smiled at another arrival for the book club and stood aside to let him pass. "You always talk such sense in our discussions. But before we go up, I thought you might like to hear what I have found out about your Latin note. Now, where did I put it?" He felt his pockets and pulled out a handsome book bound in red leather and handed it to me. I turned the spine to the light: *Suetonius Lives of the Twelve Caesars.* "I have marked the page," said Giles.

I opened the book and read a few lines. "The assassination of Julius Caesar?" I asked the bookseller.

"Exactly that," he confirmed. "Look at paragraph eighty – LXXX."

I looked down the page and slowly read aloud the complicated words. "For this reason the conspirators precipitated the execution of their design, that they might not be obliged to give their assent to the proposal. Instead, therefore, of caballing..." I looked up at Giles.

"Caballing," he repeated. "It means plotting, planning secretly – colluding, if you like. We'll note it in your vocabulary book when we go upstairs."

"Thank you," I said. I continued reading from the book. "Instead of caballing any longer separately, in small parties, they now united their counsels..."

"They now united their counsels," said Giles. "From the original Latin *in unum omnes contulerunt*. From your note."

I turned to the frontispiece of the book – it was a favourite word of mine, that my bookseller friend had taught me. Frontispiece – very elegant. *The Lives of the First Twelve Caesars, translated from the Latin of C Suetonius Tranquillus.*

"Is this writer well known?" I asked.

"Suetonius?" asked Giles. "Widely studied, you mean, or an obscure taste?" I nodded. "Well, I am told that any serious scholar of the classics would know of this book – and particularly the section on Julius Caesar. As most people know something of his life – or rather, his death, with the Ides of March and so on – it is considered a good text for teaching."

"Here at the University?" I asked.

"I thought you would want to know that," said Giles, smiling. "And my friend tells me that the Twelve Caesars are used to torment every classics scholar in the town." The bells of Great St Mary's started to chime the quarter hour. "And now we really must go up," he continued. "We do not want to earn a black mark from the president for taking our seats after he has started speaking. And hand me your vocabulary book so that I can add caballing to your list – who knows when you might need it."

Chapter Twelve

LOTTERY

George Fisher grinned at me as he raised his tankard. "You, Mr Hardiman, are a bad influence," he said before taking a long drink.

"Me?" I said in mock outrage. "I merely observed that it was a pity to spend such a fine evening in a stuffy room listening to our president's thoughts on – what was it again?"

"Mr Davison's discourses on prophecy," said the banker in a serious tone. "From his series of sermons preached in the chapel of Lincoln's Inn." He took another deep drink and then wiped his mouth with the back of his hand. "An Oxford man."

"Ah, well then," I said. "We can surely be forgiven for not wanting to hear too much of the – what was it, discourses – of an Oxford man." I took my notebook and pencil from my pocket and wrote down the word 'discourse'. I glanced up at Fisher.

"A speech, I suppose," he said. "Perhaps more along the lines of a lecture."

I nodded and wrote down the definition before returning the notebook and pencil to my pocket.

"But you are enjoying the book club?" asked Fisher.

"Oh yes," I said. "Particularly the library. To be able to take a book home and see whether I like it, without having to buy it, well."

I smiled. "And the weekly discussions are interesting, for the most part."

"Ha!" said the banker. "But not those drawn from a collection of sermons, eh?" He peered into his empty tankard. "One sermon a week is quite enough for any man, if you ask me."

"Indeed," I said. I knew that George Fisher and his family attended All Saints in the Jewry and he knew that I did not. If he had any curiosity about my faith, he kept it to himself. He signalled to the landlord and within a minute the pot boy had come to our table, delivered two more tankards and removed the dead men.

I watched the banker take a drink and then asked him a question. "Do you know much about gambling in Cambridge?" I said.

His eyebrows shot up. "Gambling? You, Mr Hardiman?"

I held up a hand, smiling and shaking my head. "Not me, no," I replied. "I reckon I used up my store of good fortune when I walked away from Boney with just this," I indicated my face. "Risking my few pounds on a wager would be tempting fate."

"Why the interest, then?" asked the banker.

"Two young men have died recently," I said baldly, "and it seems that an interest in gambling may connect them."

Fisher sat back in his seat. "Ah," he said. "A serious interest." I nodded. "As you can imagine, the University keeps a tight rein on anything within its precincts." I nodded again. "But if you tell young men that there is something exciting they are not permitted to do, then..."

"They will find somewhere to do it," I finished.

"I hear tales about rooms in inns in Chesterton, Grantchester – places just outside town," said the banker. "Your coach driver friends would know more."

"But you have never been tempted?" I asked.

Fisher shook his head. "I may be the black sheep of the Fisher family," he said, "but even the least of us is still a banker at heart.

And we bankers always prefer to control the odds when money is at risk." He caught the eye of the pot boy and signalled for two more drinks. "Although," he looked around in an exaggerated fashion, even checking under the table, "if you swear not to tell my prig of a brother I will let you into my terrible secret."

I entered into the spirit of the thing and held up my hand. "I swear," I said solemnly.

The pot boy put two more tankards on the table. Fisher took a swig and then leaned forward conspiratorially. "I have bought a ticket in the final state lottery," he whispered. He leaned back and smiled. "Well, a share in one, anyway. Ten pounds."

I shook my head. "Forgive me, but you are a fool." I lifted my tankard and then put it down again. "Ten pounds. Why, with that you could buy a cow."

Fisher barked with laughter. "And can you just imagine my sister-in-law's face, if I took a cow home with me to her fancy drawing room in Petty Cury. No, I think a share in a lottery ticket is a much more sensible purchase. And if I win one of the top prizes... Just imagine what I could do with thirty thousand pounds."

I laughed along with him. "Well, you could certainly buy a lot of cows."

Chapter Thirteen
Handkerchief

As the maid showed me into the sunny drawing room in the villa on Lensfield Road, I was surprised and pleased to see Mrs Howard reclining on the sofa, a light rug tucked around her. Standing behind her, smiling broadly, was her husband. He came across to me, his hand out, and I shook it.

"Welcome, welcome," he said warmly.

"Mr Howard," I said, "and Mrs Howard – it is a great pleasure to see you again."

"Mr Hardiman," she said quietly, inclining her head. "You will forgive me if I do not stand." She held out her hand and I walked over to her and took hold of it. It was like holding a small bird: I could feel the tiny bones and the nervous warmth. "Mr Hardiman, when my husband told me that you had a favour to ask of us, I knew that I wanted to see you myself."

"I am honoured, then," I said, and I meant it. Major William Howard had been one of the best men of my acquaintance, and bringing him home to his parents for his last months had been my final duty as a soldier. The loss of their beloved youngest son had been a cruel blow to them, and it seemed they tried to keep him with them by befriending those who had known him. I was lucky to count myself among them.

"Please do sit down, Mr Hardiman," said Mrs Howard, waving her hand towards a pair of armchairs, and her husband and I settled ourselves.

"Shall I pour, my dear?" asked Mr Howard, and when his wife nodded he busied himself with the teacups, filling them and handing them to us. He then settled back in his chair. "I hear that you are to be sworn in for a second year as constable," he said.

I nodded. "I had a letter from the Vice-Chancellor last week."

"And you have decided to continue?" asked Mrs Howard.

"Yes," I said. "I enjoy the work, and the men I work with, and the extra money..." I stopped. I had not meant to raise the subject so soon, but with the Howards I felt at ease and the words just came out.

"The extra money is useful?" finished Mr Howard. "You need not be ashamed of admitting it, Mr Hardiman. We are not so fine, Mrs Howard and I – we certainly know the value of money, and how difficult it can be to acquire it."

I smiled nervously.

"George is quite right," said his wife. "We may be comfortable now, but that was not always the case. Don't tell any of your grand university friends," she said teasingly, leaning forward as though to share a secret, "but my family is in trade." She laughed. "Only the finest of trades, mind you."

Her husband reached across and took her hand. "Mr Hardiman, if I may offer a piece of advice: if you can, find yourself a wife with a family in the wine trade. You will never want for an excellent glass of port." They smiled at each other. I smiled too, although he had given me the same advice on at least two previous occasions. It was obviously a much-cherished joke between them. "Now, please do tell us what we can do for you."

I had not imagined that I would have to explain my situation to Mrs Howard as well as to her husband, but there was no escaping it. I put down my cup and took a deep breath.

"When your son and I were in Spain," I began, "when we first arrived in '09, we were camped near a town called Talavera."

"Fetch the atlas, George," said Mrs Howard. "We shall do as we used to when William sent word of his whereabouts: we shall find it and imagine ourselves there." Her husband walked over to the bookshelf and retrieved a large volume.

"Move the tray onto the floor, would you, Mr Hardiman," he said, and once I had done so he put the atlas onto the low table. He opened it, consulted the table of contents, and then turned to the map of Spain. I leaned forward and put my finger on Talavera.

"Right in the middle," observed Mr Howard.

His wife nodded. "I remember William writing about the unbearable heat in the summer – how he longed for a fresh sea breeze," she said.

"We all did," I agreed. "We hadn't expected to stay for long, but in the end we were there for nearly a year. And while we were there, I... I formed an attachment." I darted a look at Mrs Howard, to see if she was shocked.

"William always thought it was more than that," she said mildly. "He suspected that you married the young lady."

If anyone was shocked, it was me. I sat back in my chair.

"And did you, Mr Hardiman?" asked Mr Howard kindly. "Have you a wife in Spain?"

I shook my head. "No longer," I said. "Lucia died January of '11. In childbirth."

"Oh, Mr Hardiman, how very sad," said Mrs Howard. "And the child?"

I took a deep breath – there was no point in anything but the truth. "My daughter Lucia Maria," I said. "Named for her mother and mine. She is fifteen years old and lives with her mother's people — simple, hard-working farmers." I looked from Mr Howard to his wife and back again. "And Catholic. As am I." I paused. "I will understand if, given your friendship with Mr Venn..."

Mr Howard held up a hand to silence me. "My connections with the officers of the University are matters of business. Your choice of religion is a matter of private devotion. The two have nothing to do with each other." He spoke decisively.

I took a moment to think of my reply. "It is not that I have hidden my faith," I said, "nor that I am ashamed of it. It is simply that it is of little importance to me — since I lost Lucia, and Major Howard. It plays no part in my life now, and so I do not think to mention it."

"And no more shall we," said Mrs Howard stoutly. "Now, Mr Hardiman, I am growing a little tired, but I very much want to know about this favour. Anything that my husband and I can do, you have only to ask. After your kindness to William." She smiled bravely.

"You mentioned that your family was in the wine trade, Mrs Howard," I said. "And your son talked often of his cousins in Lisbon."

"That's right," said Mr Howard. "My sister-in-law married a man whose family have been in the wine trade in Portugal for, oh, two centuries."

"He's rather a bore," added Mrs Howard, "but Grace likes the society in Lisbon, and the climate there suits her. But I am sure my sister's social engagements are of no interest to you, Mr Hardiman." She tilted her head and smiled encouragingly.

"A week ago," I said, reaching into my coat pocket, "I received a letter from Talavera. From the local priest. He says that my daughter is to be married."

Mrs Howard's face broke into a wide smile. "Oh, what lovely news to receive, Mr Hardiman. A wedding!"

Her husband leaned across the low table and shook my hand. "May I be the first to congratulate the father of the bride," he said. "Are you thinking of travelling to Spain for the wedding?"

"Oh no," I said, shaking my head. "How would I explain it to the Proctor? And I am a stranger to my daughter – we thought it best, Lucia's family and I. But she has been well cared for, I do know that." I opened the letter and read it for the hundredth time. "My Spanish is far from perfect, but Father Carrasco – the priest – says that the man she is marrying is a kind man from a respected family and that they will love my daughter as their own." I looked at Mrs Howard. "Although I have never met my daughter, every year Father Carrasco sends me news of her. He does it in memory of my wife – it is a great kindness." I sighed. "I am pleased that Lucia Maria will be settled with a good family, but in Spain the dowry is still very important. And I do not want to shame my daughter by sending her to them empty-handed."

"Of course not, Mr Hardiman," said Mrs Howard. "And I am sure that my husband would be more than happy to lend you..."

"Oh no, Mrs Howard, Mr Howard," I said, holding up my hands. "Please do not misunderstand me. I am in funds. I knew my daughter would need a dowry one day and for many years I have been putting aside what I can. I have fifty-eight pounds to give her."

"She is a lucky girl to have such a generous father," said Mrs Howard.

"It seems very little after so long," I admitted.

"Nonsense," said Mr Howard. "It will be of tremendous help to the newlyweds, I am sure. But if you have no need of money, how can we help?"

"The fifty-eight pounds is here, in Cambridge," I explained, "and I have no notion of how to send it to Lucia Maria. And I wondered whether, with you knowing a merchant in Lisbon, you had any thoughts on the matter."

Mr Howard sat back in his chair, smiling. "Of course. You were right to come to us. And I have exactly the solution. My brother-in-law regularly sends his agent to London to find buyers, negotiate terms and the like. We shall simply write to ask him when his man is next going to be in London, and then we will send the money to him there and he can take it back to Lisbon with him. The pounds can be exchanged into reales in Lisbon, and then I am sure we can work out how to get them to Talavera without too much trouble."

"And you think this route secure?" I asked.

"I shall impress upon my brother-in-law the vital importance and significance of this money," said Mr Howard. "As my wife says, he is not the most interesting of fellows, but he is what I think you would call a square cove." He raised an eyebrow at me and I nodded. "It will become a matter of honour, Mr Hardiman, for our family to undertake the safe delivery of this dowry to your family."

"George, dear," said Mrs Howard, beckoning to her husband. He walked over to the sofa and bent so that she could whisper in his ear. He left the room for a few minutes, and when he returned he handed her a small item.

"Mr Hardiman," she said. "I take it you will be writing to your kind priest in Talavera, to tell him about the money. And when you do so, please enclose this, with instructions that it is to be given to Lucia Maria on her wedding day, with best wishes and congratulations on her marriage from a friend in England who wishes her well." She held out the item and I stood to take it from her. It was a very fine linen handkerchief, carrying a light flowery scent, and with the most delicate lacework around its edges. "I made it myself, when I was first married," explained Mrs Howard, smiling. "It has witnessed our long and happy marriage," she held out a hand to her husband and he took it, "and I very much hope it brings the same good fortune to your daughter."

Chapter Fourteen

PROBABILITIES

Joseph Brown's rooms were tucked away at the top of St Clement's, just below the servants' rooms.

"Up there," said Chapman the porter, pointing. "And he's lucky to have that."

I looked at him. "Surely all tutors are allowed to live in college," I said.

Chapman sniffed. "He's lucky to be a tutor, is all I'm saying." And he was as good as his word, turning from me and sitting once more on the stool outside his lodge, arms folded.

I climbed the stairs to Brown's floor. Alongside his door, as I had seen elsewhere, one of the stones at eye-level in the wall had been painted black, and on that, written in neat white lettering, was his name: Joseph Brown Esq. I knocked.

"Come in, Mr Lawrence," called a faint voice.

I opened the door and went in. The room was small but very neat. A desk by the window was stacked with books and papers, the chair carefully pushed under it. To one side of the fireplace the alcove was filled with shelves, which were tightly packed with books. Facing the fireplace were two armchairs – old, plain and clean. A small rug on the floor was the only ornamentation to the room. A doorway at the back of the room led, I assumed, into the bedroom, and through this doorway, ducking his head, came Joseph Brown. He was wiping his hands on a small towel and stopped short when he saw me. Although, to be honest, a man of his height could hardly stop short – he was well over six feet tall, and gangly with it. He was wearing clothes as plain as his surroundings: black trousers, a simple white shirt and a slightly faded black coat that was both too short and too wide for his frame. He put the towel down on the desk and came towards me.

I held out my hand. "My name is Gregory Hardiman," I said. "I persuaded Mr Lawrence to miss his tutorial so that I could be sure of seeing you. He promises that he will make up the time."

Brown shook my hand. "'Tis just as well," he said in an accent I recognised. "Mr Lawrence is no natural student – he can ill afford to miss his work."

"Lincolnshire?" I asked conversationally.

Brown's eyebrows went up and he smiled. "Boston," he confirmed.

"So you can get home on the coach from the George, if you're up and about at three in the morning" I said. "I'm the ostler at the Hoop – all the timetables are in here." I tapped my forehead. "I am also a university constable." I looked for a reaction but there was none.

"Please, Mr Hardiman, take a seat," said Brown, indicating one of the armchairs while folding himself into the other. He smiled at me but said nothing.

"You are probably wondering why I wanted to see you," I started. "As I said, I have met Mr Lawrence, and he has told me about his... activities in Newmarket. About the wagers. And about your involvement."

"And you have come to warn me off?" asked Brown, but there was no anger in his voice.

I shook my head. "That is not for me to say, Mr Brown," I said. "How you conduct yourself as a tutor of this college is a matter for you and for Mr Vaughan – nothing to do with me."

"And yet here you are," said Brown mildly.

"Here I am," I agreed. "The Master tells me that you are a Quaker," I said.

"I am," he said mildly. To be honest with you, I was somewhat wrong-footed by Joseph Brown. I had expected him to be defensive, or evasive, or nervous. But instead he seemed entirely at ease.

I looked around the spartan room again and at Brown's plain and ill-fitting clothes. "But how is that possible?" I asked. "Surely you have not lied to the University authorities about your faith?"

"A dishonest Quaker?" replied Brown, smiling again. "The Meeting would certainly have something to say about that." He grew more serious. "When I showed an uncommon facility for mathematics at school, my father was determined that I should continue my education. Scotland was the obvious choice." He looked at me questioningly and I nodded.

"The universities in Scotland are more open to those of other faiths," I said. "Catholics, Jews, Methodists."

Brown nodded. "And Quakers, yes," he said. "But the Scottish universities do not excel at mathematics – their preference is for medicine. For mathematics, there is nowhere to match Cambridge. And being second-best is not in my nature."

"But how can you...?" I started.

Brown shook his head. "A common fallacy," he said. "If you look at the Statutes of the University – and believe me, I have – you will see that they have been very cleverly written." He sat forward, clearly enjoying himself. "In order to graduate, you must declare that you are a *bona fide* member of the Church of England." He looked at me expectantly. "In order to graduate..." he repeated.

"But not to study," I said slowly.

Brown sat back with satisfaction. "You have it, sir," he said. "And so here I am, studying with the finest mathematicians in the world – what do I care that I cannot graduate? Those who know my work know its worth."

As you know, I am something of an outlander myself in Cambridge, and perhaps Joseph Brown and I recognised this in each other. Whatever the reason, I quickly found myself warming to the man.

"But you are a tutor," I said. "How can you be a tutor without having a degree?"

"Thankfully the University has never troubled itself to address the matter too closely," replied Brown. "The appointment of tutors for a college is entirely in the gift of the head of house."

"The Master," I said. Brown nodded. "So Mr Vaughan does not mind that you have no degree?"

Brown shrugged. "He knows that my work is worthy of a degree, and he knows that I have a facility for sharing my learning with the undergraduates," he said.

"And he knows that you will be loyal to him for giving you a position," I suggested, "and that you are unlikely to be poached by another college."

Brown laughed. "You certainly do not mince your words, Mr Hardiman," he said. "But you are right: I am grateful to be here, and the Master gets a good worker."

"Which makes me wonder, Mr Brown," I said, "why you should risk your position by leading Mr Lawrence and the others astray."

In answer, Brown pushed himself up from his armchair and went into his bedroom, ducking again as he went through the doorway. He returned a few moments later holding a book. "I keep it at my bedside," he said. "It is the book by which we live." He opened it and turned forward and back a few pages, obviously looking for something specific. "There," he said. He handed me the open book, pointing to the paragraph in the middle of the page.

I took it from him and placed the book in my lap. It was obviously well-read, with slips of paper tucked into it and pencil markings in the margins. The paragraph he had pointed out to me was on a page with the heading "Liberality to the Poor" and had a double line alongside it. I read it.

"And as it has pleased the Lord to favour many amongst us with the outward blessings of this life, in so plentiful a manner that we are placed in a capacity of doing much good, and of exercising offices of Christian love and charity, to the comfort and assistance of the poor and needy; we earnestly recommend to the practice of those whom God has so favoured, the excellent advice given by the apostle: 'Charge them that are rich in this world, that they be not high-minded, nor trust in uncertain riches, but in the living God, who giveth us richly all things to enjoy: that they do good, that they be rich in good works, ready to distribute, willing to communicate, laying up in store for themselves a good foundation against the time to come, that they may lay hold on eternal life.'"

I then turned to the front of the book to read its title. *Extracts from the Minutes and Advices of the Yearly Meeting of Friends Held in London.*

"It explains the Quaker position on all manner of topics," explained Brown.

"And you believe that encouraging undergraduates to wager on horses – against the strict order of the Vice-Chancellor – can be justified by this?" I asked. I read the paragraph again. "To my way of thinking, this is telling you to share your wealth, not to wager in order to accumulate more wealth. And I cannot believe that the Quaker position, as you put it, on gambling is particularly forgiving."

"And you would be right," agreed my host. "But as a thinking man, Mr Hardiman, you will know only too well that we humans are fallible, and that none of us – or very few of us, at any rate – can live entirely within the strictures of his beliefs. Sometimes we have to... bend one rule in order to obey a more important one." He smiled at me, clearly enjoying the debate.

"The lesser of two evils, you mean?" I asked.

"Precisely," said Brown.

"And what are the evils in this case?" I asked.

"You have met Mr Lawrence," stated the tutor. I nodded. "Tell me, Mr Hardiman: if you were to tell him not to wager again, would he listen?"

"I very much doubt it," I said.

"And if I were to tell him, would he listen?" I shook my head. "The Master? Mr Lawrence's own father?" I shook my head again. "I agree," said Brown. "No matter what, Mr Lawrence will continue to wager. He is a young man with a fondness for spectacle and risk, and wagering on horses satisfies both these appetites. And if he is going to do it anyway, surely it is better that we turn it into something useful."

"Ha!" I could not help myself. "And how exactly is wagering on horses useful?" I asked.

Brown held up one finger. "Firstly, it is a mathematical exercise. Monsieur Pascal – the great French mathematician – was himself interested in gambling as it afforded him the chance to study probabilities. Before each outing to Newmarket, I task Mr Lawrence with calculating the odds and the risks. We live in exciting times, Mr Hardiman, for the mathematics of risk, and Mr Lawrence is learning a great deal. His brain is not of the highest order, granted, but give him a subject that interests him and he fares much better. Secondly," he held up a second finger, "I permit Mr Lawrence and the other undergraduates to keep only a small portion of any winnings – and of course any debts must be met in full. They know that if they object to my terms, I will inform the Master and they will face rustication or worse. In this way, they are learning hard lessons of life: that small profits are hard won, and large debts are easily incurred." He smiled at the thought. "And thirdly, and most importantly," he held up another finger and his face grew more serious, "the majority of their winnings are given to the poor. Last month, for example, Mr Lawrence's little cohort made an anonymous donation of eight pounds to the hospital fund. I insist on anonymity: it is a valuable lesson in humility to give without expectation of thanks."

As I took in what tutor was telling me, I found myself agreeing with Francis Vaughan's judgement: Joseph Brown's work was indeed worthy of a degree.

I readied myself to leave and then a thought occurred to me. "May I ask your advice, Mr Brown?"

"Of course, Mr Hardiman," he said genially.

"I have a friend who has bought a share in a ticket for the final state lottery," I began.

The tutor laughed. "You need fear no condemnation from me, Mr Hardiman," he said. "If you wish to spend your money..."

I held up a hand to stop him. "I am not humbugging you, sir. If I had bought the ticket I would admit it. But my friend is a banker," I saw Brown's eyebrows rise a little, "and as such he is canny with money. And I am wondering whether I should follow his example. I have a particular need for money just at the moment and if..."

It was the tutor's turn to hold up his hand. "Forgive me, Mr Hardiman," he said. "You have asked me a serious question and I owe you a serious answer." He sat forward in his chair. "As you no doubt know, there is suspicion that previous lotteries may have been corrupted by those organising them – keeping back winning tickets, or finding them mysteriously held by their friends. And it has been suggested that this is part of the reason for the decision to make the state lottery in October the last one. But I believe that the real concern for the government is that recent state lotteries have not been popular enough. Money is tight for many people and with ticket sales falling, contractors willing to sell lottery tickets have been harder to find. But not so with this final lottery." He smiled. "It is human nature: tell people they cannot have something, and suddenly it is the thing they want most in the all the world."

"Aye," I agreed. "My friend certainly feels that it is his last chance to make his fortune."

"And this tendency only makes it all the more foolish, mathematically speaking," said Brown, sitting back again. "First, running a lottery is a commercial endeavour, and those doing it must be paid. I am not sure of the exact figure, but it is not unreasonable to imagine that a tenth of the takings are spent on disbursements – printing the tickets, placing advertisements in newspapers, paying the ticket-sellers and so on. Second, the government also takes its slice of the takings – perhaps anther tenth. And third, as we have agreed, this final lottery will be very popular. All the tickets will be sold, and the more tickets there are in the draw, the smaller is the chance than any one ticket will win." The tutor smiled again. "It would be a kindness to your friend, Mr Hardiman, to advise him to risk his money on the horses in Newmarket rather than with the sharps in London."

Chapter Fifteen

BANKNOTES

I stepped carefully around a puddle of who knows what and into the doorway of Fisher's Bank. Its modest premises in Petty Cury were less grand than Foster's Bank on Bridge Street or indeed the banking rooms at Mr Mortlock's home on Bene't Street, but they suited me. I pushed open the door and went into the small banking office. A young clerk was sitting on a high stool behind the counter and looked up as I walked in.

"Good morning, sir," he said, putting an inky finger on the ledger he was writing in to mark his place. "How may I be of assistance with your banking endeavours today?"

I had obviously found a fellow lover of words. "I would like to see a banker, please," I said. "I need to change some coin into banknotes." I indicated my satchel, held close to my body. I had not liked carrying all my savings across town.

Like everyone working in the town, the clerk could tell at a glance where I belonged in Cambridge society – and my dark coat, neat and clean though it was, told him that I was not connected with the University. No need to disturb Mr Thomas, then – the younger brother Mr George would suffice. He put a slip of paper into the ledger, closed it carefully and slid down from his stool. "One moment, sir, and I will ascertain the presence or indeed absence of Mr George Fisher." My guess had been right. He knocked lightly on the door at the back of the office before disappearing through it. A minute later the same door flew open and there was George Fisher, grinning widely and holding out his hand.

"I thought it would be you, Gregory," he said warmly. "Stevens said that you looked like a constable." The clerk reappeared at his elbow. "His father was a porter," explained George, "and has bequeathed him a sharp eye and a deep understanding of Cambridge and its quirks." Stevens the clerk smiled shyly and returned to his stool. "Come, come," said George, beckoning me. "My brother is dining with some grandee or other and his wife is visiting her mother, so we have the parlour to ourselves."

"Thank you, Mr Stevens," I said as I walked past him.

"I am gratified to have been of some small service," he said, opening his ledger again.

George held open the door of the parlour and ushered me in. He closed the door and said quietly, "I think Mr Stevens has swallowed a dictionary. He attended St Peter's School, I believe."

"Up the hill," I said.

George nodded. "His father was determined that his son should have good prospects, and young Mr Stevens is equally determined to make his mark." He smiled mischievously. "Sometimes it is hard to keep a straight face. Now, Gregory, what's this about banknotes?" The small parlour housed two armchairs flanking a tiny fireplace, with a low table between them, and George sat in one chair and indicated that I should take the other. I swung the satchel off my shoulder and put it on my lap.

"I have fifty-eight pounds," I said. "But it is in coins. A few gold sovereigns but mostly half-crowns and shillings. It is being taken to Lisbon for me, and it would be better in banknotes. Lighter to carry – easier to conceal and protect."

"Indeed," said George, nodding. "May I?" He held out his hand and I passed him the satchel. "Weighty," he said. He leaned to retrieve a wooden tray that was leaning against the wall and placed it across his knees. "We'll count on here," he said, tipping the satchel so that the coins clattered onto the tray. "The edges will keep it all safe." And with fast, nimble movements he quickly sorted the coins into piles, counting under his breath as he went. "Fifty-eight pounds exactly," he said when he had finished. He picked up the piles of coins and dropped them back into the satchel. "I don't want to spoil the fun for Mr Stevens," he said. "He does so like to count money." He handed the satchel back to me. "It's a great deal of money, Gregory," he said, "and as you are not a customer of the bank I have to ask you a few questions about it."

I nodded. "I expected that," I said.

"How did you acquire the money?" he asked.

"I saved it," I said. "From my army pay and, since I have been in Cambridge, from my wages. I am careful with my money, as you know."

"No-one could accuse you of being a spendthrift, that is true," agreed the banker. "And why are you sending this money to Lisbon?" I hesitated. "In general terms, if you prefer," he continued. "To purchase property, for example, or to repay a debt."

"To meet family obligations," I said.

"You have family in Lisbon, Gregory?" he asked.

"Spain," I clarified. "But once the money is in Lisbon, it will be exchanged for reales and taken to... to Talavera."

The banker raised his eyebrows – he had heard me talk of my service in Spain but I had never mentioned Lucia or my daughter to him. Perhaps now would be...

"Will you go to London yourself?" he asked, and I dismissed the thought.

"London?" I repeated. "Why should I go to London?"

"Despite the irritating pomposity of my brother, Fisher's is only a country bank," he said. "There is no guarantee that an establishment in Lisbon would be happy to honour our banknotes. My recommendation would be that you take them to our agent in London to exchange for theirs – a London issuer would be more recognised."

"Who is your agent?" I asked.

"Curries," he replied. "In Cornhill."

I made a note of it. "I shall not be going, no," I replied. "I am to hand the banknotes to a friend, and he will take them to Lisbon for me. He has business in London anyway."

"And you are sure you can trust this friend, Gregory?" asked George earnestly.

"I have the word of a gentleman," I confirmed.

That evening I sat in my room, the banknotes laid out on the table in front of me. It was hard to believe that all those years of saving and planning could be reduced to a pile of paper. I picked up one of the notes and peered at the name Fisher & Son printed in ornate swirling script across the top – each curl, the banker had told me, making it more difficult for someone to make a copy of the note. The body of the note promised, in the grandest of terms, to pay the bearer on demand a sum of money. I had watched as George had carefully and neatly completed the date on each note, and at the bottom right was the signature of his brother Thomas Hall Fisher. But still, it was just a slip of paper – no heft to it at all.

I gathered the banknotes into a pile and carefully wrapped them in the piece of oilcloth that the clerk at the bank had given me, securing it with the leather lace he had also supplied. I stood and went to my cupboard, and from under my garments I took the delicate handkerchief that Mrs Howard had given me. I tore a page from my notebook and folded it around the handkerchief. With my pencil I carefully wrote *Mia querida hija Lucia Maria* on the little package, and tucked it under the leather lace. I kissed my fingertips and touched them to the parcel, and closed my eyes to conjure up my wife so that together we could wish our daughter every happiness in the world.

Chapter Sixteen

DINING

The next few days were busy at the Hoop. There were the usual coaches, of course, but as William Bird's reputation for comfortable lodgings at a fair price was spreading, we found ourselves welcoming more and more overnight guests. I had no complaints; on the contrary, it pleased me to see the stables full of contented, well-fed animals. But it meant that it was not until Saturday that I was able to send a note to Francis Vaughan asking if I could visit him. His reply came quickly, inviting me to dine at St Clement's with him on Sunday. Mrs Jacobs was torn between irritation that I would be missing my meal with her and pride that (as she put it) a lodger of hers would be sitting at high table with the Master of a college.

Vaughan laughed when I told him about my landlady's remarks. "Sometimes we have very grand dinners," he agreed, "but most of the time it is just as you see it." He gestured around the dining hall. Three tables were ranged the length of the room, leading up to the high table – rather like the stumps and bails of a cricket wicket. The benches of two of the three tables were crowded with gownsmen, bent greedily to their plates, reaching for tumblers, sharing a joke or engaging noisily in a disagreement. The third table had a clutch of gownsmen at the top end of it, nearest us, and then a length of empty benches before several place settings with no-one at them.

Vaughan caught me looking at them. "For the sizars," he explained. He pointed his fork at a young undergraduate walking between the two crowded tables, a pitcher in each hand. "They wait at table, and eat their own meal after the others." I must have looked shocked. "Sizars are offered a fine education in exchange for much reduced fees, and for performing small services for other gownsmen," he said. "Running errands, laying fires, that sort of thing. It's a marvellous opportunity for a poor lad with brains and ambition."

"You mean they are servants?" I asked. I watched as a gownsman wordlessly held an empty dish above his head, and did not even look at the sizar who took it from him and walked with it to the kitchen.

Vaughan shook his head. "Absolutely not. They are often younger when they arrive and so they stay with us for longer, but they are undergraduates like the rest." He leaned towards me and spoke more quietly. "In earlier times, they were treated meanly, that is true. Not fed properly – surviving on scraps from the table, that sort of thing. But now they have their own commons, which they can eat in peace afterwards."

I watched as the sizar returned from the kitchen with the refilled dish and placed it in front of the gownsman. Again, he was ignored. To my eye he looked like a child; small, undeveloped and with curls so pale they were almost white giving him a (no doubt deceptively) angelic appearance.

"And the gown?" I asked, indicating the sizar with my fork.

Vaughan looked at me, then at the sizar and back at me again. "The gown?" he repeated.

"The sizar is wearing a plainer gown than the others," I explained.

"It is nothing more than a uniform," explained the Master. "You know the importance of uniforms, from your own experience."

I nodded. "I do, yes," I agreed. "But the uniform is used to show seniority – who is more important, whose instructions must be obeyed. And if those who are at the bottom of the ladder start to feel that they are being held there unjustly..."

Vaughan looked at me sharply.

"Forgive me," I said, with a short laugh. "I am simply speaking my thoughts aloud – take no notice."

But Francis Vaughan was an intelligent, curious man, not given to ignoring things, and I saw him narrowing his eyes as he watched the sizar walk across the dining hall to answer the clicking fingers of another undergraduate.

After the meal, the Master and I went up to his rooms. He poured himself a generous measure of port and then looked enquiringly at me. I held up my fingers to indicate a small drink; I find port a heavy drink that often gives me a headache.

When we had both settled, we raised our glasses to each other and took a drink.

"I understand that you called on Mr Brown this week," said Vaughan.

"How did you... ah, Mr Chapman," I said.

The Master inclined his head. "Indeed," he said. "William Wickham himself could learn a lesson or two about espionage from Cambridge college porters." He sipped his port. "Did you ask Mr Brown about the gambling?"

I nodded. "I did," I said. "He was most forthcoming. And oddly persuasive."

"I thought you would like him," said Vaughan. "Not what you imagined a Quaker to be?"

"Mr Brown is not the first Quaker I have met," I replied, "but he is certainly the most..." I searched for the word. "The most cheerful," I decided on.

"And persuasive, you said," added the Master. "What did he persuade you of, Mr Hardiman?"

"He explained to me why he allows his undergraduates to gamble, and his reasoning seemed sound," I said. I outlined for the Master what the tutor had told me, and at the end of it Vaughan laughed.

"Anonymous donations," he repeated, shaking his head. "That will stick in the throat of some of them, accustomed as they are to having the whole world know who they are and how much money they have." He raised his glass. "To Joseph Brown and his clever reasoning."

As I was walking across the court towards the college gate, I saw a short figure appear from the passageway that I knew led to the back door of the kitchen. When he emerged into the light of the court, I recognised the sizar that I had seen at work in the dining hall. He walked briskly towards the porters' lodge, nodded at the man on duty, and let himself out of college.

For myself, I glanced through the small window of the lodge. Sitting at the desk was George Chapman. I knocked on the window and he slid it open.

"Good evening, Mr Hardiman," he said.

"Good evening, Mr Chapman," I replied. "The young man who just left, the sizar. Where would he be going at this time of night, do you think?"

"Mr Hodges?" he said. He leaned forward on his elbows. "Well, I can't be sure – he's a bit of a strange one. You know about his brother, of course." He looked up enquiringly at me and I shook my head. "You'd best come in." He reached up and opened the door and I squeezed into the lodge. He turned and pulled a stool from under the desk and I sat, our knees almost touching. "The young man you just saw was Nicholas Hodges. He has been a sizar at St Clement's since October last. But before that, his older brother Samuel was a sizar here."

"Is that usual," I asked, "to offer two boys from the same family a sizar..."

"A sizarship," finished Chapman for me. "It does happen, but only when the first boy cannot complete his time here – then the Master can offer his place to a younger brother, if he also has a good brain."

"I see," I said. "So why did Samuel Hodges have to leave?"

The porter looked down and shifted in his seat. "He killed himself," he said eventually. "Hanged himself, like poor Mr Fleming."

"But he would only have been a child," I said, horrified.

"Just sixteen," confirmed Chapman.

"But what on earth would make a child want to die?" I asked.

"We never did find out," sad the porter sadly. "Last summer, it was – just coming to the end of his third term. Around the time of the Pot Fair. By all accounts he was getting on well with his studies, but he was a very quiet lad – not many friends. Not any friends, really." He sighed and shook his head. "I know it's a good opportunity for these boys, being a sizar, but I do sometimes wonder."

"What do you mean?" I asked.

"Well, they're always the youngest in the college," he said, "and mostly they're a bit shy – good brains, of course, but not much in the way of, well, knowing how the world works."

"And is Nicholas Hodges like that too?" I asked.

I might have imagined it, but I am sure the porter gave a little shudder. "Oh no, he's cut from different cloth entirely. Still young, of course, and with the sadness of having lost his brother. But Mr Nicholas, there's something altogether more knowing about him."

I looked up as I heard the church bells toll. "Well," I put my hands on my knees and pushed myself to my feet, "wherever he has gone, he'll have to make it quick: that's half past nine, and the constables will be after him soon."

The last half-hour before ten o'clock is always busy in town, as the Proctors and constables complete their rounds and the undergraduates hurry home ahead of them. As I walked along Bridge Street I passed several groups of young men heading for St John's and Trinity, jostling each other and laughing as they went. From the smell of them, they had spent the evening in a tavern rather than at their books. And indeed, as I drew level with the door of the Hoop Inn, it was pulled open and another group of three men in their gowns all but tumbled into the street, clutching at each other and loudly warning themselves to be quiet. I pressed myself into the wall to let them pass; no doubt they would be casting their accounts before long, and I wanted none of that on my boots.

Once they had tottered unsteadily past me, I was about to turn into Jesus Lane when I heard a halloo. I peered up Sidney Street and saw a figure leap from the steps of the Sidney Sussex gatehouse into the road. He looked over his shoulder as though he was being chased and then hared towards me. He cannot have seen me in the shadows because he careened into me, catching me a glancing blow with his shoulder and putting out a hand to my arm to steady himself. He did not stop running, but as he turned to look at me I recognised Nicholas Hodges.

"Mr Hodges," I called after him, but he was gone, running up Bridge Street towards St Clement's.

I looked again towards Sidney Sussex but no-one was following him. At least he would be home before ten o'clock, as indeed was I. I was not surprised to discover that Mrs Jacobs had stayed downstairs to quiz me about my dinner at college.

"Here," she said, reaching for my coat as I took it off. "I'll hang that up, and then you can sit down and... ugh, what on earth have you done now, Mr Hardiman?" She turned the sleeve of my coat to show me a dark mark on it. She touched it with a finger and held her hand to the light. "Are you hurt, sir?" she asked with sudden concern. "Were you attacked on the way home?"

"Attacked? Why would you ask that?"

"This mark," she said, holding it out to show me. "It's blood – fresh blood."

And then I remembered Hodges's hand on my arm.

Chapter Seventeen
Healing

Perhaps it was the wild look I had seen in the eyes of Nicholas Hodges that evening, or perhaps it was the blood on his hand, or perhaps, as I suspected, it was what always disturbed my sleep. But after three nights of waking with a jolt, my nightshirt twisted around my legs, my mouth dry with terror, I decided that I would have to visit Mr Relhan.

Once I had seen the Hoop's overnight guests off with their mounts and their coaches, I slipped from the yard and walked the short distance to St Sepulchre's passage and the apothecary's shop. Richard Relhan had his back to the shop door, standing on a low stool in order to reach up to a high shelf behind the counter.

"Just a moment," he said without looking round, concentrating on taking hold of an elegant curved jar with both hands and carefully lowering it to the counter before stepping down off the stool. "There."

I looked at the jar. It was about eight inches high, with a wide base and an ornate steepled lid, made of white pottery with careful, clear blue lettering on it surrounded by drawings of leaves, flowers and – I peered closer – naked nymphs. I raised an eyebrow at Relhan and he smiled.

"From Delft," he explained, "in the United Netherlands. They are known for their beer and their pottery. Their medicinal jars like this," he laid a loving hand on it, "are particularly fine. I hope to buy one or two more at the Stourbridge Fair in September, depending on the price."

I bent down again and read aloud the lettering. "U Populeon." I looked enquiringly at the apothecary.

"Unguentum Populeon," he clarified. "A healing salve. Used since the Middle Ages, I believe. Made from the young buds of the black poplar. And particularly favoured for the relief of pain from haemorrhoids." We both winced and then laughed.

"I will keep it in mind," I said.

Relhan carefully pushed the jar to one side. "But you are not here today for a salve," he said. "Although I think it is not yet a month..."

"It is not," I agreed. Since I had arrived in Cambridge, I had been visiting Relhan every month to buy my tablets, which I took at the rate of two a day. As a soldier I had tried laudanum and various opium tinctures but I found their effects less predictable than the pure form that I now favoured. Relhan took a keen interest in my habit, noting down my dosage and my reaction to it whenever I brought in my little brown bottle for refilling.

I took that bottle from my pocket and put it on the counter. Relhan picked it up and shook it. "Empty," he observed. "And it is only..." he reached under the counter for his notebook and turned to the relevant page, "just over three weeks."

"Night terrors," I offered as an explanation.

"Worse than usual?" asked the apothecary, his pencil poised over the page.

I shrugged. "Not worse, exactly – the content is no worse, but the duration. I seem to take longer to wake from them."

"I see," said Relhan, making a note. "And do you find that taking a larger dose helps with that? It seems unlikely that it would."

I thought back over the past few nights. "No," I admitted. "It does not help. I hoped it would... deaden the alarm."

He shook his head. "Opium is a soporific, as you know," he said. "And more opium is more soporific. If you increase the dose, you will find it harder to wake, and meanwhile it will have no effect on what you see and what you feel while you sleep. Which cannot be pleasant." He turned to the shelves again and picked up a smaller jar. He took a black cloth from a drawer, spread it on the counter and tipped the jar so that dozens of pills rolled out onto the cloth. "I will of course supply whatever you ask for," he said, looking up at me.

"My usual amount," I said firmly.

"I think it wise," said Relhan, using his fingertip to rapidly count the tablets. He picked up the excess and put them back into the jar before using a small funnel to pour my order into my bottle. "You are aware of the other possible effects?" he asked conversationally as he pushed the stopper into the bottle. "Dry mouth. Extreme lethargy – although unlikely at this dosage. And constipation." He handed the bottle to me. "You do not want to risk that, otherwise you might have need of my salve after all." He nodded towards the Delft jar.

I put the bottle into my pocket and paid the two shillings I owed. "I shall be careful," I promised.

Chapter Eighteen

ELECTIONS

I had just refilled the water troughs in readiness for the arrival of the *Defiance* from London when a lad appeared at the door of the stable with a message for me from the Senior Proctor.

I unfolded it. *Constable Hardiman*, it said in a neat hand, *please arrive an hour in advance of your duty this evening. Yours respectfully, Nicholas Temple.*

"Is that all?" I asked the lad, turning the sheet over.

He nodded.

I walked over to where my coat was hanging on a hook, dug in the pocket for a coin and handed it to the lad.

"No reply?" he asked, disappointed.

"None needed," I said. "But if you like, you can go to Mrs Jacobs, at 12 Radegund Buildings, and tell her that I shall not be home for supper."

"12 Radegund Buildings – that's along there, isn't it?" the lad asked, pointing.

I nodded. "Last house before Butt's Green. Mrs Jacobs." I turned back for another coin. "And tell her that I said you're to have my piece of bread. I'll fetch for myself here."

"Ta, mister!" he said, shoving the two coins into his waistcoat pocket before setting off at a trot down Jesus Lane.

Knowing Mr Temple's respect for the clock, I made sure I was waiting in the Proctors' Court at five minutes to the hour. Two other constables had had the same thought and were already there when I arrived, and four more arrived in the next two minutes. We all looked puzzled.

"Seven of us?" said George Swanney.

The door opened just as the church bells started, and Nicholas Temple replied. "There should be eight of you, Mr Swanney, but Mrs Franklin has sent word that her husband is visiting his mother in Stretham and will not be back until tomorrow." He looked around the room. "No Mr Venn?" he asked.

The door opened again and in rushed the Junior Proctor. "Just in time," he gasped, as the final toll of the bell marked the hour.

"Indeed," said the Senior Proctor darkly – you will probably suspect, as I did, that he was readying himself to chastise his colleague and felt a little cheated. "Gentlemen, next month will be a stern test of you all." We waited. "There will be the proclamation of Midsummer Fair, the commencement of Commencement," he looked around the room and we duly smiled, "and not one, not two but three elections here in the town. Diaries, if you please, gentlemen."

We all reached into our pockets and took out whatever we had that served as a record of our duties and looked expectantly at the Senior Proctor.

"First," he said, "on Friday the 9th of June there is the election of the Members of Parliament for the Town. I am led to believe that in addition to Colonel Trench and the Marquess Graham, a George Pryme will also appear on the ballot paper. He is a lecturer at the University, which is in his favour, and a Whig, which is not.

There may be some posturing by supporters and discontent at the inevitable result, so we need to be on our guard on the day of the election."

"No mistaking his political affiliation," said Swanney from the side of his mouth, nodding towards the Senior Proctor.

"Indeed there is not, Mr Swanney," said Temple. "On that evening, therefore, we require six constables to be on patrol: two with me, two with Mr Venn, and two remaining all evening in the vicinity of the market square and guildhall. Volunteers, please."

I was already on duty that evening, so I put up my hand. Temple looked around the room and noted down the six names.

"Second," he continued, "from Tuesday the 13th of June to Friday the 16th of June there is the election of the Members of Parliament for the University. For those of you who have not observed this before, it works thus. There are four candidates – this year, they are Lord Palmerston, Sir John Copley, Mr Goulburn and Mr Bankes. All Tories, Mr Swanney. Only a quarter of the men who are eligible to vote live here in Cambridge, so we have to allow time for non-resident voters to come to town to have their say – which is why polling at the Senate House is open for four days. Voting closes at one o'clock on the Friday, with the result announced shortly after that. We expect no ill-discipline during this election, and so the duties will remain as assigned. However," he gesticulated towards my diary, "it would be wise to note the dates, just in case." I did as instructed.

"And third," he said, "we have the election of the Members of Parliament for the county of Cambridgeshire. This is another protracted election, with polling every day from Thursday the 22nd of June to Thursday the 29th, with only Sunday excluded. And this, gentlemen, will be a bad-tempered affair. Mr Wells has been stirring the pot again." He frowned, then looked around the room and must have seen the blank looks on our faces. "Mr Samuel Wells, from Huntingdon," he explained. "An attorney." He managed to fill the word with equal parts disgust, disdain and displeasure. "He has just recently announced his intention of calling on the day of election for the candidates to pledge themselves to support thorough reform of the Commons and repeal of the malt tax. He will not succeed, of course, but there will be some radical element," more distaste at this phrase, "who will rally to his cause and may disrupt matters. We will need to be on our guard, gentlemen. Good sense will doubtless prevail and the excellent Lord Charles Manners and Lord Francis Osborne will be returned, but any show of poor sense will need to be swiftly and absolutely quashed."

George Swanney slowly raised his hand.

"Yes?" asked Temple.

"I understand that Lord Charles is standing reluctantly," said Swanney.

"You astonish me, Mr Swanney," said Temple robustly. "I had no idea that a Member of Parliament would take a drapers' clerk into his confidence regarding his political plans."

"And no more he did, sir," said Swanney stoutly. "It's just that he is known as a man of action, and I have heard rumours that he finds political life too slow."

"Ah, well, rumours," replied the Senior Proctor, smiling unconvincingly. "If you are going to base your understanding of a man on rumours, then you will often be mistaken. Might I counsel you, Mr Swanney, to stick to your duties as a constable and leave the thinking to others."

Chapter Nineteen
GATEHOUSE

The next morning I slipped away from the Hoop in the middle of the morning and called on the porters at Sidney Sussex College. With the new gatehouse and high wall, their lodge was a much grander affair than Mr Chapman's little snug at St Clement's. I tapped on the door and walked in.

A tall, spare man was standing behind a counter and he looked me up and down.

"May I help you?" he asked, while managing to imply that helping me was the very last thing he wished to do.

"My name is Hardiman," I replied, "and I am a university constable."

"I see," said the porter, his tone a little more civil. "Are you here concerning the behaviour of one of our gentlemen?"

"Perhaps," I said. "Do you happen to know if any of your gentlemen is friendly with Nicholas Hodges of St Clement's?"

"Friendly?" repeated the man with suspicion. "In what way, friendly?"

"Ah no," I said, with a chuckle. "I am not suggesting anything of that sort. But last Sunday night, just before ten o'clock, I saw Mr Hodges leaving your college in a rush."

"To meet his curfew at St Clement's, I expect," said the porter.

"He gave the impression of being chased," I added. "Pursued. He was looking over his shoulder and ran into me. And where he touched my sleeve, he left a bloodstain. From his right hand, as though he had been in a fight with someone."

The porter shrugged but looked uneasy.

"Mr..." I began, and waited.

After a few moments, the porter said, "Baines. William Baines."

"Mr Baines," I said. "I am sure you know the duties and responsibilities of a university constable. That the Act of 1825 gives me all the powers and authorities of a constable within the precincts of the University." I looked enquiringly at the porter and he nodded reluctantly. "Now, Mr Baines, I can choose to exercise my authority by requiring you to bring every man in this college to me, one by one, to check them for wounds. Every undergraduate, every Fellow, even the Master." I paused for the porter to imagine how he might explain the situation to the Master of the college. "Or you can suggest which of your gentlemen I should see first. Mr Chapman at St Clement's assures me that nothing in a college escapes the notice of its porters. And I am sure that he is right."

Ten minutes later I was waiting in a small room behind the porters' lodge. It was simply furnished with an armchair and a table with two upright chairs, and from the remnants left on the table I guessed it was where the porters would retire to have a quick meal or a rest during the quiet overnight hours. The door opened and in came Baines with a young man. This cub was barely dressed, his shirt outside his trousers and a dressing gown draped over the lot. He looked down his nose at me and threw himself into the armchair. I remained standing and said nothing. He eventually started to shift in his chair.

"Well, Baines?" he said.

"This is Constable Hardiman," said the porter, "and this is Mr Harford."

I took my notebook from my pocket and opened it with great unconcern. "Harford?" I repeated. "First name?"

"Richard," said Baines. I wrote it down.

"You can go now, Baines," said Harford, waving his hand dismissively at the porter.

"Please remain, Mr Baines," I said. "I need a witness to our discussion."

The porter looked uneasy but stayed where he was. Harford's eyes darted from me to Baines and back again.

"Mr Harford," I said. "Where were you on Sunday evening at just before ten o'clock?"

"Here, of course," said the undergraduate. He sat upright in his chair. "And if any of your lot," he jabbed his finger in my direction, "says otherwise, he's a liar."

"Your eye," I said, pointing towards it with the end of my pencil, "what happened there?" There was a cut above his left eye, and the skin around it had ripened nicely into a livid bruise.

Harford put his hand to his eye. "I tripped and caught it on the corner of my desk," he said.

I scratched my chin. "Tripped and fell, eh?" I asked. He nodded. "I'm not convinced," I continued. "With this," I indicated my own face this time, "I've become something of a student of facial injuries. Mine's from a sabre. Right-handed. Downwards, from a man on a horse." I mimed the action. "And yours," I leaned forward and looked more closely at him. He sat further back in the armchair. "Yours is from a fist. Right-handed. Upwards, from a smaller man." I mimed the action, and Harford flinched. "And I have an idea who he might be."

"Don't see how you can," said Harford rudely. "As I said, I tripped and caught myself on my desk."

"Do you have any reason to go to St Clement's?" I asked him.

"The church?" he asked.

"The college," I said.

He shook his head.

"No Fellows to meet?" I asked. "No friends among the undergraduates?"

Harford shook his head again. I thought I heard Baines open his mouth to speak; I glanced at him but he said nothing. I made another note in my book and then closed it and put it into my coat pocket.

"You should see an apothecary about that," I suggested, pointing at Harford's eye. "Get a soothing salve. And move your desk."

"Can I go now?" he replied, pushing himself up out of the armchair.

"You may, Mr Harford," I replied. "Thank you for the information." I patted my pocket where I had put the notebook.

Harford looked wary, glancing from me to the porter, and then left.

"And what was it you wanted to tell me, Mr Baines?" I asked conversationally as we returned to the gatehouse.

He looked sharply at me and then sighed. "Ah, I thought you might have noticed that." He stopped. "Mr Harford was lying to you about St Clement's. The lad whose body was found in the privy. They knew each other, Mr Harford and him."

"How well did they know each other?" I asked.

"Oh no, nothing like that," said the porter, shaking his head. "It happens sometimes, of course, but not these two. But they were good friends. The lad from St Clement's – Pearson, was it – came here to dine a few times, and Harford went to St Clement's in return."

"Pears," I said.

"That's it," said Baines. "Mr Pears. Shocking business."

"I suppose Mr Harford was distressed by his friend's death," I suggested.

The porter thought for a moment. "I'm not sure that distressed is the right word. More... frightened. He's not been out of college much since it happened."

Chapter Twenty
SWEETS

William Bird's plan to poach stagecoach business from the other inns in Cambridge was canny. Coach drivers who pulled in at the Hoop would receive a free meal and a tankard of ale, as well as a private room for their overnight stay. And if you have ever shared a bed in an inn with a snoring, stinking stranger, you can imagine why that might tempt them. With some of the best drivers in the country working the routes to Cambridge, it was a canny offering: a stagecoach owner would sooner change the inn he used than lose a decent driver. There was already talk of a new early service going to London via Royston, and although I knew I would curse the early start on frigid winter mornings I was happy to see William doing well. My contribution, which was no hardship at all and indeed I would not have had it any other way, was to make sure that every horse that came into our yard received the best possible care. I hope you won't think me boastful if I say that anyone who once brought their horse to the Hoop would refuse to stay anywhere else in Cambridge after that.

Someone else whose fortunes rose along with the Hoop's was Jamie. After the death last year of George Ryder, the inn's cook, I had been worried that his replacement would not take kindly to having a simpleton washing the pots in his kitchen. But Seth

Young, the new man, had a soft heart and – more importantly – a wife with a younger brother cut from the same cloth as Poor Jamie. And so Jamie stayed on, master of the kitchen sink, whistling tunelessly to himself as he plunged his hands into the water and stacked the dishes carefully to dry. These days he also kept a newspaper propped up on the shelf over the sink. Not that he could read much of it yet, but the pot boy would bring him any paper that he found left in the parlour and Jamie would proudly point it out to me. I would nod, smile, and say (as I always did), "One day, Jamie – but we mustn't run..." and he would finish (as he always did), "before we can walk". With his appetite for adventure, we were now working our way through Doctor Parkinson's *Dangerous Sports*, which warned against all manner of reckless behaviour – Jamie was particularly taken with the engraving showing an unfortunate boy killing his sister while playing with a pistol. And he longed to read the story of Robinson Crusoe, having once seen a thrilling handbill for a stage production in London. But for now at least, Jamie still enjoyed the pleasures of childhood, and his real weakness was for sugary treats.

After each lesson Jamie would close the book we were reading and put it carefully into the pocket of his apron. Then he would look around the yard casually, trying not to let his eyes stray to me. Or, more accurately, to the left-hand pocket of my coat. For he knew that in there I kept a bag of whatever Mr Byford had been selling for a tempting price in his confectionery shop in Bene't Street. Jamie's favourites were barley sugar twists, with their simple flavour, but over the months I had brought him cinnamon tablets (he wrinkled his nose at the strong smell), ginger tablets (flapped his hand in front of his face as the heat reached his tongue), peppermint sticks (valued for their long life) and even Pontefract cakes (met with curiosity and then delight). Today's offering was new: lemon barley sugars.

I let Jamie think he was fooling me with his pretend indifference. Then I made as though to stand, patting my coat pockets as I did so.

"Ah, wait a minute," I said, and his eyes lit up. "I nearly forgot. Mr Byford thought you might like these."

I took the brown bag out of my pocket and untwisted it. I held it out to Jamie. He delicately put his hand in and took out a single sweet. He sniffed it and then put it into his mouth, tasting it carefully. His eyebrows lifted in surprise.

"Barley sugar," I confirmed, "but with lemon in it. A bit more sour, I think."

He nodded and continued sucking, moving the sweet from one cheek to the other.

"Good?" I asked. I popped one of the sweets into my own mouth, and indeed it was – very good. "Two more for later, and the rest for the next lesson," I said, as I always did.

And as he always did, Jamie took a spotlessly clean cloth from his back pocket, laid it across his hand, took two sweets from the bag, and carefully wrapped them up before putting them back into his pocket.

"I shall tell Mr Byford that you approve," I said. Jamie nodded enthusiastically. "Have you ever been to Mr Byford's shop?" I asked.

"Mother and me went once," he said.

"Mother and I," I corrected automatically.

"Mother and I," he repeated. "We saw through the window." He swept his arms to indicate a great view. "Shelves up to here." He reached as high as he could. "Jars and bottles. Wooden boxes too. There was a..." he flattened his hands to show a surface at the height of his waist. "Like in the parlour."

"A counter," I said. "Where Mr Byford serves his customers. But you didn't go in?"

Jamie shook his head. "Mother said not to, not with no money."

"Very sensible," I said.

"And it was too busy," he added. "Four of them in there. Boys, I said, but Mother said they was from the University. Black coats. But they was boys."

"Were," I said. "They were boys."

"Yes," agreed Jamie.

Boys from the University, I thought to myself: perhaps sizars. It was time for me to learn more about these child gownsmen.

Once Jamie had gone back to the kitchen, I checked that all was ready in the stables for the horses that would arrive later in the afternoon and then I walked across town to Bene't Street. Mr Byford's shop was in the middle of a row and, as Jamie had remembered, had a large window. Shelves in the window showed a selection of things to tempt passersby, including a pair of cakes with gaudy pink icing, tall glasses flanked by fruits (in the warmer months, Mrs Byford made cooling fruit ices) and several delicate bowls filled with sweets. There was plenty of interest in the window, and a regular trickle of customers went into the shop itself.

To appear less conspicuous – a very useful word, that, which I am glad to have learned – I let myself into the churchyard opposite the shop and busied myself looking at gravestones. All the while, I kept half an eye on the front of Byford's shop. I had only an hour to spare, and half of that had gone – and I was just reminding myself that of course a watched pot never boils – when I saw Nicholas Hodges hurry into Bene't Street from the direction of the market. He stopped outside Byford's shop and looked around; I quickly turned away. When I turned back, he had gone. But thankfully I could see through the window that he was in the confectioner's;

as I watched, Mr Byford handed him a paper bag like the one in my own pocket. Just as Hodges walked back into the street, his name was called and he turned to look. Another young lad in the same plain black gown was trotting towards him from Trumpington Street. A sizar from another college, I guessed; he'd be easy to describe to porters, with that shock of ginger hair barely contained by his cap. The two of them met, spoke for only a moment, and then walked back in the direction of the market. I slipped out of the churchyard and followed them.

Although some of the stallholders had packed up and left, the market was still busy. The sellers of fresh foods were keen to clear their stalls and were calling out their best prices, and this brought in customers who were happy to take what was left in order to save a few pennies. As the two sizars wove through the narrow gaps between the stalls and the shop-fronts, I was able to all but catch up with them. They emerged from the market and paused at Hobson's fountain, cupping their hands and taking a drink. I positioned myself on the other side of the fountain and did the same, thereby hiding my face. I could tell from the pitch of their conversation that they were having a disagreement.

"And I say it's too soon," said one.

"What's the benefit in waiting?" asked the other. "Every day that he goes about his business, enjoying himself, clicking his blasted fingers..."

"I know, I know," said the first. "It sticks in my craw too. But if we act too soon someone will begin to suspect."

"I don't care about that," spat his companion.

"You should," was the reply. "If they hang you, then what will become of your mother?"

The warning had obviously hit home. I stepped back from the fountain and could see Hodges, head down, walking quickly in the direction of St Clement's, while the lad he had met was walking back through the market, and broke into a run as the bell tolled the hour.

"What do they think I am, a valet?" grumbled George Chapman. By now, I was no longer surprised when I came home to find the porter of St Clement's sitting in my landlady's kitchen. He and Mrs Jacobs, although still not – at least in my hearing – using each other's Christian names, had struck up a friendship. Both widowed and childless, they were a good match, particularly as neither of them demanded much in the way of witty conversation.

They both looked across at the door as I came in. Chapman was sitting at the table, a newspaper in front of him, and Mrs Jacobs was at the stove.

"Ah, Mr Hardiman," she said. "Have you time to take an early supper with us before you go on duty?" She uncovered a pot and bent to look at its contents. "There is enough for three."

I shook my head. "I'll just have something cold," I said.

"There's a nice loaf," she said. "And in the pantry you'll find some cheese. From Mr Rutledge in Trumpington Street. On your recommendation, Mr Chapman." She nodded at the porter, who leaned back in his chair and hooked his thumbs into his belt.

"The cook at St Clement's won't buy his cheese from anywhere else," he said grandly. "And if it's good enough for Mr Vaughan, it's good enough for us."

I had my back to them, putting together my cold plate, but I noted his use of the word 'us'. I suspected that before too long I would be seeing Mr Chapman over breakfast as well as supper.

I sat at the table, balanced a piece of cheese on a corner of bread and took a bite. Landlady and porter watched me, and I nodded.

"Very good," I said, swallowing. "So who is treating you like a valet, Mr Chapman?"

He sat forward again and folded his arms. "You remember Mr Fleming, the undergraduate who..." he put a hand to his own throat.

"Of course," I nodded.

"After he died," continued the porter, "his bedmaker parcelled up his clothes and books and we sent them home to his family." I nodded. "His mother has written to the Master and said that something was missing – a black coat. Now," he leaned forward again, "you might think that the bedder could just have another look, find the coat and give it to me to send on. But no." He looked at Mrs Jacobs and she shook her head in sympathy. "The bedder – silly woman – has taken it into her head that there is something ghostly in that room," he fluttered his fingers in the air to suggest flying creatures, "and she refuses to go in. And all the other bedmakers have taken fright along with her. So guess who has to do it?"

"You, Mr Chapman, that's who," said Mrs Jacobs stoutly. "And you a porter. It's beneath your dignity, that's what it is."

"If you want, Mr Chapman," I said mildly, "I'll come to St Clement's tomorrow morning and I can have a look in Mr Fleming's room – see if I can't find that coat for you."

"There now," said Mrs Jacobs with a smile. "That's much more suitable. I'm sure a university constable is the one to be looking for things, not a college porter."

"That's an excellent notion, Mr Hardiman," said Chapman. "I am much obliged."

And I knew he was. He had once confessed to me, on a particularly foggy night when all sound was deadened and wraiths seemed to curl around every corner, that he had a great fear of ghosts, and I suspected that he shared the bedmakers' unease.

Chapter Twenty-One

COAT

The following morning I made sure that the stalls were all cleaned and the water buckets filled and then, as I had promised, I walked over to St Clement's. George Chapman was waiting for me and beckoned me into the lodge.

"'Tis good of you to do this, Mr Hardiman," he said.

You might think that I would tease the porter about his discomfort, but I was in no position to judge him. I have my own ghouls, as you know, which choose to visit me while I sleep. And no doubt Mr Chapman's fears were as real to him as my battlefield spectres are to me.

"Before we go up, Mr Chapman," I said, "could we have a word?"

The porter pulled out a spare stool for me, and we sat.

"Mr Chapman," I began, "do you remember the night you found Mr Fleming in his room?" I took out my notebook and turned to the relevant page.

"Not likely to forget, am I?" he replied. "I wish I could, but it comes into my dreams sometimes, seeing him hanging there." He shuddered.

"Indeed," I said. "But when I arrived, Mr Fleming was on the floor. And the Master said," I read from my notes, "the porter and a kitchen boy had cut him down. The porter, that was you?" I looked up at Chapman.

"That's right," he agreed.

"How did you come to be in Mr Fleming's room?" I asked.

"A message had come for him about his tutorial the next morning being a half-hour earlier than usual and I thought he would need to know, so I delivered it instead of putting it in his pigeonhole for him to collect," he said.

"And the kitchen boy?" I asked.

"When I went into Mr Fleming's room and found him, I knew I'd need help," said Chapman. "I leaned out of the window and saw Thomas – the kitchen boy – in the court, and shouted down to him to run and get a knife from the kitchen and bring it to me." I nodded at him to continue. "I stood by Mr Fleming and tried to take his weight, holding him on my shoulder. I thought that if I could take the pressure off his neck... Thomas arrived with the knife and stood on a chair to cut through the sheet but, well, it was too late."

"We know you did all you could, Mr Chapman," I said. "But can you remember: once you had Mr Fleming on the floor, what did you do?"

The porter paused, thinking. "I took the... noose from his neck – pulled it off quick. Then we sat him up, hoping it might help. But nothing. So we laid him down again and I sent Thomas back to the kitchen – he looked green and I didn't want that mess to clear up as well. Then I went to tell the Master and he sent me to find you."

"Do you recall seeing Mr Fleming's coat?" I asked.

The porter shook his head, then frowned. "Actually, yes. It was there, on the floor next to him, balled up. Before he left, Thomas put it under Mr Fleming's head. But it looked uncomfortable, so I got a cushion from the chair instead. I can't remember what I did with the coat – just pushed it to one side, I suppose. Funny how we think of these things, isn't it – Mr Fleming was beyond caring about cushions, I'm sure."

—ℓℓ—

We climbed the stone staircase to the first floor and the porter hesitated outside the door to Fleming's room.

"You can leave me here, Mr Chapman," I said. He gave a tight nod and walked off down the stairs. I turned the handle and walked in.

The room had been carefully cleaned, and I am certain that anyone who was unaware of what had happened there would have felt nothing unusual in it. The bed was made, the furniture was polished and straightened. I opened the wardrobe – a twin of the one in Joshua Pears's room – and it was empty. The desk had been cleared, the Argan lamp filled, and the cupboard beside the bed was bare. I stood in the middle of the room and looked about me, thinking. Recalling what the porter had said, I dropped to my knees and looked under the bed. And there, against the wall under the head of the bed, was something dark – it looked as though the bedder had swept under the bed and instead of catching whatever this was had simply pushed it further away with her broom. I lay flat on my stomach and reached as far as I could, and managed to catch hold of the item. I pulled it out. It was a dusty, crumpled black coat.

I sat back on my heels. With something of an effort and gripping the edge of the bed – my knees are not what they once were – I got to my feet. I shook the coat out: it was very grubby and would certainly need cleaning before we could return it to Mrs Fleming. I laid it on the bed, smoothing it out to check for any damage that might need repairing. And as I did so I realised that there was something in the right-hand pocket. I felt inside it and pulled out a folded piece of paper, obviously torn from a notebook. I opened it and turned it to the light. On it were written just four words: *In unum omnes contulerunt*. They now united their counsels, I thought to myself, and was pleased that I had remembered.

I went straight to the Master's rooms and thankfully found him alone, writing letters at his desk. "Encouraging the great and the good to send their sons to St Clement's," he explained, looking up at me with a tired smile. It fell from his face as he saw the expression on mine. I wordlessly handed him the note. He read it. "Dear God," he said, his shoulders slumping. "Another one. Where did you find it?"

"I went back to Mr Fleming's room," I explained. "I felt sure I had missed something. A coat was under his bed, pushed right back into the corner. And that was in the pocket."

"How did it get there?" asked the Master.

"The paper, or the coat?" I asked. "Hard to be certain. Obviously the killer put the note in the pocket, intending it to be found."

Vaughan sighed. "The killer," he said flatly. "As we feared: you think that Fleming was murdered?"

"What else can we think now?" I asked, gesturing to the note.

The Master was on his feet, striding around the room and frowning as he tried to make sense of this. "But the noose," he stopped, mimicking putting one around his own neck, "Fleming hanged himself."

"That is how it appeared, yes," I agreed, "but perhaps that is what we were meant to think. But then," I was thinking aloud, "why leave the note? Why bother to make it look like self-murder if you're going to leave a note saying that you killed him?"

The Master returned to his chair and sat down heavily into it. He stared out of the window above his desk.

"And why put the note in the pocket and then shove the coat under the bed," I continued. I took out my notebook. "Mr Vaughan," I said. "Mr Vaughan," I said again, when he did not answer.

He turned his head slowly to look at me. He was ashen. "Dear God," he said again. "What am I to tell Fleming's mother? That we have to dig up her son's body to have another look at it?"

"If we can find the killer," I said, "and he confesses, then there will be no need to examine the body."

"Is it the same killer?" asked Vaughan, a note of hope in his question. "The same as Pears?"

"It seems likely," I said, "with the note. But..." I hesitated.

"Yes?" prompted the Master.

"The two victims – Fleming and Pears," I said. "They must have had something in common, for the same person to want to kill them both. Can you think of anything?"

"Fleming and Pears," repeated Vaughan. "They came up at the same time. They were both due to graduate this July. But beyond that, I would not have thought they moved in the same circles." He shook his head. "Not at all, no. Fleming was a mathematician of some ability, serious about his work. God-fearing. While Pears," here the Master shrugged and gave a small smile, "was not. Mr Pears cared more about his outward appearance than either his brain or his soul. They would have known each other, of course, but I am certain they would not have liked each other."

***

After dinner that night I made an excuse to Mrs Jacobs – saying I had a sore head and wanted to rest my eyes – and went up to my room. The truth was that I wanted to think carefully about what

I had heard, and my landlady was incapable of sitting quietly. To keep my head clear, I even decided to forgo my evening dose of opium and hoped it would not affect my sleep.

Two undergraduates dead. One a clear murder – after all, no man takes himself to the privy and then stabs himself violently and repeatedly, and no knife was found with the body. The other seemingly a self-murder, but the discovery of the note in Fleming's coat pocket suggested otherwise. That the two deaths were linked was beyond doubt; the notes were the link. But the two victims – what had they in common, apart from being undergraduates at St Clement's? As the Master himself had said, they were cut from seemingly very different cloth: one a dedicated and able student, the other simply passing time until he could take up whatever position his family could find for him. It was hard to imagine that they were more than the barest of acquaintances, let alone that they both knew the same person well enough that he would want to kill them.

I reached for my notebook and turned to the jottings I had made when I had taken the first note to Geoffrey Giles. They all contributed to one. All what? All deaths? But surely two would not count as *all* – that would be they *both* contributed to one. Were there to be more deaths? Or did it refer to all killers? But in that case, the one to which they all contributed would be the death – and we already had two of those. It was most puzzling.

Chapter Twenty-Two

Acquaintance

The sizars' room was nothing like those occupied by the fellow commoners, and even scholars – with the college offering them financial help – had their own bedrooms. But at the top of the stone staircase, tucked under the roof, was the small room shared by two of the five sizars at St Clement's. In the middle of the room, where there was a simple table and two chairs, a man could stand upright. The ceiling quickly fell away to either side and two stump beds were pushed under the slopes. Against the far wall was a cupboard with a wash bowl and jug on it. I glanced all of this over the shoulder of Nicholas Hodges, who was standing in the doorway of the room with his hands on his hips. He was a good four inches shorter than I am, but he still managed to tilt his head so that he was looking down his nose at me.

"Yes?" he said in an unfriendly tone.

"Mr Hodges?" I asked. "Mr Nicholas Hodges?"

"And you are?" he replied.

"My name is Hardiman," I said, "and I am a constable of this University." I watched his face carefully but he did not seem alarmed. "As such, I am helping the Master to find out what he can to understand – to explain – the death of Joshua Pears. Mr Pears' mother, at least, surely deserves to know what happened to her son. And to start with, I am talking to every man living in college."

Hodges hesitated for a moment and then stood to one side. "You are welcome to come in, Mr Hardiman, but sadly I will be of no use to the Master or to Mrs Pears. I knew who her son was, of course, but we were not…"

I walked into the room and sat in one of the chairs, taking out my notebook and pencil.

"Not friends, Mr Hodges?" I asked.

He shut the door and sat down opposite me. "You know that I am a sizar," he said. I nodded. "And Pears was a fellow commoner. A man of means. Financial means rather than academic means, that is. I doubt he was even aware of my existence." He could not keep the bitterness from his voice, and I was reminded of how young he was. "I served him in hall. That was the extent of our acquaintance, Mr Hardiman."

I made a note. "And the other sizar who shares your room." I indicated the two beds with my pencil. "Did he know Mr Pears any better?"

"Will?" he laughed. "Will Mason is even poorer than I am. Even further beneath the notice of Pears and his kind." Suddenly serious, he leaned forward and grasped my arm. "You've no need to worry Will about this. He's… delicate. Easily alarmed. And, as I say, he did not know Pears either." He sat back again. "I am sorry for Mr Pears's mother and sister, of course, and I would help if I could, but there is really nothing I can tell you, Mr Hardiman." He smiled, but it was an empty smile.

The door to the room opened and Hodges jumped to his feet. "Will," he said unnaturally loudly. "This is Mr Hardiman, a university constable. Come to talk to us about Joshua Pears. I have told him what I can – that we never knew the poor man, except to serve him in hall. Isn't that right, Will?"

I stood and looked at Will Mason. He was taller than Hodges and thinner, with nervous hands that clutched each other, and his eyes darted from Hodges to me and back again. They were most unusual eyes: one was blue and the other green.

"Mr Mason," I said. "Is that right?"

He looked at Hodges again before answering. His voice cracked and he tried again. "It's as Nick says, sir," he confirmed. "Only in hall."

I closed my notebook and smiled at him. "Then I shall trouble you no more, Mr Mason," I said. I turned back to Hodges. "Thank you both."

It was only as I was reading my notes after dinner that evening that it occurred to me: if they were not acquainted, how did Hodges know that Pears had a sister?

Chapter Twenty-Three

Lionheart

"Hello again, Mr Mason," I said, stopping alongside the sizar as he looked into the window of Woollard's grocery shop on Trinity Street. "How fortuitous to run into you again." In fact I had followed him from St Clement's. "Mr Hardiman," I said. "Constable."

Mason looked uncomfortable. "I must..." he started, looking about him.

"I am pleased to have met you like this," I continued, "as I wanted to ask you a little more about Mr Pears."

"But Nick – Mr Hodges – told you," he said, looking down at his feet. "We know nothing about him."

"It is always a mistake, I think," I said gently, "to let another man speak on your behalf. After all, what it suits him to say might not suit you." I was quiet for a moment. "Shall we have a little talk, Mr Mason? I know somewhere we will not be seen."

I took his elbow and we walked a few doors down to Nicholson's. I ushered him in ahead of me. Geoffrey Giles was behind the counter, sorting through books and ticking them off in a ledger.

"Mr Giles," I said, "could we possibly borrow your back room for a few minutes?"

Giles looked up and smiled. "Of course, Mr Hardiman," he said, "as long as your young guest does not mind a certain degree of homely chaos."

Mason smiled shyly at the bookseller and shook his head. I led him through the shop and pulled aside the heavy curtain concealing the door to the parlour. As Giles had warned, the room was far from tidy, with piles of books on every surface and covering most of the floor. Thankfully the two sagging old armchairs were used by the shop staff during their breaks and so did not have time to acquire their own burdens of books. I sat in one and Mason took the other.

"Now then, Mr Mason," I said, taking out my notebook and opening it. "Mr Hodges told me," I read from my notes, "that Mr Pears was a man of means who was unaware of his – Mr Hodges's – existence. Mr Hodges served him in hall, nothing more. And the same goes for you. He was quite sure that you did not know Mr Pears except by sight, from serving him in hall." I looked up at Mason. "Is that right, Will?"

Mason looked miserable. He stared down at his hands in his lap, and nodded.

"Tell me, Will," I said, "what do you think of Nick Hodges?"

His head jerked up and he blinked. "Think of Nick?" he asked.

"It's a simple question," I said. "You have shared a room with him for, what, eight months now. I'm sure you look out for each other. Keeping each other out of trouble – that's what friends do, isn't it?"

To my surprise, Mason burst into tears. Not great sobs, to be sure, but a closed-face sort of crying, wiping angrily at his cheeks with the back of his hands.

I leaned forward and put a hand on his knee – he was skin and bone under his worn black trousers, which I had noticed were a couple of inches too short for him. "Don't upset yourself, lad," I said. "Have you a handkerchief?" He shook his head and I reached into my own pocket and handed him mine. He took it and balled it into his eyes before blowing his nose. "That's better," I said. "Now, what do you want to tell me?"

"It's Nick," he said. I nodded. "He has these... wild ideas," continued Mason. "Things he reads and ideas that stick in his head." He tapped his own forehead with his finger. "They stick in there, and then it's all he can talk about. It can be a bit frightening."

"What sort of ideas?" I asked. But I had jumped too soon – Mason went quiet. "Sometimes," I started again, "people can be carried along with someone else's ideas because they want to please that person. They don't want to lose them as a friend. Like," I cast around in my memory, "like Richard the Lionheart."

Mason tilted his head to one side. "Richard the Lionheart?" he repeated.

I shrugged. "Well, I'm sure that not all the barons wanted to go off on crusade for years," I said, "leaving their families and homes behind. But they wanted to stay friends with the King and to please him, and so they did as he suggested and headed off to the Holy Land. Some of them might have thought it was a bad idea, risking their lives like that, especially after the earlier crusades."

"I don't think I would have gone," said Mason.

"But if Nick Hodges asked you to, would you?" I asked.

Mason was silent for a long minute. "D'you know about his brother?" he asked suddenly. "Nick's older brother?"

I nodded. "Samuel, wasn't it? I was told that he was a sizar at St Clement's first, but that he killed himself and his place was offered to Nick."

"But do you know why he killed himself?" asked Mason urgently. I shook my head. "Because they made his life a misery. They teased him for being poor and tormented him with foolish demands and orders and never gave him a moment's peace. He was shy, Nick said, and quiet. But they wouldn't leave him be."

"Who is 'they', Will?" I asked gently. But he clamped his lips shut and shook his head. "If you tell me, Will, perhaps I can help."

He shook his head again. "I shouldn't have spoken to you. Nick will be angry if he finds out – you mustn't tell him." He stood up and looked around as though hunting for the way out. "If you tell him, he'll make me leave the Liberators." He tugged open the door, pulled the curtain aside and ran from the shop. I followed him out of the parlour.

Giles winced as the shop door slammed shut behind Mason and then turned to look at me.

"What on earth did you say to him, Mr Hardiman?" he asked with amusement. "It was as though he had the Devil on his heels."

I threw up my hands. "I have no idea," I said. "He's a nice lad, but caught up in something, I think. Troubled."

"They're young, sizars," said the bookseller. "Clever, of course, and hard-working, but still very young."

"How did you..." I started. "Ah, the gown."

Giles nodded. "When you've been here a bit longer, you'll be able to recognise them all. The gowns, the hoods, the trims – all slightly different. It's like a Cambridge code." He smiled. "Are you on duty this evening?"

"I am, yes," I said. "I try to take other evenings apart from Wednesday, so that I can attend the book club. Will you be there this week?"

"I plan to be, yes," he replied.

"Until then," I said. Just as I was pulling open the shop door I remembered something. "Does the word Liberators mean anything to you, Mr Giles?" I asked.

The bookseller frowned as he thought. "Liberators?" I nodded. "You know, it does sound familiar, but I just cannot recall. Leave it with me."

Chapter Twenty-Four
PILEUS

I patted my pocket and pulled out the note that had been delivered to me at the Hoop that morning, and re-read it. *Dear Mr Hardiman*, it said, *I have tracked down a reference to the Liberators. I do not wish to commit more to paper, but if you are indeed attending our book club this evening, I will explain everything. With best regards, Geoffrey Giles.*

I made sure to arrive early at the Black Bull, as I wanted to catch Mr Giles on his way in. I knew I would not be able to concentrate on the business of the meeting until I had spoken to him. And evidently he felt the same, as it was still twenty minutes to the hour when I spied him walking towards me from the direction of his shop.

"Mr Hardiman," he said happily, holding out his hand for me to shake. "We were of the same mind. Shall we treat ourselves to a little refreshment before we go upstairs?"

I held open the door of the inn and we went into the parlour. A few tables were busy but I pointed to a small one flanked by two armchairs and we walked quickly over to it before it was nabbed by anyone else. The pot boy, obviously eagle-eyed and thinking of his tip, was there almost before we were.

"Madeira for me, please," said the bookseller. It was not my usual tipple but with a long evening ahead of me it would be unwise to have a bigger drink. I indicated that I would have the same. The two small glasses arrived and we raised them to each other.

"Well, this is most welcome," said Giles, licking his lips. "I am playing truant, you know." He smiled mischievously. "On most Wednesdays I close the shop and then race home to prepare dinner for my father and get him into bed before coming here. But today," he took another grateful sip of his wine, "today Mrs Phipps next door said that she would take a plate round for him and then send in her husband to help him up the stairs and into bed. It's very kind of them." Knowing the bookseller as I did, I felt sure that the kindness was more than warranted. And indeed, he continued. "I wrote a recommendation for their boy, when he wanted a position at the University press. He's no genius, but he knows his letters and he's a hard worker by all accounts." He looked around him and then seemed to remember something. "But you're not here to listen to me rabbiting on about my domestic arrangements, Mr Hardiman." He leaned forward. "You asked about the Liberators, after that young sizar bolted from the shop."

"I did, yes," I said, nodding.

"Far be it from me, Mr Hardiman, to enquire into your work – your work as a constable, I mean," said the bookseller, "but suffice it to say that I think you may be looking in the right direction."

I reached into my pocket and took out my notebook and pencil.

"The note you brought me a little time ago," continued Giles. "The one with the stains on it." He dropped his voice on the word 'stains'. "I told you that it was likely a quotation from Suetonius, from his *Caesars*." I nodded. "Well, the Liberators were the assassins of Julius Caesar – that is the name they gave themselves, and it has stuck. Brutus — one of the main assassins, as you know — even had coins minted showing his head on one side and two daggers on the other, along with a cap called a *pileus* that was worn by freed slaves. The implication was that Brutus and the others had liberated the Roman citizens from a form of slavery under Julius Caesar."

I looked up from scribbling in my notebook. "*Pileus*?" I asked.

"P I L E U S," said the bookseller. "Close-fitting, no brim, made of felt. Like the top of a mushroom — now also called the pileus for that reason." He smiled with satisfaction — I knew he loved words as I did.

"So anyone studying the *Lives of Caesar* would know about the Liberators?" I asked.

"I am not certain that it is in the original Suetonius," said Giles, draining the last drop from his glass, "but yes, anyone reading about the assassination of Caesar would certainly stumble upon it. And now we must leave Ancient Rome and turn our attention to the future, Mr Hardiman. I believe that this evening's lecture concerns electromagnetism."

Chapter Twenty-Five
Robbery

The knocking at the front door was loud enough for me to hear it from my room on the top floor, which was fortunate as I was alone in the house. Mrs Jacobs and my fellow lodger Mr Carey had gone to church, and with no coaches calling at the Hoop on a Sunday, I was just thinking about stretching my legs with an outing to Chesterton. I put on my coat and walked quickly down the stairs, calling, "Coming, coming," as I went. The knocking stopped. I pulled open the door and there, one hand against the wall to steady herself, was Agnes Grantham.

"Thank goodness you're here, Mr Hardiman," she said. She stood upright and put her hand to the small of her back.

"You'd better come in," I said, standing to one side, "unless you're worried about..." I gestured into the street to indicate the other houses.

"If some old maid is sitting behind her curtains looking for something to gossip about," she said, "she's too late." She indicated her belly. "I can barely fit through the door as it is."

"Not quite, "I said, pointing at the kitchen and shutting the front door behind her, "but when I went to Newmarket with Charlie, he told me you were expecting your first."

Agnes walked into the kitchen and looked around her. Approvingly, I thought. I indicated one of the chairs and she sat heavily into it.

"Well, Mrs Grantham," I started.

"Please just call me Agnes," she said. "It's bad enough being the size of a cow, without feeling as old as the hills. Mrs Grantham is my mother-in-law."

"Agnes, then," I said. "I can't imagine that you have urgent need of an ostler, so have you come to see me as a constable?"

She put her hand to her mouth and chewed the corner of a nail. "More of a friend," she decided. "A useful and sensible friend." She paused for a moment. "There's been a robbery – at Barker and Eaden's yard, where Charlie works."

"Ah well, a robbery at a town premises – that's something for the town constables, not a university constable," I said.

"I know that, Mr Hardiman," she said, shifting in her seat. "And in the usual run of things, that's what would happen. But Mr Barker, he's blaming Charlie – says he didn't lock the office door when he left yesterday. Says he's going to let him go without a recommendation. After four years – no recommendation. And with this one on the way." She put a hand on her belly. "And you know Charlie, Mr Hardiman – he's careful. He says he did lock the office."

I put up a hand to stop her. "The office, you said?" She nodded. "That's where the robbery was – the office, not the warehouse?" She nodded again. "So the thief was after the takings, not the stock."

Agnes leaned forward and tapped her finger on the table. "That's the strange thing, Mr Hardiman. There was no takings in the office. And everyone knows that. Saturday morning, regular, Mr Barker takes the week's money to the bank to pay it in."

"So if there was no money on the premises, and if the warehouse wasn't touched," I said, "what did the thief want?"

"Charlie said that the only thing missing is the latest book of orders. But why would anyone want that? If anyone wants to know who Barker and Eaden's customers are, they have only to follow the cart around town." She reached across and put her hand on my wrist for a moment. "I was hoping you could go and see Mr Barker. Talk to him. Ask him not to let Charlie go without a recommendation." She pushed herself to her feet. "I know Charlie wants to move on anyway, but with no recommendation – Cambridge is a small town, Mr Hardiman."

"I make no promises, Agnes," I said, standing as well. "I don't know Mr Barker, and he might not appreciate me sticking my nose in. But if you tell Charlie to come and see me this afternoon at the Hoop – three o'clock – I'll have a word with him and decide what's best." I walked with her to the front door. "I'm surprised he sent you this morning, instead of coming to see me himself."

Agnes flashed me a quick smile as she turned sideways to go carefully down the three steps to the street. "He doesn't know I'm here, Mr Hardiman. But if I left it to him, he'd just mull on it for days and then it would be too late. I'll just tell him that you've heard about the robbery from someone else and want to hear his side of it."

Not for the first time, I wondered how many men thought they were making their own decisions, blissfully unaware of the strings being pulled by the women in their lives.

At three o'clock that afternoon I cast a last look around the empty stalls at the Hoop; now and then a guest would arrive on a Sunday evening, but it was unusual. Nonetheless, I liked to have everything ready just in case, and I knew that Monday would bring at least eight horses from the two regular coaches. I went out into the yard and waited, turning my face to the sun and closing my eyes. As purple shapes danced behind my eyelids, my mind drifted to Talavera and the white, shining heat I had felt there. A few moments later I heard trotting footsteps. I opened one eye to see Charlie Grantham in his Sunday best trousers and shirt with a faded work coat thrown over the top.

"Shall we go into the parlour, Charlie?" I asked. "I am sure the cook can prepare us a pot of coffee. Or maybe a small tankard of something?"

Charlie smiled cheekily. "I won't tell Agnes if you don't."

"I doubt there is much you can hide from that clever wife of yours," I said. Charlie looked at me sharply but said nothing.

Once we had settled in the parlour, a tankard in front of each of us, I smiled encouragingly at Charlie. "I saw Agnes this morning," I said.

Charlie nodded. "She mentioned she'd seen you in town," he said. "She told you about the robbery, then."

"She did, and about Mr Barker's reaction to it," I replied.

He leaned forward and put his hands around his tankard, gazing into it as though looking for an answer. "I can't make sense of it," he said. "Why break into the office when there is no cash there? Everyone in town knows that the clerk takes it to the bank on Saturday morning – has done for years, decades p'raps."

"Agnes said they took an account book," I said.

"That's right: just the one. They made a mess of the place – pulling stuff out of drawers, overturning furniture, even broke a window."

"A window in the door?" I asked.

Charlie took a drink then shook his head. "I wish they had," he said. "But there was no damage to the door. That's why Mr Barker blames me: I was the last to leave yesterday and he said I didn't lock up properly, but I did, I know I did. I even made a joke of it to Mr Powell." He looked miserable.

"Mr Powell?" I asked.

"The clerk at Barker and Eaden's – in the office," he said. "He needed to go to some appointment or other yesterday afternoon, and he asked me to lock up for him and take the key to his lodgings. I was pleased to be asked, you know. Thought it showed they trusted me."

"And did you return the key to Mr Powell as arranged?" I asked.

"I did," replied Charlie. "To his lodgings in Northampton Street. He asked whether I had checked that the door was locked, and I said that it was safer than the county gaol." He leaned forward and looked at me earnestly. "I know I locked that door, Mr Hardiman. I turned the handle to check. It was locked." He took a drink. "You know I've been looking for a new position anyway, but I can't go without a recommendation. Cambridge is a small town." It was exactly what Agnes had said.

"And that's why it won't matter so much," I said. "Plenty of people know you, and even without a recommendation they'll know you're a good man."

Charlie smiled at me, but it was watery.

"So after making all this mess, the thief took just one thing: an account book," I said.

"The most recent one," added Charlie. "That's why Mr Barker is so upset, I reckon."

"Why's that?" I asked.

"It's the one with the unpaid accounts in it," said Charlie with a sad laugh. "You remember I told you about Mr Barker offering tick to all and sundry." I nodded. "Well, it's all in that book – who owes him what. Dates, amounts – everything. And without it, he says..."

"He can't collect anything," I finished.

Chapter Twenty-Six
CLERK

I had a disturbed night. First I was going over the robbery in my mind, trying to make sense of it. And when I did finally fall asleep, one of my regular nightmares came to visit. The one with the wounded Frenchie and the dying horse. I was relieved to escape the house and walk in the cool morning to town.

Almost every stall was already occupied when I arrived at the market just as the bell of Great St Mary's struck a quarter to the hour. As I waited outside Barker and Eaden's premises on the corner of St Mary's Street and Market Hill, the air was filled with the noise and smell of clucking chickens in the poultry market. A woman with sunburned cheeks and sleeves pushed up to reveal strong, brown arms held a bird out to me by its legs, expertly twisting her wrist to evade its sharp beak. I shook my head and she turned back to her stall, shoving the chicken into a wooden crate.

A young man came around the corner, stepping carefully to avoid the mucky water and heaven knows what else on the cobbles of the market place. He nodded at me, his eyes darting quickly to and then away from my scar, as he walked round me to the door of the Barker and Eaden's office and took a key from his pocket. He unlocked the door and pushed it open, but as he went to close it behind him, I put out my hand and stopped it. He looked at me, a slight frown on his face.

"May I help you?" he asked, sounding unhelpful. "The office will open at eight o'clock sharp, if you have business with Barker and Eaden's." He tried to close the door again.

"I think you would prefer to hear what I have to say before any customers arrive," I said. "About the robbery. My name is Constable Hardiman." Yes, I know what you are thinking: he would assume I was a town constable. But I was not lying, and if he had asked what sort of constable I was, I would have told him.

Alarm crossed the man's face, but he tried to hide it and stood to one side to let me into the office. He indicated a chair against the wall but I shook my head. He took off his hat and put it on the stand, then walked over to the window to raise the blind. Everything had been tidied in the office, and even the broken window had been mended. I pointed at it.

"I see you have had the glazier in," I observed.

"One cannot appear in disarray to one's customers," he said. "We have some very superior people calling into this office."

"And some very rough ones," I said. "Thieves, for instance."

"Most unfortunate," agreed the man. He took up his position behind the counter. "And now, Constable Hardiman, we have five minutes until I have to open the office. I don't see what else I can tell you, as I spoke to your colleagues when they called at my lodgings on Saturday evening."

I took my notebook from my coat pocket. "If you could give me your name, sir, just to be certain that I am speaking to the right man." I looked at him with a smile.

"Mr Thomas Powell," he said.

I wrote it down and then turned back a page and pretended to read from it. "Is it right, Mr Powell," I asked, "that you have a porter called Charles Grantham in your employ here at Barker and Eaden?"

"We do, yes," he replied.

"Well, at least he told the truth about that," I said, smiling to myself as I made a tick mark in my notebook. "You will forgive me, Mr Powell. It's just that I spoke to this Mr Grantham, and he claims that he was given the key to this office on Saturday afternoon, with instructions to close up and lock the door at four o'clock."

"That's right," said the clerk a little impatiently. "I gave him the key myself."

"You, Mr Powell?" I asked. He nodded. "Is that usual practice, Mr Powell, for a warehouse porter to be left in charge of locking the office?"

"Mr Grantham," he replied smoothly, "is a long-standing and trusted employee of this business. I myself had an appointment for which I could not be late, and so I asked Mr Grantham if he could take charge of the key for me."

"And Mr Barker and Mr Eaden," I asked, "were they happy with this arrangement?"

"As I explained to your colleagues," said Powell, looking pointedly at the clock on the wall, "Mr Barker and Mr Eaden were both in London on Saturday, meeting a supplier and staying away overnight."

"Convenient," I said quietly. The clerk looked at me sharply. "Convenient," I repeated, "that you should have," I checked my notes, "a long-standing and trusted employee like Mr Grantham." I made my face as bland and open as I could.

"Indeed," said Powell, "which made it all the more disappointing when he let us down."

"Ah yes," I said, consulting the blank page of my notebook again. "He failed to lock the door, and that is how the thief or thieves entered the office."

The church clock struck the hour. "Indeed. And now, constable, I am afraid I will have to ask you to leave. I have my work to attend to."

"Of course," I said, standing. "Just to be clear, Mr Powell. Mr Grantham told us that after he had locked the office, he returned the key to you at your lodgings. Did he say anything to you then, about having checked that the door was locked?"

The door to the office opened and we both turned to see a grey-haired man in dark clothes and an academic gown.

"Ah, Bursar," said Powell in what I had once read described perfectly as honeyed tones. "We have your order, I believe." He looked at me and I smiled genially but made no move to leave. After a moment he answered. "Not that I recall, no."

"Thank you, sir," I said, and I left Barker and Eaden, closing the door quietly behind me.

Chapter Twenty-Seven
RESPONSIBILITY

"Thank you, Joe," I said, handing over two shillings. I had grown fond of the lad and whenever possible I used him to run my messages. This one had taken him most of the afternoon, as I had told him to wait outside St Clement's until Will Mason appeared and then bring him to the Hoop. I had written a short note for the sizar, to persuade him to come: *Mr Mason, please attend me at your earliest convenience on a matter of urgency and delicacy. Yours, G Hardiman, University Constable.*

Joe's eyes shone as looked up at me. "Two twelvers!" he said. He jerked his head towards Mason. "D'you need me to take him back again?" he asked.

"No, thank you, Joe," I said. "Mr Mason will make his own way home once we have spoken."

Joe gave the sizar a long look and then tucked the two coins down the front of his waistcoat and scampered out of the yard.

"Mr Mason," I said. "There is a pot of coffee and a plate of excellent fruit loaf waiting for us upstairs. Shall we?" I find that few young men can resist the offer of cake. I led him through the stables and up the ladder to the loft. When we had moved from the Sun to the Hoop, William Bird had donated two armchairs to the ostry, and these were a sight more comfortable than the old upright chairs I had used before. To go with them I had a small table, and as requested Poor Jamie had brought up a pot of coffee from the kitchen and wrapped a cloth around it to keep it warm. Alongside it was a plate covered with another cloth.

"Sit, sit, Mr Mason," I said, taking my own seat and leaning forward to pour two cups of coffee. I lifted the cloth on the plate and offered the fruit loaf to the sizar. He took the largest slice and bit into it hungrily.

I opened my notebook. "On the 12th of June you told me about the Liberators," I said.

Mason's eyes widened. He swallowed quickly. "No, no," he shook his head. "I told you nothing."

"You said that if Mr Hodges found out that you had spoken to me, he would make you leave the Liberators." Mason looked as though he might cry. "I have said nothing to Mr Hodges," I said, "but I have been making my own enquiries into what the Liberators might be. It's interesting, isn't it, how history can repeat itself."

"It's just a name," said Mason.

"Ah, but that's not the whole story, is it?" I said. I reached for a slice of fruit loaf and pushed the plate towards Mason. He took another piece. My mother used to say that feeding growing boys was like shovelling coal into a cellar – no matter how much you put in there, it was never full. "I'm not an educated man, as you can see," I said, waving my arm to indicate our surroundings. "I grew up on a farm in Norfolk. The local vicar taught me to read, and I'm still learning." I reached into my coat pocket and took out my vocabulary book. "Whenever I hear a new word, I write it in here. See." I opened the book and showed it to him. "Elephantine – that was in a newspaper last week. Like an elephant." I put the book on the table. "Mr Giles at Nicholson's is a friend and he helps me as well. I often take him things I don't understand. So when you said something about Liberators, I had never heard of them, and I asked Mr Giles." I waited.

"My father was a rector," said Mason eventually. "He taught me to read. From the Bible and the newspaper – turn and turn about. God and mammon, he called it." He smiled at me then, but sadly. "He died when I was twelve. My mother started looking for an apprenticeship for me, but the Archdeacon said that with my brains I should aim higher. And he knew about sizarships, and here I am." He shrugged.

"I am sure it would please your father to see you keeping up with your studies," I said. "But he might worry about you going around with a group calling themselves the Liberators. Mr Giles told me that they were the men who conspired to kill Caesar. If they all stabbed him at once, they reasoned, no single one of them would be the murderer."

By now, Mason was looking thoroughly miserable. I sipped my coffee and waited.

"Nick was kind to me," he said quietly. "When I arrived. He had been told by his brother how it all worked. Where to sit, who to avoid, how to address certain people." He looked at me with wide eyes. "There was a lot to learn."

"I can understand that," I agreed. "I still feel like a stranger here myself sometimes."

"So when he asked for my help, I didn't like to refuse," continued the sizar. "He said he just wanted to scare them. Scare them like his brother had been scared."

"Samuel must have been very scared," I said. Mason nodded. "The porter at St Clement's told me that he killed himself," I continued, "but no-one knew why."

"Nick knew," said Mason. "It was because of them – how they treated him. Worse than a dog, Nick said. Ordering him about, tripping him up, going into his room and taking his things. Making him polish their boots."

"Why?" I asked.

Mason shrugged again. "Because they could, I suppose. Nick thought they were jealous of Samuel – of his cleverness."

"So they made his life a misery, and Mr Hodges thought he'd do the same for them," I suggested.

Mason nodded. "We'd hide their gowns so that the constables would catch them improperly dressed, and spill ink on their papers, and piss in the water jugs before putting them out in the dining hall." I thought back to my visit, and Mason caught my eye. "Not on High Table, sir."

"I'm grateful," I said.

He flashed me a quick smile before turning serious again. "I'd do some of it and he'd do some, and there are two other sizars from other colleges, and they did some as well."

"Does one of those other sizars have bright red hair?" I asked.

"That's John Coleman," said Mason. "From St Peter's College. You can imagine the ragging he gets for that hair. Once three Petreans held him down and tried to set fire to it, to see if it could burn any brighter – he was terrified. So Nick suggested he join us, like the Liberators in Rome, just as you said: if we all did some, we shared the responsibility." He paused and looked miserable. "But soon it wasn't enough for Nick," he said. "And when he told me what he wanted to do next, I said no. I couldn't do that, I said."

"Kill someone, you mean?" I asked, thinking to lance the boil. Mason looked down at his hands folded in his lap and nodded. "But Nick could do it, could he?" I asked. A few moments, and then another nod. "Nicholas Hodges killed Joshua Pears in the privy at St Clement's. He stabbed him with a knife." A few more moments, and then a smaller nod.

"Why didn't you go to the Master? Or to the Proctors?" I asked.

"Nick said that he would tell them I was involved – in all of it," he said. "And he said that I could still do my part as a Liberator if I just kept my mouth shut. So I did." He looked up at me and he was crying. "I know it was wrong, I do. I wanted to tell someone, but then there was Harford and Nick said that was an end of it."

"Mr Harford at Sidney Sussex?" I asked.

"Yes," said Mason. "He and Pears were friends, and when Pears invited him to St Clement's, Harford was... well, he was just as nasty as Pears, so Nick said he was fair game. Nick walloped him to show him he was serious, and Harford took fright – he hasn't been back to St Clement's since. So I said to Nick, well, that's that then: with Pears dead and Harford warned off, then the rest of them will think twice. And he agreed." He looked at me pleadingly. "He agreed, Mr Hardiman."

"That's as may be, Mr Mason," I said gently, "but Mr Hodges has killed two men. We cannot just let that pass."

The sizar looked surprised. "Two men?" he repeated. "No, Mr Harford was hurt, but nothing more. Just the eye." He indicated his own face, then blushed.

"I am well aware of my appearance," I said. "No need for embarrassment. But I did not mean Mr Harford – I'm talking about Edward Fleming."

"The one who hanged himself?" asked Mason with genuine surprise. I nodded. "But that wasn't Nick. It can't have been. He would never do that, not hang a man, after the way Samuel..." His voice trailed off.

"Are you sure?" I asked. "There are other details that suggest that both men were killed by the same person – or people."

"As sure as I can be," said Mason. "Nick has nightmares about people hanging, about nooses and all that – I hear him shouting and then crying. I really don't think he could..." He shook his head and then looked up at me. "And how would he manage it? Nick is small like me – fast, and strong, but small. And wasn't Mr Fleming a tall man? How would Nick get him up there?" He pointed at the rafter above our heads.

And he was right. Even if Fleming had already been dead or dying, how could Hodges alone have manhandled him into the noose?

Chapter Twenty-Eight

Accomplice

When Geoffrey Giles had first suggested I join the Bull Book Club, and indeed had generously used his influence to support my admission, I had not known how valuable a part of my life it would become. The library was a treasure trove, that's true, and the lectures were often most interesting (and sometimes not). But with its determination to attract thinking men who liked to hear different opinions, it brought together – and you must forgive me – the most useful people. For instance, on this evening I knew that, unless he was ill, I would find Mr Henry Eaden at our meeting. Still a young man, making his way in the wine trade in Cambridge, he had also seen the benefit of making influential friends – and was sharp enough to steer clear of the Rutland Club at the Eagle Inn. Not that there's anything wrong with that club, I should say – simply that it is a Tory stronghold, and no wine merchant can afford to upset all the Whiggish wine drinkers.

As luck would have it, the evening's lecture helped my cause. The topic was the latest edition of Mr Capper's topographical dictionary of the United Kingdom that had been published the previous year, and the club had just acquired a copy for the library. And after the lecture we were invited to view some of the maps, which meant that members stayed to chat rather than disappearing off into the night. After explaining my plan to Mr Giles, I waited by the door until I saw the wine merchant coming towards me.

"Mr Eaden," I said, holding out my hand. "My name is Gregory Hardiman."

"The university constable," he said, shaking my hand.

"One of them," I admitted.

"No need to look worried," he said, smiling. "I have a good memory for names and details – important for a salesman, I think."

"And a constable," I agreed.

"I assume you wish to ask me something, Mr Hardiman," he said, "but perhaps we could talk outside – it's a warm evening and I find the room a bit close." He held out his arm to steer me. "After you."

Once we were standing in the street outside the inn, Eaden took a deep breath and rolled his shoulders back. "Ah," he said, "that's better. Now you have my full attention." And he turned to look straight at me, ignoring a call of farewell from a couple of other members heading away up Trumpington Street.

"It is about the robbery at your office on Saturday last," I said.

The wine merchant looked puzzled. "But surely that is a matter for the town constables, not the University," he said.

"It is, yes," I said. "But I have been asked to look into it by a friend. Agnes Grantham."

"Grantham?" repeated Eaden. "Charlie's mother?"

"Wife," I said. "When he told her what had happened and that he is to be dismissed without a recommendation, she came to me. We both used to work at the Sun. She is expecting their first child."

He folded his arms. "I am sorry for her, of course, but if we tolerate the sort of carelessness..." He stopped as I held up my hands.

"I am sorry to interrupt you, sir," I said, "but I think that perhaps there is another explanation." I waited and he gave one quick nod.

"Charlie says that he did lock the office, and that he returned the key to Mr Powell, your clerk."

"Yes," said Eaden. "But everyone agrees that whoever was in the office and stole the accounts book had a key – there was no damage to the door or the lock. So Charlie must have left it unlocked."

"Not necessarily," I said. "I have spoken to both Charlie and Mr Powell. And they both confirm that the key was returned to Mr Powell at his lodgings at about six o'clock on Saturday. And although returning the key does not prove that it was used to lock the door, Charlie distinctly remembers Mr Powell asking him whether he had indeed locked the door. And Charlie made a joke of it, saying that the office was locked up tighter than the county gaol." I could see that Eaden was thinking about what I was saying. "Charlie's a good man, Mr Eaden," I continued. "He takes his responsibilities seriously."

Eaden nodded. "He always has done, yes," he agreed. "But might he have had an accomplice – someone who persuaded him to leave the door unlocked for them?"

"Possibly, yes," I allowed. "But it makes no sense. If someone wanted the office left open so that they could steal from it, why would they take only a ledger? Why not something valuable – the keys to the warehouse, for instance, so that they could steal all your stock? And if Charlie was the accomplice, why go to all that trouble – why not just ask him to take the ledger for them?"

"That's very true," said Eaden. "The question we should be asking, I suppose, is who would want to steal the ledger?"

"Precisely," I said. "And I have an idea – but you might not like it much. Would you be free to meet me at your office early tomorrow morning, sir? At eight o'clock?"

Chapter Twenty-Nine

Ashes

The next morning I went to the Hoop earlier than usual to give myself time to see to the horses and the stables before meeting Mr Eaden. When I heard the church bell tolling a quarter to the hour, I washed my hands, put on my coat and walked into town. At five minutes to the hour, I was waiting outside the door of Barker and Eaden. And at one minute to the hour, Mr Eaden appeared, raising his hand in greeting as he walked towards me across the market. He unlocked the door and ushered me in.

"I won't open the blinds," he said, "in case it entices an early customer. Now, Constable Hardiman, how can I help you? You promised me an unpleasant idea."

"How long has Thomas Powell worked for you?" I asked.

"Powell?" repeated Eaden. "Oh, a year I should say — perhaps a little longer."

"And is he a good employee?" I asked.

"I think so, yes," said Eaden. "That said, I do not have much to do with him. I deal with suppliers, and simply leave my orders in that tray." He indicated a wooden tray at the end of the counter. "I rarely speak to Powell — he makes sure that the orders are paid for promptly."

"And the other side of the business – the customers?" I asked, making notes as I went.

"That is Mr Barker's domain," he replied. "He has a good touch with people – they like him."

"We both know that there was that unfortunate business last year," I said, "with colleges being over-charged for their orders. Was that down to Mr Barker?"

Eaden flushed a little. "That was down to our inexperience, I am afraid," he said. "It was a mortifying lesson but one that we have learned. And learned well: we are scrupulous about our charging now. Indeed, we took on Powell to make sure of it. Surely you do not suspect him."

"If I can be completely candid with you, Mr Eaden," I said, and he nodded. "My reasoning is that the ledger was stolen because it has information in it that someone wants to hide. The only people who know precisely what is in that ledger are you, Mr Barker and Mr Powell. If you are confident that Mr Barker is now on the straight and narrow…"

Eaden interrupted me. "I would stake my life on it," he said.

"And if we assume that you are as baffled by the disappearance of the ledger as I am…"

Eaden nodded vigorously. "Of course."

"Then," I said, "I am afraid we have to consider Mr Powell. And I would suggest that we need to visit him at home."

Eaden glanced at the clock on the wall. "If we leave now, we can probably catch him before he sets off for work," he said.

A quarter of an hour later, after a brisk walk through town, across the Great Bridge and into Northampton Street, we were standing outside Mr Powell's lodgings. It was a large house that had seen better days, with flaking paint and rotting woodwork. There were three storeys with irregular windows and a lopsided dormer under a bowing roof of small tiles. I knocked on the door and a small scowling girl opened it.

"We are here to see Mr Powell," I said.

She pulled the door open wider and pointed up the stairs. "Up there," she said. "Next floor. Number three."

I went up the stairs first with Eaden following me. When I glanced down the little girl was watching us, arms crossed. Catching my eye, she disappeared into the parlour and shut the door with a bang behind her.

There were four closed doors leading off the landing. I knocked on the one with a number three drawn on it in chalk. It was opened almost immediately by Thomas Powell with an irritated look on his face.

"I have told you, Mrs Palmer," he was saying, but stopped when he saw me and, over my shoulder, Henry Eaden. He recovered quickly. "My apologies," he said in a friendlier tone. "I thought it was my landlady enquiring about the rent. But why are you... I mean, is there a problem at the office, Mr Eaden? I was just on my way." He reached up to the hook by the door and took down his coat.

"If we could have a word before you leave," I said.

Powell hesitated, then replaced his coat on the hook and stood to one side.

"You will forgive my accommodation, gentlemen," he said. "I live a bachelor life, and I was not anticipating guests."

The room was tidy enough but sparsely furnished and lacking homely touches. There was a single bed, the covers pulled up, and a small table under the window that served as a desk, to judge by the papers and books piled on it. By the fireplace was a low armchair. "I am afraid I cannot offer you any refreshment, Mr Eaden," he said.

Eaden shook his head. "There is no need," he said. "Constable Hardiman just wanted to talk to you again about the robbery – at the office."

I watched Powell as Eaden said this, and the clerk's eyes darted to the fireplace and then back again. "Of course," he said smoothly. "Anything I can do to help."

I walked across to the fireplace and looked into the grate. There was some ash in it. I squatted and dipped my finger into it. Paper.

"It is unusual to burn a fire in the summer, Mr Powell," I observed.

"I feel the cold," he said. "And I was getting rid of some old newspapers."

I looked about me, and propped up against the armchair was a ledger. I reached for it and stood up.

"Is that our ledger?" said Eaden with surprise.

"Some of it," I said, opening it. The front was stamped with the name Barker and Eaden. But most of the pages were missing – torn from the spine and, I assumed, burned in Powell's grate. I handed it to Eaden, who turned it over in his hands disbelievingly.

"What have you done, Mr Powell?" he asked. "Or, more importantly, why?"

"Discommuning," said Mrs Jacobs with authority. "'Tis a terrible threat for a Cambridge business. My poor Walter lived in fear of it. Not that he ever did anything to deserve it, of course."

I had heard enough stories of Mrs Jacobs's late husband to know that he was second only to the angels in goodness and beauty.

"And apparently Thomas Powell too," I said, trying to tell from the mysterious smells wafting from the stove what might be for dinner. "It turns out that he was letting gownsmen run up debts at Barker and Eaden."

"Tsk tsk," she tutted. "The Vice-Chancellor would not like that at all, not one little bit. Let a gownsman run up debt and that's you, discommuned. And no gownsman allowed to do business with you again."

"Indeed," I said. "And when Powell realised that the debts would not be cleared by the end of term and all would be revealed, and most likely the business would be discommuned, he decided that all he could do was destroy the records of the orders and try to cover up the shortfall with some clever accounting."

"Well, I hope Mr Barker and Mr Eaden have shown him the door," she said. "Especially after he tried to shift the blame onto poor Charlie Grantham."

"They have indeed," I said, "and they have promised Charlie a pay rise to make up for doubting him."

"That will come in handy with the baby," she observed as she reached for a plate and ladled my dinner onto it. "Irish stew," she said, and I had little choice but to believe her.

"Will Powell be sent to prison?" she asked, filling her own plate and sitting at the table.

"I doubt it," I replied. "Mr Eaden is persuaded that he was naive rather than criminal – he believed the gownsmen when they promised to clear their slates."

My landlady shook her head. "He must be a ninny – letting young men have wine on tick. Mr Eaden is lucky he still has any business – or wine – left."

Chapter Thirty

DIGNITY

"It's good of you to take my place, Mr Gilbert," I said.

"Adam," he said, holding out his hand for me to shake.

"Gregory," I offered.

"It suits me too," he said. He smiled cheekily. "There's this girl, see. I'm trying to show myself off a bit." He puffed out his chest and put his hands on his hips. "She's only seen me as a waterman, in my filthy work clothes, stinking of the river. But in this," he took the cloak from the hook and swirled it around his shoulders, "in this, well, I'm a swell and no mistake."

"Very dashing," I agreed, handing him his hat. "But all the same, I'm grateful."

"Don't mention it, Gregory," he said, leaning forward to take a closer look at himself in the glass. "When I saw that I wasn't on duty for the proclamation, I was disappointed – but it's worked out perfectly now." He turned to look at me. "You don't fancy the fair yourself?"

I shook my head. "I'm not that keen on crowds and anyway, I've been to the Pot Fair before."

"So have I," he said, "but not like this – not part of the show of it all, I mean." He grinned.

"Don't beam like that when you're processing," I reminded him. "The Proctors won't like it. Dignity at all times."

"Dignity," he repeated, winking at me. He looked down at himself. "Poor girl," he said. "She doesn't stand a chance."

―☙☙―

What I had said to Adam Gilbert was true: I was perfectly happy to forgo the duty of attending the proclamation of Midsummer Fair. But in all honesty I had another reason for wanting to be in town while nearly everyone else was not.

I could see George Chapman frowning as he tried to decide where his loyalty lay, and I fancied I knew what he was thinking. On the one hand, he should insist on having the Master's permission before allowing me to search a gownsman's room. On the other hand, he knew that I would have a good reason for asking. And on that same hand, he feared that if he vexed me I would make it awkward for him to press his suit with my landlady. I had no such intention, but I was happy to let him believe it. With a sigh, he jerked his head in the direction of the sizars' room.

"Be quick about it," he said. "If anyone finds you in there, I'll say you sneaked past me."

"Understood," I said, and walked away before he could change his mind.

The sizars' room was as I remembered it. Hodges and Mason were obviously tidy by nature, as both beds had the covers pulled up. I walked over to the cupboard; on top of it, the jug was standing neatly centred in the wash bowl. I opened the doors and inside was their small collection of clothes, carefully folded. I pushed my hands between the layers, looking for I knew not what, and found nothing. I closed the cupboard and turned around to look at the room again. For two undergraduates, they showed few signs of study: the table was bare. But then where would I keep my belongings in such a room, with no shelves on its sloping walls? I walked to one of the beds and got to my knees to look under it. As I had thought: a small wooden trunk, about eighteen inches long, a foot wide and the same high. I pulled it out and sat back on my heels to open it. In it were four books, all in poor condition, all – I turned them to the light – about mathematics. This was Mason's trunk, then; Giles had told me that he was always asking for the latest books on geometry. I put them on the floor and looked again into the trunk. There were two notebooks; I glanced through them and they contained, as far as I could tell, lecture notes and calculations – one notebook completed and the other in current use. Apart from that, the trunk held a pair of boots wrapped in cloth, a winter coat of good stuff, and a small battered box of much-loved tin soldiers. I replaced everything and pushed the trunk back under Mason's bed.

There was a similar trunk, slightly larger, under Hodges's bed. Indeed, this one had the initials SWH painted on the lid – I guessed that it had been bought for the older Hodges boy and then passed to his brother. It contained a few more books, although equally battered, and I could see from them that Hodges's interest was in the classics. I looked at them one by one, and Giles had been right. On the spine of one, a much-read blue volume with scuffed corners, was written *Suetonius De Vita Caesarum Libri*. I put everything else back into the trunk and then went to the table and sat down with the book. The title page began with Latin, but thankfully was also in English: *The Lives of the Twelve First Roman Emperors, Writ by C Suetonius Tranquillus; with a Free Translation, Wherein Due Regard Has Been Had to the Propriety of the English Tongue*. I turned to a random page, and the text was set out in two columns: Latin on the left and English on the right. What a clever idea, to help with the learning of a language.

I returned to the front of the book. Giles had said that the Liberators were the assassins of Julius Caesar, so that was the story I needed to read – and luckily the very first words of the very first chapter of the book were "Julius Caesar". I turned the pages, stopping whenever I saw a mark in the margin or an underlining, as I guessed those would be significant to Nicholas Hodges. Nothing seemed relevant until, suddenly, there it was. Paragraph 80 contained that strange word that Giles had made me write in my notebook, and the sentence was underlined with a forceful, heavy black line as though done over and over again: "Instead of caballing any longer separately by two or three together, they now united their counsels". A couple of words were left alone before the underlining started again: "the people themselves being not at all satisfied with the current state of affairs". And then the black line almost bit through the page: "declaring against the tyranny they were under, and calling out amain for some to assert their cause against the usurper". "Amain" was not a word I knew, so I took my vocabulary book from my pocket and made a note of it to ask Giles later. I also wrote down the phrases that had been underlined. And in the column of Latin, there it was, with a thick dark frame drawn around it by Hodges, and a vertical line in the margin to mark the spot: *in unum omnes contulerunt*. I turned to the next page, and the only mark was a box drawn around a name: Cimber Tullius. Again, I made a note of it. Just then I heard the bell toll; I had no idea when one or other of the sizars might return to their room. I quickly leafed through the rest of the pages of the chapter but there was nothing of note. I put the book back into the trunk, slid it back under the bed, and glanced around the room to make sure that there was no evidence of my visit.

I had intended to go to the inn to check on the horses but I now knew I needed to see Giles so that I could understand what I had read. When I reached Nicholson's I peered through the window but I could not see him; there was another man at the counter. I was about to give up when the curtain to the back of the shop was pulled aside and Giles appeared. He caught sight of me and smiled, beckoning me in.

"Mr Jones," he said to the man behind the counter. "I shall take over now – you may go for your break."

Once we were alone, I took my vocabulary book from my pocket. I explained where I had been – the bookseller raised an eyebrow but said nothing. And I described what I had read.

"Ah, the Clarke translation," he said approvingly. "Not the most recent – 1732, if I am not mistaken – but superb for students seeking to improve their Latin. A schoolmaster, so he knew the difficulties."

"It was certainly helpful for me," I said. "I found the passage you mentioned, about caballing together. It was underlined, along with these phrases." I opened my vocabulary book and pointed to it. Giles read in silence.

"Well, he's upset about something, your sizar," he said wryly. "Feeling oppressed. Oh, and amain. Not much used these days – as I say, Clarke is not the most modern translation – but it means with great force, or energetically." He took a pencil from under the counter and wrote the definition down for me in my book. "And what's this – Cimber Tullius?"

"Hodges had drawn a box around the name," I explained. "I have never heard of him."

"According to Suetonius," said Giles, "he was the Liberator who struck the first blow. He was a Roman senator, of course, and, like all of them, once part of Caesar's inner circle. But Caesar had exiled his brother – Publius, I think he was called. And Plutarch suggests that the presentation of a petition to Caesar to ask for Publius to be brought back to Rome was the excuse Tullius used to approach… Why, whatever is it, Mr Hardiman?"

"Do you mean," I asked slowly, "that one motive Cimber Tullius had for murdering Caesar was revenge for ill-treatment of his brother?"

"As much as we can be sure of these things after so many centuries, well, yes," said Giles.

Chapter Thirty-One

Mayhem

It was one of those early summer days that make a man glad to be alive. I had finished sweeping out the stables and spreading fresh straw in the stalls, and after splashing water on my face and arms I sat on the stool in the corner of the yard and turned my face to the sun. Jamie would be finishing his pots soon and would be keen to read more of Doctor Parkinson's dreadful warnings. I must have dozed off; I woke when a shadow fell across me and there was Jamie. He fetched another stool and sat down next to me, carefully inspecting his hands to make sure they were clean before he took the book from his apron pocket. As he did so, a piece of paper fell to the ground. I bent to pick it up and saw that it was covered with pencil shading.

"That's a trick Nat showed me," Jamie said.

"Nat the pot boy?" I asked.

He nodded and pointed at the paper. "If someone writes something and then takes their paper away, if you do this with pencil," he mimed scribbling, "on the paper underneath, you can see what they wrote." He looked at me, his eyes shining. "It's magic, Nat says."

"No," I said, "it's just because..." I saw the expression on Jamie's face and changed my mind. "No, Nat's probably right. It is magic."

After Jamie's lesson, as he liked to call it, I put on my coat and walked to St Clement's as fast as I could. Given what I had discovered in the sizars' room, I had to speak to Francis Vaughan. I turned into Thompson's Lane and saw George Chapman standing outside the college gate, looking anxiously up and down the street.

"Good afternoon, Mr Chapman," I said as I walked towards him.

"Has he sent for you, Mr Hardiman?" he asked, looking past me. "Has the Master sent for you?"

I shook my head. "I was hoping to see him," I said, "but why would he want to see me?"

"It's Mr Hodges," said the porter, leaning towards me and dropping his voice. "He's gone."

I knocked lightly on the door to the Master's rooms and went in. Francis Vaughan was sitting in one of the armchairs; his head was in his hands, but he looked up as I walked across to him.

"Good afternoon, Master," I said.

"Mr Hardiman," he replied flatly, indicating that I should take the seat next to him. "What an infernal mess."

"Mr Hodges, you mean," I said.

"All of it," said Vaughan.

"Have you spoken to Mr Mason?" I asked.

The Master shook his head. "Mason told the porters that Hodges had left college before dawn this morning, when he was missed at breakfast, but I have not spoken to him, no." He looked sharply at me. "You think I should?"

"I think we both should," I replied. "And after that, I have more to tell you about Nicholas Hodges."

Ten minutes later William Mason was sitting nervously in the Master's room, his clasped hands between his knees. He looked from Vaughan to me and then down at the floor.

"Now then, Will," I said gently. "It seems that Nick has gone missing and we need to work out what has happened." He said nothing. "Did you see Nick go to bed in your room last night?" I asked.

Mason nodded without looking up.

"But when you woke up he had gone?" I asked.

He nodded again.

"Do you know what time he left?" I persisted. "Did you hear anything?"

"It was getting light," he said quietly. "I half-heard him and thought he was going to the privy. When I woke up properly he wasn't there and I thought he had gone to breakfast."

"So he left between dawn and breakfast," I said to the Master. I turned back to Mason. "Did you know that Nick was going to run away?" I asked.

Mason shook his head without looking up.

"But you are not surprised," I continued. "You thought he might, didn't you, Will?"

He shrugged.

"Mr Mason," said the Master, not with anger but certainly firmly. "Mr Mason, look at me, if you please." The sizar did so. "That's better. Now, tell me why you had an idea that Mr Hodges might absent himself from college without permission."

Mason glanced at me and I nodded.

"After I spoke to Mr Hardiman last week," he began, then stopped and cleared his throat. "After that, I came back to our room here at college. Nick – Mr Hodges – was there, and he was acting strangely again. It reminded me of what he was like before... before Mr Pears. Wild – not making much sense. But then he calmed down and was himself again, and I was relieved. But then yesterday, he started again, raving almost. Striding up and down the room, talking all sorts of nonsense. And then I saw it." He stopped and closed his eyes for a moment. "He had it in his hand and he was turning it over and over, and then holding it out, and testing it – lunging forward and back." He stopped again, for longer.

"Good heavens, man," said Vaughan. "What did he have in his hand?"

"A knife," said Mason miserably. "Not a kitchen knife – a dagger. Short, with a thin blade and a black handle."

Vaughan looked at me in horror. "The coroner said that such a knife was used to kill Pears. It was never found."

"I thought he had thrown it in the river," said the sizar. "He told me he had – that's why I believed him when he said there would be no more. Like I told you, Mr Hardiman. He promised there would be no more. But now the knife has gone – he's taken it with him. He hollowed out one of the legs of his bed as a hiding place for the knife, and I looked there and it's gone."

The Master was looking from me to Mason and back again with wide eyes. "You knew? You both knew that Hodges killed Pears?"

"I was coming to speak to you today..." I started, but stopped when I saw the thunderous look on his face.

"You," he said, pointing at Mason. "Return to your room now and stay there: I will send for you when I am ready to speak to you again." The sizar scrambled to his feet and walked quickly from the room, banging the door in his haste to pull it shut behind him. The

Master stood and walked towards his window, then to the desk, then back to the window.

"Mr Vaughan..." I began, but he held up a hand to silence me.

He paced around the room for perhaps three minutes, occasionally glancing at me but mostly looking at nothing, just working thoughts around in his head. Finally, he came and sat down again.

"Now, Mr Hardiman," he said in a low voice, "you will tell me everything you know about Mr Hodges."

And I did.

"We must go to a magistrate," said the Master once I had finished speaking. "He can then issue a warrant and the parish constables will look for Hodges. It is out of our hands."

I shifted forward in my seat. "If I may, Master," I said.

"What is it?" he asked, irritation in his voice.

I remembered what he had once confided in me, about St Clement's being a poor college and needing to attract undergraduates who could pay higher fees. Having a murderer in residence would not help.

"If we go straight to a magistrate," I said, "the Proctors will be vexed at having been excluded. They will feel slighted. Perhaps the Vice-Chancellor too." Vaughan looked sharply at me. "I have had more time than you to think about this," I continued. "If the Proctors suspect that I have been acting on my own authority, I will certainly lose my job."

"And if they suspect that I have been instructing you," added the Master, "I may lose mine."

"I doubt it would come to that, sir," I said, "and I would certainly deny that you were involved."

Vaughan's face softened a little. "I am grateful, Mr Hardiman," he said. "I do not like the subterfuge, but I know that you are much more use to St Clement's as a constable than as an ostler."

"Subterfuge?" I asked.

The Master gave a single barking laugh. "You and your words. Trickery, misrepresentation. French, I should imagine. Here: pass me your book and I shall write it for you." I did so, and it seemed to restore the kindness between us.

"What I suggest, sir," I said as he wrote, "is that you report the matter to the Proctor. Say that Mr Hodges has run off, and that in searching his room for a possible explanation you have come across the marks in the Suetonius. This, together with the note found with Mr Pears, has made you fear that Mr Hodges is involved. The Proctor and the Vice-Chancellor can then take the matter to a magistrate, and the correct process can be followed."

Vaughan handed my vocabulary book and pencil back to me.

"They would have to go to a magistrate, then?" he asked. "It could not be kept in the Vice-Chancellor's court?"

I knew he knew the answer and was asking out of desperation, but I shook my head anyway. "I have checked," I said. "The University charter. The Vice-Chancellor's court has jurisdiction in all University civil and criminal proceedings except treason, felony and mayhem. I am not sure whether murder is felony or mayhem or both, but it is certainly beyond the reach of the Vice-Chancellor."

"So be it," said Vaughan, passing a hand across his eyes and looking more tired than angry. Then he suddenly sat upright. "But does this mean that Hodges killed Fleming as well? The notes – they were the same. Dear God."

I shook my head. "I thought so too, but now I am not sure. The notes suggest the same killer, yes, but there are more reasons against it." I looked at the Master and he nodded wearily. "First," I said, "Mason told me that Fleming was not one of the men who bullied sizars – on the contrary, Samuel Hodges even mentioned in a letter to his brother that he had been comforted by Fleming. Second, Nick Hodges has a horror of hanging, as that is how his brother died – he is unlikely to choose it as a way to kill someone. And third, Nick Hodges is short – too short to hang a tall man like Fleming on his own."

"Are you telling me, Mr Hardiman," said the Master slowly and carefully, "that St Clement's is home to not one but two murderers?"

"Possibly," I had to admit. "But there is nothing to suggest that whoever killed Mr Fleming is also a St Clement's man. He could have visited from outside college."

"You have spoken to the porters?" asked Vaughan. "Asked them about visitors on the day of Fleming's death?"

I nodded. "If you are willing to trust me a little longer, Master," I said, "I am sure I can find out more. In the meantime, when you report the Hodges matter to the Proctor, perhaps do not mention Fleming at all. After all, as far as the University is currently aware, he simply hanged himself."

Chapter Thirty-Two

Northampton

"Well, it's quite a grisly business, Mr Hardiman," said Mrs Jacobs conversationally as she tended to the pots on the stove. I had been in two minds as to whether to tell her about Nicholas Hodges, but I knew she was no gossip and, to be frank, I needed all the help I could muster. And when I arrived home and found the porter from St Clement's in the kitchen with my landlady, I decided that three heads were better than one.

"It is, Mrs Jacobs," I said, "and given the state of mind of Mr Hodges, and given that we assume he has a dagger with him, it could become even more grisly."

"So you need to find this young man quickly," she said, bending to dip a spoon into a pot and taste its contents. "Right, we're ready. Plates, please, George."

George it was now, not Mr Chapman. I caught the porter's eye and he blushed. He moved to stand beside Mrs Jacobs with the plates in his hands, and as she reached for each one he handed it over. She then put the filled plates on the table and we sat to eat. Mr Chapman's praise for the food was not as lavish as in the past, but it was a passable meal of herrings and potatoes. When we had finished, Mrs Jacobs leaned across the table, taking our plates from us and stacking them.

"Take out that notebook of yours, Mr Hardiman," she instructed, "and we shall make a list of everything we know about Mr Hodges. That might help us imagine where he has gone."

"A good notion, Mary… Mrs Jacobs," said Chapman, catching my eye and correcting himself.

I wiped my mouth and reached over to take my notebook and pencil from the pocket of my coat, which I had hung on the back of the door. I turned to a clean page and wrote "Nicholas Hodges" at the top of it. Below that, I wrote: aged 15, sizar, classics, Suetonius, brother, revenge, Liberators, dagger.

My landlady tilted her head to read what I had written. "Where is he from?" she asked. "Might he not go home?"

"Possibly," I said, "although I imagine he would not want to bring trouble to his mother's door."

"Not necessarily to his own home," clarified Mrs Jacobs, "but to a town or village that he knows. Somewhere he feels safe."

"Northampton," said Chapman as he picked at his teeth. "When he arrived, and his brother before him, the trunk had a return label for an address in Northampton."

I added Northampton to my list.

"What did he take with him?" she then asked. We must have looked blank, because she continued. "A dagger, yes," she pointed at my notebook, "but not his trunk, because that's still in his room. Did he take any clothes at all – or just the ones he stood up in? That will tell you whether he planned to go, or just ran away in a panic."

"I don't know," I admitted. "I could ask Will Mason."

"The lad who shares his room," explained Chapman to Mrs Jacobs.

"I called in on Mason after I had left the Master this afternoon," I said. "I was wondering what had made Hodges leave so suddenly – why go now, drawing attention to himself, with the end of term only a week away? And Mason said that they argued yesterday evening as they were getting ready for bed. Hodges may have thought that he was losing Mason's loyalty – that Mason might sacrifice him to save his own skin."

"That will be it, then," said Mrs Jacobs decisively, pointing at me with the bread knife she was wiping on a cloth. "No planning – just an escape. He's probably hiding under a hedge somewhere between here and Northampton."

"There's the *Rising Sun*," said Chapman suddenly.

"I beg your pardon?" replied my landlady.

"The coach – goes from the George on Bridge Street," he said.

"Monday, Wednesday and Friday mornings at six," I confirmed. "Birmingham, via Northampton."

Chapter Thirty-Three
STONE

The next morning I rose early and walked into town and along Bridge Street to the George Inn. It was a handsome building with large windows overlooking the street, and as a church bell struck half-past five, I walked into its yard. As I had expected, it was full of activity. The *Rising Sun* was standing ready, with two lads loading boxes and sacks onto it and a third giving the bright red and yellow paintwork a final dust and shine. I walked over to the stable door.

"Rob?" I called softly, not wanting to startle the horses. "Are you there?"

"Upstairs," came the reply. "With you in a minute."

A ladder in the corner of the stables led up to the ostry, where Robert Parkin lodged. As I watched, his boots appeared and he climbed down.

He looked surprised to see me. "Gregory?" he said. "Is there a problem at the Hoop? I've no animals to spare, I'm afraid. These four are from the southbound mail, and those are just heading out with the northbound."

"No, no," I said. "Nothing like that."

Rob opened one of the stalls, slipped a halter over the neck of the horse and handed the rope to me. "He's the lead – take him into the yard for me and I'll bring the next."

I did as he asked and one by one he brought the horses out of their stalls and backed them into the traces, taking the lead animal from me at the end and putting him in his place. Taking two each, we worked our way around the horses, checking hooves, legs, straps and bits. When he was satisfied that everything was in order, Rob nodded and we walked away from the coach, sending one of the lads to fetch the driver.

"Now then, Gregory," said Rob as we sat on two upturned crates at the side of the yard. "You can tell me what this is about. I can't imagine you roused yourself at this hour just to help me."

"I'm looking for someone," I said. "There's a young lad gone missing from one of the colleges."

"Kitchen lad?" asked Rob, scratching his neck and yawning.

I shook my head. "An undergraduate – a sizar."

That caught his attention. "One of the young charity lads?" he asked.

"If you like," I said. "He's in a bit of trouble at the college and has taken it into his head to run off."

"During term?" asked Rob, surprised. "He'll be in the suds for that."

"He will," I agreed. "And the longer he's gone, the worse it will be. Now, we know he's from Northampton. And chances are..."

"He'll be heading home," finished Rob. "And you're hoping he'll be on that." He nodded his head towards the coach.

"I am," I said.

"Any sign of him yet?" asked Rob, indicating the passengers who were starting to gather in the yard. There was one young man, two more of middling years, and a husband and wife with grey hair, stooped backs and far too many bags and bundles. I shook my head.

"Well, if he's not quick, he'll miss it," observed Rob. "Here's the driver."

I looked at the man who had just come out of the inn and into the yard. "That's John Topham, isn't it?" I asked.

"It is indeed," agreed Rob. "A good man – experienced. Light on the strings and sparing with the whip." He stood and went over to speak to Topham and the two shook hands. I could see Rob shaking his head, and knew that he was telling the driver that there was nothing to be worried about with any of the animals. The passengers climbed into the coach – the young man on the roof and the others inside – and the driver stepped up onto the box. There was no sign of Nicholas Hodges. Rob stood back as Topham lifted his whip and touched it on the rump of the lead horse and the coach lurched forward and slowly turned out of the gates. The church bell tolled the hour and Rob and I smiled at each other – it is very pleasing when a coach is so punctual.

I bid farewell to Rob Parkin and walked back to the Hoop; I would have to think again about where Nicholas Hodges might have gone. It was a busy morning, with several overnight guests at the inn all demanding their mounts be ready at the same time. I barely had a moment to myself before the *Defiance* had to be seen off to London and the *Fakenham Day* to Swaffham. Once they had gone, my stomach was growling loudly and I was just heading to the kitchen when I heard running footsteps and someone calling, "Ostler! Ostler!" I turned to see a young lad skidding into the yard.

"Mr Hardiman?" he asked.

"That's me," I replied.

"I've a message for you from Mr French at the King's Head," he said.

Jacky French is ostler at the King's Head Inn on Sidney Street. As you have probably realised, the horsemen in Cambridge all know each other.

"Hand it over, then, lad," I said.

"Nothing written, sir," said the boy. "Just this: driver of *Blucher* says driver of *Rising Sun* attacked by passenger near Huntingdon. Driver hurt, passenger dead." His eyes shone. "It's a good message, isn't it, sir? I'm to take it to all the ostlers."

"You'd better be on your way, then," I said, digging into my pocket for a coin and putting it into his outstretched palm. He looked down, closed his hand over the coin, smiled broadly, saluted me with the other hand, and hared out of the yard.

I was not far behind him as I all but ran along Bridge Street and into Sidney Street, ignoring the curious looks of those I passed. I ducked into the yard of the King's Head, skirted the *Blucher* which was being cleaned in readiness for its return to Huntingdon that afternoon, and reached the ladder leading up to the ostry. A lad filling a bucket from the pump looked up and called over. "If you're after Mr French, he's in the parlour with Mr Williams the driver," he said. "He's shook up."

"Thank you," I replied, and headed indoors. The parlour was at the front of the building, looking out into the street, and there were three tables occupied. Sitting at one of them were two men: I recognised Jacky French, and guessed from his high boots and the shock on his face that the other man was Williams the coach driver. Jacky glanced up and saw me, and beckoned me over.

"Pull up a chair, Gregory," he said. "This is Isaac Williams, driver of the *Blucher*." The driver looked at me, his face bleak, but held out his hand for me to shake. "And this is Gregory Hardiman, ostler at the Hoop. I told you I've sent word to all the ostlers, so that they can pass on word to the drivers – we want to make sure they hear the true story, not whatever rubbish they print in the newspapers. Don't want to spread panic about a gang of young ruffians attacking drivers, do we?"

A pot boy stuck his head around the door of the parlour. "A jar of coffee, strong as you can," said Jacky. "Three cups." The pot boy nodded and disappeared.

"We'll have the coffee first and then think about some food. Tell Mr Hardiman what you told me," Jacky told Williams.

The driver looked at me but said nothing.

"What I know," I said, "is that the *Rising Sun* left the George at six this morning, bound for Birmingham. I saw it leave myself – John Topham driving. And just now I received a message saying that the driver had been injured and a passenger killed." Still nothing from Williams. "I know you're tired, Mr Williams, and shocked, but as Jacky says, it's as well we know the truth of what happened."

The driver sighed. Just then the pot boy arrived with the coffee, and we spent a few minutes filling cups and taking sips and commenting on how welcome the hot drink was.

"It was about three miles south of Huntingdon," said Williams suddenly. "On the Great North Road. I could see a coach pulled over to the side."

"What time was this, Mr Williams?" I asked.

He gave me a puzzled look. "About half-past eight," he replied. "I left Huntingdon at eight."

"Thank you," I said. "You saw a coach pulled over."

"Yes. I knew it was the *Rising Sun* from the livery," he said. "Red and yellow – very distinctive. And as I pulled alongside, the dragsman shouted at me to stop. He was standing by the horses. And it's as you said: it was John Topham." He paused and swallowed hard. "John was holding his arm, here." Williams demonstrated, using his right hand to take hold of the top of his left arm, just below the shoulder. "I could see it was bleeding. Someone had tied a kerchief around it, but the blood was coming through." The colour had drained from the driver's face and he looked as though he might faint.

"Are you upset by the sight of blood, Mr Williams?" I asked.

He nodded and put a hand to his mouth. "Always have been," he said with a gulp. "My wife makes a joke of it, but I just can't." He closed his eyes and shook his head.

"Many people find it distressing," I said. "Let's not dwell on that. So you stopped your coach and went over to help, I assume."

Williams took a deep breath. "I did, yes. The passengers – five of them, four men and one woman – were standing on a little bank at the side of the road. A little way from them was a shape on the ground, covered with a blanket – I could see from the feet poking out that it was a man. Well, a boy really."

"And did Mr Topham tell you what had happened?" I asked.

Williams, nodded. "The boy had been sitting outside, next to John – Mr Topham. He didn't have much with him, just a small bag. He'd climbed on when the coach was going up the hill just the other side of the Great Bridge – told John he had overslept and John took pity on him. And they fell to talking; John likes company when he's driving. The boy said he was going home to Northampton because his mother had been taken ill. John asked what his job was in Cambridge, and the boy said he was an undergraduate at St Clement's College. John asked if he had a letter of permission from the Master, and when the boy said he had forgotten to bring it, John told him that he would have to put him down in Huntingdon." Williams looked at Jacky and then me. "We all know we're not permitted to take gownsmen out of town during term without written permission."

"And then what happened?" I prompted.

"At first, John said, the boy seemed to accept it. But about five minutes later he reached down into his bag and pulled out a knife – a small, sharp, nasty thing, John said. And he told John that if he tried to put him down in Huntingdon he would stick him with it. And John laughed."

"Laughed?" said Jacky.

"He said he was so surprised, he couldn't help himself," explained the driver. "It made no sense, anyway. The coach had to stop in Huntingdon for the horses – they couldn't keep going just because this boy said so." He shook his head. "But there was no reasoning with the lad, and he made to stab John. Now John's quite a big fellow, so he put the strings in one hand and slowed the horses, and with the other arm he tried to push the boy away. They wrestled, the boy got one good hit with the knife," here the driver went pale again, "and then the coach went into a rut and the boy was thrown out. John managed to stop the coach and ran back, but the boy was dead. Hit his head on a stone in the road. One of the passengers helped John carry him to the side of the road, and a gentleman riding past agreed to take the news to Huntingdon and send for the constables and a doctor. I passed a few minutes later – John just wanted me to bring the news here. To tell the Master of St Clement's."

Chapter Thirty-Four

COMMENCEMENT

"Hodges dying could not have happened at a worse time," said Francis Vaughan, showing unusual ill-temper. After I had left the King's Head, I had returned to the Hoop to welcome the two coaches arriving in the middle of the day – one coming from London and one heading there – and then gone to St Clement's with the sad news. The death of Nicholas Hodges would be a matter for the Huntingdon constables and coroner, but notifying his family of the loss of a second son while under the care of St Clement's would be an uncomfortable duty for the Master. Still, I was surprised at his irritation.

He caught my eye. "Forgive me, Mr Hardiman," he said. "You must think me callous. But this time of year does not show me at my best." He sat down heavily in his armchair and sighed deeply. "I am not sure when the solemn conferring of degrees turned into this, this… circus of festivities, but there it is."

"Ah," I said. "Commencement." The Master dropped his head into his hand and groaned. "The Proctors have been talking about it for weeks," I continued. "They even have a chart on the wall, to make sure that we all know where we have to be every day."

The Master looked up. "Arrival of the families and other guests from Friday," he said, ticking off items on his fingers, "Commencement Sunday sermon at Great St Mary's – lengthy, no doubt, but let us hope uncontroversial – followed by the usual fashionable promenade on the Backs, all of us decked out like peacocks. Commencement Ball at the Town Hall on Monday evening, with gentry and clergy from the whole of East Anglia showing off their plain daughters in hopes of snaring a wealthy gownsman. Time permitting," he emphasised the words, "degrees will be sealed and delivered at the Senate House on Tuesday. And throughout it all, I am required to be in my festal gown, on show, and frittering college funds on entertainments for our guests." He paused to draw breath. "The cook is already spending beyond his budget, the wine cellar is looking sadly unimpressive, and the porters are complaining – in advance, mind you – that the guests lodging with us here in college will be ungrateful, demanding and stingy with their tips." He smiled thinly. "If there were a potion I could drink to fall asleep for a week, I would take it now."

"Then you are not going to be happy to hear what else I have to tell you, Master," I said.

"I rather feared that," he replied. "Out with it, Mr Hardiman."

"There can now be little doubt that Nicholas Hodges murdered Joshua Pears," I said. "He attacked the coach driver with a knife that was almost certainly the one he used on Mr Pears, and the books in his room show that he was using details from the life of Julius Caesar – or, more accurately, his death – to justify what he was doing. And when Mr Mason told him that the game was up, he fled."

"The coach driver," asked Vaughan, "is he badly injured?"

I shook my head. "A painful wound, apparently," I said, "and he'll not be able to pull on the reins for a while, but no lasting damage."

"Thank heavens," said the Master. "I should hate to add a third victim to Hodges's tally."

"Ah, well, now," I said. "Mr Fleming. I do not believe he was murdered by Nicholas Hodges."

The Master closed his eyes slowly and took a deep sigh. After a moment, he looked at me. "So it is as we feared," he said sadly. "We at St Clement's have been at the mercy of two killers. One was Nicholas Hodges. And the other? Do you know his identity?"

"Maybe," I said. "I have a theory – a suspicion. Well, I have an explanation and a motive that make sense to me. I just need to test them to be certain. But I need to be quick about it."

The Master looked at me sharply. He was an intelligent man and had immediately understood. "A University man, then – one who is about to disappear at the end of term. You have nine days, by my calculation."

"You're the mathematician, sir," I said, pushing myself to my feet.

"I may be," agreed Vaughan, "but it does not take a mathematician to know that nine days is not very long."

At the meeting of the Bull Book Club that evening, all talk was of the ongoing election for the Member of Parliament for the county. After four days of polling, which those in the know agreed had been remarkably dull and uneventful, the rankings of the three candidates remained unchanged. Lord Charles Manners was in the lead and expected to be returned, followed fairly closely by Lord Francis Osborne. But what was exercising the members of the club was the unexpectedly good showing of the late addition to the ballot paper: Mr Henry Adeane of Babraham.

"Well, it has certainly ruffled the Rutland feathers," said my friend George Fisher with some satisfaction. No-one can live in Cambridge very long without learning of the influence of the

Dukes of Rutland and their circle – indeed, Lord Charles Manners is the younger brother of the current Duke of Rutland. And there are those who feel that that influence amounts almost to a stranglehold on Cambridge, dictating who can make important decisions and who will benefit from those decisions. I suspect George Fisher may be among those who would like to see that influence challenged.

"Has it?" I asked. "But I understood that Lord Charles and Lord Francis are both set to be returned."

"Oh yes," said Fisher, waving his hand dismissively. "But times are changing. Adeane comes from an old and respected family, to be sure, but he is ploughing his own furrow. His father may have been a Rutland man, but Henry most certainly is not – and declares it quite freely. Gregory," he leaned forward conspiratorially, "I believe that there is a rising spirit of independence in Cambridge. And a growing number of us are pleased to see some credible opposition to the status quo."

"The existing state of affairs," I said.

"Precisely," agreed the banker.

Just then a man entered the room waving a sheet of paper. "Today's results!" he called. The room fell silent as he read aloud. "One hundred and seventeen votes cast today. The totals so far, after four days of voting, are as follows. Lord Charles Manners: one thousand three hundred and eighty-six. Lord Francis Osborne: eight hundred and seventy-three. Mr Henry Adeane: six hundred and eight. Polling will close tomorrow at noon."

Fisher turned back to me. "There were more than forty votes cast for Adeane today. He won't win this time, but his day will come. Put that in your notebook, Gregory: that on the 28th day of June 1826 I, George Fisher, banker of this parish, predict that Mr Henry Adeane will one day represent Cambridgeshire in Parliament."

And only four years later his prediction came true – but that's a story for another day.

Chapter Thirty-Five

Angel

I will be honest with you: when I agreed to be a university constable, I had little idea of the nature of the job. The hours suited me, and I was happy to do my part to keep order in the town. But I had not realised quite how much prinking and processing there would be. And I dislike both prinking and processing. I like my clothes to be clean and well-fitting, made of sturdy material, but beyond that, I cannot see the point of worrying about them. The University, on the other hand, likes nothing better than dressing up, so that each man can tell from the colour of another's gown or the shape of his hood precisely where he belongs. The Proctors are no exception, and as a constable I must accompany them to all manner of services, events, occasions and ceremonies that have nothing at all to do with keeping order. And I hope you will forgive me for saying that I find it irksome.

As I was not appointed until late July last year this would be my first Commencement, and I could see from the chart drawn up by the Proctors that it would be a busy week. The official proceedings start on Saturday, with not one but two Congregations – formal meetings of the governing body of the University, with enough gold, scarlet, fur and braid on display to rival the King's Court in London. With both Proctors on duty, several constables are needed

– and William Bird has reluctantly given me leave from the Hoop for the day. I can tell you – as I told William – I would far rather be rubbing down the horses and reading with Poor Jamie than roasting in my uniform in the Senate House while listening to endless pronouncements in Latin. Commencement Sunday brings a long sermon at the University church, again with full regalia, followed by a grand dinner hosted by the Vice-Chancellor. On Monday there will be two more Congregations and, in the evening at the Town Hall, the ball that Francis Vaughan had mentioned. And all of this before the actual business of Commencement on Tuesday, when various advanced degrees are awarded in a solemn (and long) ceremony in the Senate House. The general festivities continue, with gatherings and entertainment, until term ends on Friday. George Chapman, who has lived through many a Commencement week, says that those who think of Cambridge as a sleepy backwater for the training of clergymen would be shocked to see it for those seven days.

I don't want you to think that I am a kill-joy; although I prefer the quieter life myself, I am happy to see others enjoy themselves with music and dancing and dining, if that pleases them. But the loss of normal routine coupled with the arrival of so many extra people would make it harder for me to find the killer of Edward Fleming. I could only hope that on the day before the start of what the Master had called the circus, the man I needed to see would keep to his usual pattern.

The parlour of the Angel on Market Street was much busier than on my last visit, which I suspect was thanks to the crowds in town to hear the result of the election for the Member of Parliament for the county. I stood just inside the door for a moment, blinking in the gloom after the bright day outside. Once my eyes had adjusted I could see that there were no tables free and I had to stand by the bar, my shoulder turned to the door to prevent anyone spotting me as soon as they walked in. The harried landlord slid a tankard across the counter to me, swept my coins into the drawer, and gesticulated to the pot boy to take some drinks to a table. I lifted the tankard to my mouth and casually looked around the room. No sign of him. I drank as slowly as I could but after twenty minutes my tankard was empty. Even space at the bar was popular, and I indicated to the landlord that I would take another drink. Just as it arrived, I heard someone call, "Richard – over here!" I turned to see a young man waving from a table, and Richard Lawrence walking towards him. I abandoned the tankard and moved swiftly to the table, where Lawrence had just taken the seat offered to him by the young man.

"Mr Lawrence," I said.

He looked up at me. After our last conversation when we had discussed Fleming's green ledger, he was slightly more civil to me – but only slightly. "Mr Hardiman," he said.

"Constable Hardiman," I corrected him. At this, the young man who had called Richard over stood up and melted away into the crowd. I took his seat. I beckoned to the pot boy, told him to bring over my tankard from the bar, and ordered another for Lawrence. The gownsman looked at me warily but said nothing. The two drinks arrived and we both took a sip.

"I want to talk to you about Edward Fleming," I said. I took my notebook and pencil from my coat pocket and turned to a clean page. I wrote the date at the top of it.

"Again?" said Lawrence, irritation in his voice. Now it was my turn to say nothing. "But I have told you all I know," he continued after about a minute of silence.

I turned back a few pages in my notebook. "Let me see," I said. "Ah yes, you called me an ugly hobnail – which is certainly true. And you said that Mr Fleming was gambling on horses at Newmarket, which is also true. You confirmed that he kept a ledger of this activity – the bets, the stakes, the odds and so on – and I know that such a ledger exists."

Lawrence looked uneasy, but he was determined to put me in my place. He drained his tankard and got to his feet. "As I said, *Constable* Hardiman, I have told you all I know."

I caught hold of his wrist and squeezed tightly, pulling down on it to force him back into his seat. "I am growing tired of your posturing, Mr Lawrence," I said. "And unless you want me to drag you out into the street and haul you before the Proctors right now, I suggest you stay here until I tell you that you can go."

Lawrence slumped back like a peevish schoolboy.

"That's better," I said. "Now it's my turn: let me tell you what I know." I turned back a few more pages in my notebook. "You're a clever young man, aren't you, Mr Lawrence?" I looked at him and he shrugged. "The trouble with being a clever young man here in Cambridge," I continued, "is that you are not the only clever one. Edward Fleming was also clever. And so is Joseph Brown."

"My tutor?" asked Lawrence sharply. "What has he to do with this?"

I continued reading from my notebook. "Mr Brown has very kindly explained to me," I said, "about the mathematical challenges he sets his students. How he uses wagers to explain probability and prediction. Far too complicated for me to understand, but I can see the principle of the thing." I looked up at him. "But for a man with Mr Brown's brain, Mr Fleming's ledger is like a child's primer: simple and plain to read. And he tells me that you have been cheating."

Lawrence sat forward, his face flushed. "I have never..." he began.

I held up my hand. "Well, perhaps cheating is too strong a word. But you do gather information that you choose not to share with others, in order to make sure that you have the advantage."

"That's not cheating: that's just being thorough," grumbled Lawrence.

"If you were a professional gambler, perhaps," I allowed, "but for a man who is supposed to be engaging in an academic exercise alongside other undergraduates, it's pretty sharp behaviour." I looked down at my notebook again. "At my request, Mr Brown has compared the information in Mr Fleming's ledger with that reported in the newspapers before and after the meetings, and has spoken to friends of his connected with the racecourse. And his view is that you have not been telling your fellow gownsmen everything you know about the horses. He has written down his findings for me." I took a folded piece of paper from the back of my notebook and opened it out on the table, flattening it with my hands. "Now, let me read this to you so that I get it right." I looked up at Lawrence and he shrugged again. I continued. "'At the Second October Meeting in Newmarket last year,' says Mr Brown, 'a horse called Magistrate had a set-back the day before his race. It was not reported in the newspapers, but there were rumours on the racecourse and the odds lengthened. I assume Lawrence heard these rumours, but when he actually saw the horse he was impressed by its form and backed it at the early long odds.'" I looked up at Lawrence. "I hope this makes more sense to you than it does to me." He looked bleak but gave a curt nod. I continued reading what the tutor had told me. "'Seeing the improvement in the horse, the men at the betting posts shortened the odds. When the horse won, Lawrence collected the winnings on behalf of the group. But,' and I think this is the important detail, Mr Lawrence, 'it is the shorter odds that were reported in the newspapers, and it is the shorter odds that Lawrence reported to the group and that were recorded in Fleming's ledger. Lawrence thereby made extra profit for himself, having actually placed the bet at longer odds.' At least, that's what Mr Brown thinks." I looked up and folded the paper again, slipping it back into my notebook.

"And if I did? What of it?" sneered Lawrence.

I took a long drink from my tankard and looked at him over the rim of it. Then I said, as casually as I could, "Have you heard of Suetonius, Mr Lawrence?" He stood up so quickly that his chair toppled over. He barged his way past several men, who turned to scowl at him, and made for the door. Just as he reached it, George Chapman stood up from his stool and stepped smartly in front of the door, blocking the way out.

"Thank you, George," I said as I caught up with them.

Lawrence looked from me to Chapman and back again. "My father is in town," he said quickly. "Here for Commencement – he has money."

"I'm sure he does, Mr Lawrence," I said. "Lodging in Cambridge during Commencement is an expensive business."

"No," he continued urgently. "You don't understand. He can pay you – both of you." He looked at Chapman and smiled. "Enough so that you won't have to be a porter any more. Or a constable." He turned to me, his eyebrows raised.

"I'm not sure about you, Mr Chapman," I said, tilting my head to one side, "but I can't hear too well in this busy parlour. I could have sworn I heard this young man attempting to bribe us, but surely he would not be so foolish." I chuckled and George Chapman copied me.

"That would be most unwise," said the porter.

"It would certainly suggest a guilty conscience," I agreed. "But then a murderer should have a guilty conscience."

"Murderer?" stuttered Lawrence. "Murderer?" By now, the parlour had fallen quiet and all eyes had turned to us. "But I have not murdered anyone. He was dead already."

Chapter Thirty-Six

DISHONOURABLE

Henry Lawrence was not at all as I had imagined him. When Richard Lawrence made his clumsy attempt to bribe me, I assumed he had learnt such tricks at his father's knee, but far from it. Henry Lawrence – summoned to St Clement's by an urgent note from Francis Vaughan – was as dignified and honourable as his son was slippery. The Master of Lawrence's own college would have to know soon enough, but for the time being St Clement's seemed as good a place as any to find out exactly what had happened before we turned the matter over to the town constables and the magistrates.

Vaughan had arranged four chairs around his table. He took one, I another, and the Lawrences, father and son, completed our group. I could see some similarity between them, but in his darker colouring I guessed the boy favoured his mother. Henry Lawrence had sandy hair and the ruddy cheeks and pale blue eyes of a country boy, but I had been told that he was a lawyer with a fine London firm. Surprisingly perhaps, given what I have seen of lawyers, he was quiet and listened carefully first to the Master and then to me as we outlined what we had discovered and what we suspected about his son. Less surprisingly, he took neat and careful notes of everything we said, occasionally holding up a hand to halt us as he wrote.

When we had finished, he turned to his son. Richard Lawrence sat pale in his chair, all bravado gone. "Now then, Rick," said his father. "You must tell us the truth. You know I will brook nothing less. It will go badly for you if you lie to me. And I always know when you are lying." He waited, his pen poised. "Now, sir, if you please," he said sternly.

"Fleming..." started his son. He shut his eyes for a moment and swallowed hard. "Fleming realised what I was doing. Just as you said, Constable Hardiman." He nodded at me. "The difference between the odds – pocketing the difference."

"Dishonourable behaviour, Rick," murmured his father. "Disappointing."

Richard Lawrence bit his lip, perhaps to hold back tears. "I went to his room to have it out with him. I offered him a cut." He glanced at his father, who said nothing. "But he wouldn't take it. He said he would tell the others – that he would tell Mr Brown and then I would be rusticated. We argued."

"Argued?" I asked. "Or fought?"

"I know what you think," said the gownsman, "but it wasn't like that. We tussled – grappled. I was trying to grab the ledger – I thought if I could get rid of that, then it would be his word against mine and perhaps..." He shook his head. "It was foolish. And then he just collapsed."

"Collapsed?" repeated Vaughan. "Fainted, you mean?"

Richard Lawrence shook his head. "More than that – his eyes went up into his head, and he was shaking, sort of flapping his hands." He made the motion with his own hands. "Then he fell onto the floor and I didn't know what to do. I... I just watched him. And he made this horrible choking sound," he closed his eyes at the memory. "Just for a few seconds. And then he was dead."

"The falling sickness," I said. "When I was a boy, a young woman in the village died of it."

"But you did not run for help, Rick?" asked Henry Lawrence.

"I was scared," said his son quietly. "People would ask why I was in his room and what we were arguing about, and how he had died – they would think what you all think."

"But to watch a man dying and not go for help." His father shook his head sadly. "We have indulged you too much, your mother and I. We have bred a selfish creature with no care for anyone but himself. May God forgive us."

"But he was dead, pa," protested Richard. "I checked: I used a glass to look for breath, and I felt his wrist and listened to his heart. No-one could have helped."

We were all silent for a moment. Then I asked, "What did you do next, Mr Lawrence?"

The undergraduate put his hand to his mouth as though he could not bear to let the words out. He spoke through his fingers. "I tied the cord from his dressing gown around his neck, threw the end of it over the beam, and pulled him up. Then I moved the chair to make it look like he had hanged himself." He jumped up from his seat and ran to the fireplace, where he was violently sick. Vaughan stood and went to his desk and poured a tumbler of water. He walked over to Richard Lawrence and handed it to him. The undergraduate wiped his mouth with a handkerchief and drank the water, nodding his thanks to the Master.

"Sit down," said his father. "You can clean up that mess later."

Richard returned to his chair. "Will I be hanged for murder?" he asked, looking first at me and then at his father.

"No," said Henry Lawrence decisively. "He died while you were fighting. Manslaughter. Unlawful killing without premeditation or malice." A lawyer through and through, then. "You will plead guilty to manslaughter and you will serve a short term of imprisonment. Between two and six months, depending on the judge."

"But pa," said his son, turning to him with pleading eyes.

His father held up his hand. "I do not make the laws, Richard. You have done wrong and you will be punished. Your mother and I taught you right from wrong, and if you choose to ignore our teachings, then you must pay the price." He softened a little. "We will stand by you, Rick – we will not disown you. But neither will we prevent the proper application of the law to your actions."

"To that end, sir," I said, "I would like to ask your son about the note he left in Mr Fleming's coat."

"A note?" said Henry Lawrence. "What note is this, Rick?"

"I can't," the gownsman said quietly. "Mr Hardiman, I can't." He shook his head, folding his lips in on themselves.

"A man must own his actions," said his father. "However shameful they may be."

We waited. After a minute, Richard Lawrence started to speak quietly. "When Joshua Pears was killed, we all heard about the note left with him."

Of course: a thrilling detail like that would not stay secret for long in the gossipy world of the University.

"And I thought," he continued, speaking more quickly now, "I thought that if everyone assumed that the same person had killed Fleming, then I would be safe."

"How did you know what the note looked like?" I asked. "The exact words on it?"

"I bribed one of the coroner's men," he replied, looking down at his hands. "He let me look at the note."

"And the coat?" I asked. "How did you manage to put the note into Mr Fleming's coat?"

"When he first collapsed," said Richard Lawrence, "I took it off him – I thought it might help him breathe more easily. I did try, pa," he said urgently. "When I went back to Fleming's room, to look for somewhere to leave the note, somewhere that might have been missed when his room was first examined, I looked under the bed and there was the coat. So I put the note in the pocket and pushed it back under the bed. And hoped that someone would find it."

Chapter Thirty-Seven

RESULT

I was just finishing my early supper when there was a knock at the door.

"You finish that, Mr Hardiman," said Mrs Jacobs, pointing at my plate. "I'll go."

She returned a moment later with a folded piece of paper and handed it to me. "From Mr Vaughan at St Clement's," she said. "No reply needed."

I wiped my mouth and my fingers and opened the note. *Mr Hardiman*, it said. *I have today met with the Vice-Chancellor. He is in agreement that the matter of Mr Lawrence is outside his jurisdiction and he is to refer it to the magistrates. Your name has not been mentioned. Thank you, as ever, for your invaluable and discreet assistance in this matter. With sincere good wishes, Francis Vaughan.*

"Something wrong at the college?" asked my landlady, reaching past me for my empty plate.

"Not at all," I said. "On the contrary: a good outcome."

When I reached the Proctors' Court I found that I was again paired with George Swanney. He was already there, checking his reflection in the glass. I sat on the long bench against the wall so that I could lean forward and buff my boots – the Senior Proctor always inspected us carefully, and would comment if he saw dust on them.

"No surprise with the election result, then," I observed. "Lord Charles and Lord Francis have been returned."

Swanney looked over his shoulder at me. "Of course," he said. "The Duke of Rutland would not have it any other way. I ducked out of the shop to hear the results and some of the speeches." He came and sat beside me. "I have nothing against the two men personally, you know. Manners fought in the wars, I believe, and Osborne is as active as his health permits. But it cannot be right – it cannot be healthy – for one family's interests to direct – to dictate – the government of a county for so long. Manners has represented Cambridgeshire for twenty-four years, brought back time and again by freeholders who like a steady diet of King, constitution and Protestantism."

I thought of what George Fisher had said to me. "I believe you are not the only one who feels that way," I said.

Swanney looked at me sharply. "Do you mean..." he started, but the door opened and in strode Mr Temple.

"Gentlemen," he said, looking at us both sitting on the bench. "You are university constables, not housewives sharing receipts. Stand, if you please, so that I may inspect you."

As we were returning our capes to their hooks at the end of our patrol, George Swanney pressed a note into my hand.

"It is my address," he said. "When all this fuss," he gestured at the chart on the wall, outlining the events and attendant duties of Commencement, "is over, perhaps you would like to come to my home for supper. My sister is an excellent cook, although I take care never to tell her that – she needs no encouragement to think well of herself."

Chapter Thirty-Eight

IMPERFECT

I cannot have been the only person to breathe a sigh of relief on the 7th of July, which marked both the end of term and the closing of the Midsummer Fair. Certainly when George Chapman had called round for supper he had been worn out, falling asleep in the chair by the stove. Mrs Jacobs had brought her sewing in from the sitting room to keep him company, and I caught her gazing fondly at him.

The next morning I walked along Jesus Lane towards town. It was a beautiful day, growing warmer by the minute, and I turned my face to the sun. I would have eight horses to rub down this noon, four heading north and four heading south; they would be dripping with sweat in this weather, and very thirsty. After that, I had decided, I would come home to wash properly, rather than just tipping a bucket over myself in the corner of the yard. I was going to have supper with George Swanney and his sister, and as he worked in a drapers' shop he was sure to prize a clean and neat appearance.

It was perhaps fitting that George Swanney lived above a milliner's shop. I knocked on the door in Silver Street and heard someone running down the stairs to answer me. Swanney opened the door with a smile and beckoned me in.

"Welcome, welcome," he said, standing to one side. "Your hat can go there," he pointed to a rack. We walked up the stairs and into a bright, airy room that made the most of its large window jutting out over the shop below. There was a faded but comfortable-looking sofa against the wall, flanked by two small tables, each of which had two or three books on it. My fingers itched to pick them up and see what they were, but I clasped my hands behind my back. Two armchairs – one larger and one smaller – stood with their backs to the window, I guessed to make the most of the light. A fireguard with an embroidered panel protected the room from dust and draughts from the chimney.

Swanney walked over to a small cabinet and opened the door.

"Would you care for a glass of hock?" he asked.

"I would, yes," I said. He poured two glasses, handed one to me and raised his own.

"Your good health, Mr Hardiman," he said.

"And yours, Mr Swanney," I replied, raising my glass. "Although perhaps we should be Gregory and George when we are not under the stern eye of the Senior Proctor."

"Stern is one word for it," said George, smiling. Just then there was a crash from the room to the rear of the apartment and a woman's voice said, "Blast it!"

"My sister," said my host by way of explanation. "Please excuse me. Do make yourself at home." He waved his arm to indicate the room and then disappeared through a door leading to the back. I took another sip of the wine, which was unexpectedly good, and walked over to one of the small tables. I put down my glass so that I could pick up the book on the top of the low pile. It was a tattered old thing, just clinging onto its cover, and bristling with slips of paper. I turned to the title page. "A Vindication of the Rights of Women," I read quietly aloud, "by Mary..." I looked again at the unfamiliar name.

"Wollstonecraft," said a woman's voice behind me.

I jumped – perhaps it was impolite to look at someone else's choice of reading. I closed the book and turned around.

"Of all the books to leave lying around, Kate," said George, coming out of the kitchen.

"Why?" said the woman stubbornly. "It's what I happen to be reading at the moment."

"It's what you always happen to be reading," said her brother. He smiled at me apologetically. "She must know it by heart now, and I'm not far behind her, given how much of it she reads out to me."

"It's better for you than those silly adventure stories you choose," she replied, nudging him.

"Our guest is not here to watch us squabbling," said George, holding up his hands in surrender. "So. Now. Mr Gregory Hardiman, may I present my sister, Miss Catherine Swanney. Kate, this is Mr Gregory Hardiman."

"You're often the distance man to George's sprinter, I am told," said Miss Swanney, smiling at me. I looked for any sign of distaste or fear in her face, but there was none. No doubt her brother had warned her about my scar but still, people are usually taken aback.

"I am," I admitted, "although your brother is so swift that I am rarely needed."

"Yes, we're nippy in this family," said Miss Swanney. "Long legs."

Without meaning to I glanced down at her skirt; when I looked up she was smiling at me. I felt myself blush.

"Why don't you gentlemen take a seat while I finish in the kitchen," she suggested. "Ten minutes to go."

"I hope you are hungry, Gregory," said George as he pointed me towards the sofa. "Kate feeds me as though I were twins." He sat in the larger armchair. "But none of it is ever wasted; anything we can't finish is taken to the corporation almshouses."

"This is a very comfortable room," I said, looking around me. "Light. Welcoming."

"It is one of the advantages of working at Mr Warwick's," said George. "Once a year he allows staff to choose any fabrics and so on at a reduced price. I flatter myself that I have a good eye, and Kate is talented with her needle, so between us we manage well."

"Have you lived here long?" I asked.

"About six years," he replied. "When our parents were alive, and our younger sister Sarah, we lived out in Newnham. But now it is just the two of us, and with my work being in town, it made sense to move here."

The door to the kitchen opened and Miss Swanney's head appeared. "Table, please, gentlemen," she said.

We did as we were told and sat opposite each other at the small dining table. The kitchen door opened again and Miss Swanney reversed into the room, a steaming plate of food in each hand. George jumped up quickly and took one from her, putting it in front of me. She put down his plate and then returned to the kitchen for her own. I rose to my feet and waited for her to seat herself before I sat down again. George had put the hock bottle and a jug of water on the table and busied himself topping up our glasses.

"Start, start," said Miss Swanney, pointing at my plate. "It's much better hot."

I looked down at my plate. There was a generous rump steak with a dark sauce, boiled potatoes in their own white sauce, and both carrots and runner beans. It smelt wonderful. I sampled each in turn, and they were delicious. I looked up with a smile.

"I told you," said George, attacking his own meal.

"You are an excellent cook, Miss Swanney," I said.

"It's all a matter of organisation and chemistry," she replied.

"I once knew a lecturer in chemistry," I said. "Mr John Galpin. He studied gases, I believe." And in my head I asked myself why I was trying to impress this woman. I looked at her as she ate. She shared her brother's dark hair and pale skin, and they both had a strong nose and a wide mouth. She was not pretty, exactly, but she had a pleasing face – open, and intelligent. She glanced up from her plate and caught me staring at her.

"Does it pain you, Mr Hardiman?" she asked. "Your scar?"

"Kate!" said her brother.

"Are we supposed to pretend that it is not there?" she asked. "Make Mr Hardiman think that that we are, what, ignorant, or unobservant?"

I laughed. "No-one, Miss Swanney, could ever accuse you of being either ignorant or unobservant. And no, it does not pain me. It did, at first – the injury itself, of course, and then the healing and the scarring. The skin pulled, and itched terribly. But now," I put down my knife and raised my hand to my cheek, "now, no: it is simply part of me."

***

By the end of the meal, I knew that I had made good friends. George Swanney was excellent company, telling amusing stories about customers at the shop and asking me about life at the Hoop. But his sister was easily his equal. She was quick-witted and curious, jumping from her seat to grab a book or a newspaper to read something to contribute to our discussion, and taking a full part in any debate. We talked about war and education and custard and exploration, and it was with great surprise that I glanced at their long-case clock and realised the time.

"That was a delightful evening," I said, hauling myself to my feet from their comfortable sofa. "Thank you for taking pity on this battered old bachelor."

"Not so old, if you don't mind," said George. "We're of an age, I believe. Men in our prime." And he puffed out his chest comically.

"And not so battered either," added his sister. "Imperfect, to be sure, but you wear it well."

And I was more pleased with her half-compliment than I could ever have imagined.

Chapter Thirty-Nine
Assizes

It was a hot day and we constables were certainly regretting the weight and warmth of our cloaks, but there was nothing for it: the Proctors were required to attend the assize sermon at St Mary's church and then process to the Shire House, and we had to go with them. At church the preacher read from the Book of Zechariah about the flying scroll, which seemed to me to have little to do with the work to come – although there was something about stealing, so perhaps I just needed to pay more attention. After that we accompanied the two Learned Judges (they were capitalised like that on the Proctors' wall chart) to the Shire House. Our solemn procession through the muck and noise of the market was one of those comical contradictions of Cambridge life.

Lord Chief Justice Best took charge of one court and Mr Justice Bayley the other, while the great and the good of Cambridgeshire were sworn in to serve – as they always did – on the grand jury. When the jury had taken their seats in his court, his Lordship said that he regretted to observe from the number of prisoners in the calendar that Cambridgeshire and Cambridge have more than their fair share of crime. This, he suggested, proved that greater vigilance was needed from the police, and he encouraged the jury to report to him any suggestions they might have for improvements in local policing. At this, all eyes turned to Mr Mortlock in the jury, and he had the good grace to look slightly uncomfortable: his family and friends had supplied all of Cambridge's mayors for the past four decades.

At the end of his remarks his Lordship formally released the Proctors and constables from their duty at court, but we none of us moved. We knew that the first business of the day would be the trial of the eight men accused of riot and assault in November last. For those of you who may not be aware of the event, on the 5th of November last year there was a disturbance in Cambridge between townsfolk and undergraduates. The Proctors and some other University officers – including the four constables on duty on the night (I was not one of them) – tried to calm things, but were themselves turned on and assaulted. Eight men seen to be in the heart of the disturbance were arrested and charged, and now they were to stand trial.

The eight men were brought into court, shuffling together in the dock and looking around for familiar faces in the crowd. They seemed pitiful specimens to me, but surviving on the meagre rations and squalid conditions of the county gaol for eight months would make a scrub of the finest gentleman. The clerk of the court read aloud the names of the eight and one by one they pleaded not guilty: John Redhead, Charles Willimott, Samuel Bowman, James How, William Glover, Robert Burrows, Charles Edwards and James Raby.

The case was brought on behalf of the University by Henry Storks, who stated that the University was anxious to protect its officers from the insults to which they were frequently exposed during riotous assemblies, especially upon public occasions. "Hear, hear," said several people.

The first witness to speak was the man who had been Junior Proctor at the time of the incident, Henry Venn. He was a clergyman, and I had heard him deliver a very moving evening lecture in Great St Mary's on the evils of the Atlantic slave trade. He confirmed that on the evening in question, at about half-past nine, he had been summoned to the Senate House where he came across a crowd of perhaps three hundred men, both gownsmen and townsmen. He then heard loud shouting from the Market Hill and set off in that direction with Mr Joshua King, a Moderator. (The University is full of unfamiliar terms; the Moderators assist the Proctors in the assessment of examinations.) They were walking along St Mary's Passage when they heard someone say, "Here they come – now for it!" Two men rushed from the crowd in fighting attitude, fists raised, and one of them struck Mr Venn a hard blow upon the temple, forcing him to take a few steps back. Mr King was meanwhile struggling with a townsman who was secured and identified. Mr Venn called out that he was a Proctor, and the gownsmen started to disperse but the townsmen did not.

Mr Venn said that he then walked along Trinity Street and found several gownsmen cowering in the doorway of the Sun Inn; he managed to get them away but they said that others were hiding in the yard of the inn. A mob of townsmen forced open the gates to the yard with great violence, surrounded the gownsmen and Mr Venn, and he was struck and kicked several times. The gownsmen fled and Mr Venn and Mr King assured the townsmen that no undergraduates were left. The townsmen then started to insult the two officers, asking if they had put all their babies to bed. Mr Venn and Mr King walked back towards the market, and the mob of townsmen followed them, hissing and booing, and pelting them with mud, dirt and stones. Mr Venn finally reached safety at his own college, Queen's. In response to a question from Mr Storks, he confirmed that he was in the crowd for about three hours, that he could only estimate the number at three hundred, and that the crowd was very dense.

Both Mr King and the Senior Proctor at the time of the incident, Mr Temple, corroborated the testimony of Mr Venn.

Several witnesses were then called to identify the prisoners and their part in the incident. Constable Samuel Cockerell had seen Samuel Bowman strike Mr King. Other witnesses had seen James Raby throwing stones near the Sun Inn, Charles Edwards being active in the crowd, John Redhead hitting the Junior Proctor twice, James How hitting a gentleman three times near St John's College, Charles Willimott pushing about in the crowd, and Robert Burrows and William Glover being very disorderly.

A Mr Kelly appeared as counsel for Mr Willimott and started speaking, but before he could finish Lord Chief Justice Best raised his hand and said that he too thought the evidence against Willimott was slight. He looked at Mr Storks, who promptly agreed to an acquittal for Willimott. The judge then summed up the evidence and turned to the jury, who immediately returned their verdict, acquitting Charles Willimott and finding all the others guilty. A couple of people in the court called out "Shame", but they were quickly shushed as everyone waited to hear the sentences. An usher walked to the dock and beckoned to Willimott, who shook hands with two of the men he was standing with before climbing down into the well of the court.

The Lord Chief Justice looked down his long nose and fixed his eyes on the seven men still standing in the dock.

"This is a complicated case," he said in a clear voice that carried an echo of his childhood in Somerset. "There are shades of difference in your guilt but," and here he paused, "you all took part in this cowardly and dastardly conduct. You selected the Proctor and Moderator, who were alone and unprotected, as the objects of your spite and your malevolence. This uncivilised behaviour will not be tolerated. Your sentences are as follows." I saw two men near me lean forward; they both had notepads and pencils and were obviously reporting the case for the newspapers. "John Redhead: twelve months in gaol. James Raby: six months. Samuel Bowman and James How: three months. William Glover, Charles Edwards and Robert Burrows: one month. At the expiration of your terms of imprisonment, you are each to enter into a recognizance to keep the peace for three years. And if you fail to do so, you will be required to pay a surety of fifty pounds. Take them down."

I looked across at the Proctors and they both seemed satisfied with the outcome. They rose to their feet, inclined their heads at the judge, waited for people to shuffle out of their way, and left the court accompanied by all the constables except me. Also on the morning's list for sentencing was Richard Lawrence. I looked around the court and saw Henry Lawrence, pale and neat, a notebook open on his lap. He must have sensed me looking at him, as he turned to meet my gaze and gave a little nod. I nodded back.

We had to sit through two more cases: a hard-faced, stiff-backed woman who pleaded guilty to one indictment of fraud (confined for two months) and a mild-looking man who admitted committing bigamy (fined one shilling and discharged, as neither of his wives had wanted him punished). After that, Richard Lawrence was led to the dock and looked over at his father before turning to face the judge. The charge of manslaughter was read aloud to him, and he said quietly the single word, "Guilty". The judge looked at him for a long moment before passing down a sentence of three months in gaol. Richard bowed his head and was led from the dock. I looked again at his father, who gave me a short nod before standing and making his way out of the court.

"Three months in prison," said Francis Vaughan unhappily, shaking his head. "And the loss of so much more."

I had, as requested, gone to St Clement's after returning my equipment to the Proctors' Court. It was too late for me to see the *Fakenham Day* off to London from the Hoop, and as a consequence I had missed my midday meal. My stomach growled.

"Forgive me, Mr Hardiman," said the Master. "Thoughtless of me." He leaned out of his window and looked down into the college court. "You, lad!" he called. "Find Mr Wells in the kitchen and tell him to send up a plate of cold meats."

He turned back to me. "Sit, sit," he said, gesturing to the two armchairs. "Too hot for coffee, I think – perhaps a glass of ratafia?" I shook my head. "I agree: terribly sickly. Hock, then."

"Diluted, please," I said.

The Master poured two half-glasses of wine from the decanter and topped them up with water from a jug. He carried them over and put them on the low table between us.

"Three months," he said again.

"The conditions in the town gaol are not what he will be used to," I observed. "Not as bad as in the old gaol, I am told, but still..."

"A far cry from this," agreed Vaughan, waving his hand around to suggest the college, with its comfortable rooms, quiet court and well-stocked dining hall.

"But Mr Payne is a good man," I said. "The gaoler. A fair man who keeps to the rules. And Mr Lawrence's father will know how to make his son's stay as bearable as it can be."

There was a quiet knock on the door and in came Wells, the Master's footman. He was carrying a tray on which was laid a plate covered with a cloth, with a heel of bread wrapped in another cloth alongside it. He went to hand the tray to Vaughan, who shook his head and pointed to me.

"It's game pie," said the footman, "and some cheese."

"Thank you," I said, taking the tray from him. He bowed and left. I uncovered the pie and used the knife to cut off a corner – I tried not to gobble it, but I was very hungry. The Master smiled indulgently as I wiped crumbs from my mouth. I swallowed. "What did you mean by the loss of so much more?" I asked. "For Richard Lawrence."

Vaughan's smile disappeared. "Well, he cannot return to the University," he said. "And even with his father's connections, he will struggle to make his way in London." He looked at me. "Do you think he might do well in the army?" I was drinking my wine and I choked a little, my eyes watering. "Surely the army is not so picky these days?" he asked.

I shook my head. "No, no – it's more that Mr Lawrence might be a little... soft for such a life," I said. "Although three months in the town gaol will certainly knock the corners off him. And the army is a grand life for a young man in search of adventure."

The Master nodded thoughtfully. "I shall write to his father and suggest it. Perhaps if I were to ask Mr Brown to prepare a short recommendation for young Richard, mentioning his academic achievements and his, let's say, commercial skills." He sighed. "If only young men would think of the consequences before they acted – but then I suppose there would be little exploration or invention. And perhaps no marriage at all."

Chapter Forty
Hazard

"I hope you don't mind my asking to come with you again," I said to Charlie Grantham as I helped him load the last boxes onto the cart in the yard of Barker and Eaden. After such a busy and exhausting few weeks, I felt in need of some relaxation away from Cambridge. The weather was fine, the July Meeting at Newmarket was being advertised in the newspapers, and so I had made plans for my excursion.

"Not in the slightest," said Charlie. "On the contrary: I like the company, and I can kip on the way home." He winked at me. "And kip is what I want more than anything these days."

"Ah yes," I said, giving Major's harness a final check and stroking his velvet nose while he sighed. "I heard the good news a few days ago, from Mrs Bird. A girl, I believe, and hale and hearty. Congratulations to you." I reached across and shook his hand.

Charlie climbed up onto the cart. "Marianne," he said proudly. "Mary for my mother, and Anne for Agnes's."

I climbed up alongside him. "A very pretty name," I said. "And a very pretty baby too, I am sure."

Charlie pulled a face. "They all look like piglets to me, babies – but I don't say that to Agnes, o'course."

"Very wise," I said. "I am a little surprised that you're still working for Barker and Eaden, after that unpleasantness last month."

"Talking of that, Agnes and me, we can't thank you enough," said Charlie, looking across at me.

I waved his thanks away. "I knew there had to be a mistake," I said, "and it just needed uncovering. I'm glad Agnes thought to ask me for help. But I thought it would make you even keener to move on."

"It has," admitted Charlie. "But the extra money they offered is useful right now, and it means I can take my time finding something better. And on days like today, well, it's not that bad." He smiled.

I had to agree with him. Unlike on our previous visit in April, it was light for our entire journey to Newmarket. The sun climbed in the sky ahead of us as we followed the same route through Teversham and Bottisham. Just as we neared Newmarket we heard hooves coming up fast behind us and a man on horseback galloped past, kicking up dust. Major looked over his shoulder at us and Charlie laughed.

"I swear he's wondering what's the rush," he said, pointing at Major. "When he's tethered on Cambridge Hill, overlooking the course, I sometimes catch him staring at the racehorses. Then he looks at me and, no word of a lie, he shakes his head."

"They're smart animals, horses," I said. "I daresay he feels sorry for them, running around with men on their backs whipping them, while he's munching on grass and listening to the birds. Isn't that right, Major?" And the horse whinnied in reply.

As we slowed to turn in onto the heath, I turned to Charlie.

"D'you mind if I leave you here?" I asked.

"You're not watching the races?" he asked, pulling the cart to a halt.

"Not this time," I said as I jumped down. "I want to go into town and see what else there is."

"Taverns," said Charlie with authority. "A great many taverns."

"So I have heard," I said. "What time will you be setting off home?"

Charlie reached behind him for his satchel and took a newspaper from it. "The last race is at a quarter past five, so shall we say five o'clock? Anyone who wants any drink will have bought it by then."

"I'll make sure I'm back in good time."

Three-quarters of an hour later I was in the high street of Newmarket, and what a sight it was. It was a broad thoroughfare, sweeping down the hill from the heath, grand buildings on either side, and filled with men on foot, on horses and in every manner of coach and cart, from rough wagons to elegant phaetons. I had expected everyone to be making their way to the courses, but plenty seemed to be going in the other direction. I looked at the large brick building opposite me and there was that name again: the Rutland Arms. I turned my back on it and walked along the street until I found the place I was looking for: the Black Bull. When I told William Bird I was going to Newmarket, he said he had heard that the beer was well kept at the Black Bull and that the landlord, Vincent Finton, was an honest man in a town with plenty of rogues.

I walked through the narrow archway – it was so narrow that the daily mail coach would need to swing wide into the street to be able to pass through it. But the yard itself was long and wide, with rooms overlooking it on one side and a high wall on the other.

At the far end of the yard was another gateway; I walked towards it and peered out, and there was the market place. I ducked back into the yard and went indoors in search of the parlour. It was already busy, I guessed with men filling their bellies before heading up the hill to the races in the afternoon, but I managed to find a small table for myself. A pot boy appeared at my elbow.

"Ale and pie?" he asked.

"What sort of pie is it?" I asked.

"Not horse, if that's what you're thinking," he replied wearily. "It's pork – made by Mrs Finton this morning."

"Ale and pie it is, then," I said. "And bring me a second piece of pie to take with me, if you would."

With a new baby at home Agnes might not have made a damper for her husband, and even if she had, Charlie and I would probably be grateful for a bite on the way home.

William Bird was right: the ale at the Black Bull was good. And Mrs Finton's pie was very tasty. I took the second piece, which had been carefully wrapped in a piece of paper, and put it into the pocket of my coat. I left some coins on the table and walked out into the yard. Rather than go back to the High Street, I went through the rear gateway into the market. It had just gone noon and most of the stall-holders were packing away into the carts that now blocked all the lanes leading to the market place. I squeezed myself between them, turning without plan into any small alleyway that presented itself. It was some time since I had explored a new place. A scrawny girl of about seven was standing in an open doorway and cast a practised eye over me, taking in my plain, serviceable coat and my battered face. She held out a hand.

"Spare a coin, sir?" she asked.

I put my hand in my pocket and felt the pie. I pulled it out. "Here," I said, handing it to her. "Have this instead."

She snatched it from me, unwrapped it and took a big bite. A toddling boy, naked and grimy, appeared at her side and reached up; she broke off a hunk of pastry and passed it to him. They both stared at me, chewing and silent. I smiled and walked on. The alleyway became, if possible, even more cheerless. Despite the July sunshine it was dank, and the smell was foul. I was relieved to spy a turning to my left, and I walked quickly along it until I found myself coming out into the light again. I took a deep breath. Opposite me was another tavern: the Fox and Goose. I crossed towards it, thinking to have a refreshing drink, but I stopped in my tracks when I heard something. I turned my head and listened, and it came again. "Please. Help." I had heard enough – more than enough – dying men, and this plea was given with someone's last strength. There was an alleyway alongside the tavern and I walked down it, glancing over my shoulder – it was exactly the sort of place where a robber would lie in wait for a man looking for a quiet place to relieve himself. And from the stink of it, plenty had done that. A few yards in, I saw him: a figure slumped on the floor, trying to haul himself into a seated position. He saw me too, and put out a hand. "Please, help me," he said again.

"I'll do my best," I said, crouching down next to him. "Where are you hurt?"

"Chest," he said with some effort. "Knife."

"Can you stand, do you think?" I asked. "It's too dark here for me to help you." I took his arm and put it around my neck and then reached around his waist. I braced myself to pull him upright, but he was much lighter than I expected and I managed it easily. We walked slowly back towards the tavern, me all but dragging him and him wincing at every movement.

As we reached the street I saw a man and called out. "Hi there, you, sir!" He stopped. "This man is injured. I am a constable. Can you go into the tavern and ask for someone to come out and help us?"

He stared for a moment and then did as I had asked. Just then the man in my arms gave a small sigh and fainted. I quickly laid him on the ground and pulled up his shirt. There was a great deal of blood spreading across his chest and down towards his trousers, but no apparent wound. It must have been a small blade. By now, half a dozen people had gathered and were gawping at us.

"Out of my way, if you please," I heard a woman say, and I looked up to see a young woman in an apron pushing her way towards us. "You," she said, flapping her hands at the other onlookers, "back indoors or on your way. Or I'll send word to your wives that you've nothing better to do on a working day than come to my tavern." They did as they were told.

"I need a basin of water," I said, "and a clean cloth. And a tot of brandy."

"I'll see to it," she said, and went back inside. I liked that she wasted no time asking questions. A minute later she returned with all three items and crouched down beside me. The man on the floor groaned and his eyes flickered open.

"It's you," he said softly. "Constable Hardman."

"Hardiman," I corrected and looked at him again. It took me a moment to place him, but it came. "Mr Harford," I said.

"Can he stand?" asked the woman.

I shook my head. "Best not," I decided. "He has a knife wound somewhere and has lost a lot of blood."

"A friend of yours?" she said, putting one hand behind Harford's neck and with the other lifting the tumbler of brandy to his lips. He took a sip and then coughed. She waited and gave him another drink.

"I know him," I said. "He lives in Cambridge. Like me."

"Stetchworth," said Harford quietly.

I looked at the woman. "That's a village near here," she said. "About three miles south."

"Is that where your family is, Mr Harford?" I asked.

He nodded and then fainted again.

"We'll take him indoors," said the woman decisively. "The parlour will be too busy, but we can put him in my room and call the surgeon. I'm Ellen May – my father is the landlord." She stood up. "You, and you," she said, pointing at two men who were walking past. "Help the constable carry this man inside. One of you under each arm and one for the legs – and be careful, he's badly hurt."

An hour later, I was sitting in the parlour of the tavern with Miss May, lifting a tankard to my lips and finding that I needed two hands to steady it.

"Shock," I said by way of explanation.

"Mr Peck is an excellent surgeon," she said. "And if he needs assistance, we have two veterinary surgeons we can call." I looked at her, startled, and she smiled. "You looked so worried – I wanted to make you smile. Forgive me." She smoothed down her apron. She was about twenty years old, I would guess, with a neat figure and a round, open face. Her pale red hair was pulled back into a neat bun and her grey eyes missed very little. They certainly caught me staring at her, and I looked away quickly.

"How do you know Mr Harford?" she asked. "Is he a constable as well?"

"Oh no," I said. "I met him when I was..." I searched for the right word, "enquiring into young men gambling on horse races."

"But he is not..." she said quickly and then stopped. "I mean, I assumed he was gambling but not on the horses."

"Why on earth do you say that?" I asked.

"When I was taking off his coat," she said, "I found these." She reached into the pocket of her apron and handed me two dice, now a bit grubby. "I assumed he was playing hazard somewhere in town and someone objected to him winning."

"Hazard?" I repeated. "In Newmarket? I thought all the gambling was on the horses."

She pinched her lips and shook her head. "If only that were the case. But when you have hundreds – sometimes thousands – of men in town who enjoy gambling, there are always those who will take advantage. They set up tents on the heath, and tables in back rooms – or just a bench on a street for the pea and thimble men. And that's just for the working men. For the gentry, every fine house in Newmarket offers gaming in the evenings – hazard, whist, roulette."

"No wonder the young men from the University want to come here," I said, half to myself.

"Is that where he's from?" she asked.

I nodded.

"We've seen more gambling than ever in the past months," she continued. "I put it down to the lottery."

"The lottery?" I asked.

"The end of the state lottery," she said. "Last draw in October, isn't it? Once that's gone, how is a man to make a quick fortune?" She smiled sadly.

I left Miss May in the parlour and went up to see Mr Harford and the surgeon Mr Peck. The latter was rolling down his sleeves as I walked in.

"You the father?" he asked.

I shook my head. "I believe his family is in Stetchworth," I said.

"Best send for them," he said. He must have seen the look on Harford's face. "He's not going to die, but he needs care. And a proper wash."

"A long, thin knife, I thought," I said. "I was a soldier – I've seen most types."

"He's been lucky," said Peck, putting on his coat and picking up his bag. "A deep wound, but missed the heart and lungs. Plenty of blood lost – the pale face – but he's young, strong, he'll fix soon enough. I've cleaned it, put a compress on it. Change it twice a day. And you," he turned and spoke to Harford, "no riding, no running – four weeks." He turned back to me. "His address." He held out a piece of paper. "I'll send my bill."

"Thank you, Mr Peck," I said, "but could I trouble you to give that to Miss May and have her send for his father? I want to have a word with Mr Harford."

The surgeon nodded once and left.

I looked around the room and picked up a stool and placed it next to the bed.

"Now then, Mr Harford," I began, "before your father arrives, I think we need to have a little talk."

Harford said nothing but nodded.

"It may be outside term," I continued, "but I suspect that you should not be here in Newmarket. You should be at home with your parents. What have you told them?"

He shrugged and grimaced.

"Careful," I said. "Don't move more than you need to, while the wound closes." I waited, but he said nothing. I sighed and folded my arms. "Ah well, you're right. You don't have to tell me anything. But as a university constable I am obliged to report the matter to Mr Chafy; he's the Master of your college and he will have to know." I stood up. "He and your father can discuss it and decide what to do next. As it is outside term, it may not be rustication, I suppose." I turned to go.

"No, wait," gasped Harford.

I looked back at him, cocking my head.

"Sit down again," he said. "Please."

I did so. I felt in my coat pocket and took out my notebook and pencil. I waited.

"This," he said eventually, pointing at his chest, "it's nothing to do with the gambling."

I held up a hand. "Let's start at the beginning, Mr Harford," I said. "Where do your parents think you are?"

"Cambridge," he said. "I told them I was staying at college for another week to finish my reading."

"And did you plan to come to Newmarket, or was it by chance?" I asked.

"I planned it," he said. "I knew about the hazard tables and I've always had good luck with dice. I told a friend at college and we arranged to come together, but he lost his nerve and went home, so I came anyway."

"When?" I asked.

"Yesterday," he replied. "I came on the mail coach, in the late morning. And while I was waiting for the coach I had a feeling someone was watching me. He must have followed me here."

"Someone was watching you in Cambridge?" I said. "Who?"

"Will Mason, of course," said Harford. "I knew he would try again."

―――

"You look worse than I do," observed Charlie Grantham as we pulled out onto the road. "I was going to ask you to take the reins while I had my kip, but maybe it should be other way round."

When I had made my way back to Cambridge Hill, I had given Charlie quite a fright. My clothes were dirty and bloodstained, and I was puffing from walking fast to get back in time. His first thought was that I had been set upon by footpads, and he'd quickly grabbed a wooden cudgel from under his seat. When I had caught my breath and had a good long drink, I had told him a little of what had happened to me – that I had come across an injured man and had helped him. I did not mention who that man was, or the most disturbing thing of all: that Will Mason had tried to murder him.

"No, no, I'm fine," I protested. "A quiet walk home with Major is just what I need. You settle down in the back and I'll wake you when we reach Cambridge."

It sounds generous of me, but the truth is that I wanted time alone with my thoughts. I wanted to force myself to remember everything I could about Will Mason. I wanted to plan what we should do about finding him. And I wanted to work out why, every time Miss May came into my mind, I found myself comparing her to Miss Swanney.

Chapter Forty-One
STILETTO

I had barely slept a wink. Seeing Harford's injury and hearing his cries of pain had stirred all sorts of memories, and the old horrors played out behind my eyelids. Besides, it was a warm and muggy night and not a breath of breeze moved through my room, no matter how wide I opened the window.

Mrs Jacobs cast concerned glances at me as she served my breakfast. When I had arrived home the previous evening, it had taken me a while to quieten her enough to understand that the blood on my clothes was not mine. But then she had had the good sense to leave me alone, although I know it cost her dearly to bite her tongue. Things were different this morning.

"Now then, Mr Hardiman," she said, sitting down opposite me. "I heard you walking about in the night, so I know that whatever happened yesterday has upset you."

I took my time, preparing a forkful of food, putting it in my mouth, chewing slowly and then swallowing. I wiped my lips. "It has, Mrs Jacobs," I said.

"But you said the young man will survive," she said. "And your shirt and coat will be good as new once I've finished with them. They've been soaking overnight in soapy water and a dab of alcohol on the worst stains..." She trailed off as I shook my head.

"It's not the clothes," I said. "And he will survive, yes." I closed my eyes for a moment. "What is upsetting me is that I could have prevented it happening at all."

"You?" said Mrs Jacobs, frowning. "How?"

"I know the lad who attacked him – who tried to kill him," I said. "And if only I had…"

"If wishes were horses, beggars would ride," said Mrs Jacobs decisively. "Did you know he was going to do this?" I shook my head. "Well, then – you can't spend your life imagining what every person you meet might do in the future," she said. "You're an ostler, not a fortune-teller."

Despite myself, I smiled. "You're right about that, Mrs Jacobs," I said. "And if I don't get to the Hoop sharpish, I won't even be an ostler for much longer."

We both stood.

"I find it best in life, Mr Hardiman," she said in a kindly tone, "not to worry too much about the past, about things you cannot change. Much better to try to make things better now."

Mrs Jacobs was right, of course. And after I had given the horses their breakfast and checked over the ones that were setting off first thing and cleaned out the stalls ready for the arrival of the *Defiance*, I walked into town. Cambridge has two cutlers, and I went to the larger of the two: Mr Henry Peters just alongside Great St Mary's. With it being a warm day, Mr Peters had his shop door open and was working just inside in his shirtsleeves, sharpening a knife on the stone that he turned by pressing on the foot treadle. The noise was piercing and I had to wait until he paused to check his progress, feeling the blade with a practised flick of his thumb, before I could get his attention.

"Mr Peters," I called.

He looked up and smiled. "May I help you?" he asked, putting down the knife, wiping his hands on his apron and coming to the door. "We have some fine scissors and shears recently arrived from Sheffield. Or perhaps a new razor?" He gestured to the fine display in his window. Up high, against a black velvet board to show them to advantage, their blades glinting, I saw a row of daggers.

"My name is Gregory Hardiman," I said, "and I am a university constable. We have had some trouble with young men causing injuries with knives, and I need someone who knows about such weapons."

"You're talking about the boy stabbed at St Clement's," said the cutler. It was not a question. "I wondered when someone would come to see me. But you said injuries, so there has been more than one incident." It was pleasing to find that a man who sold sharp items had a sharp mind. "Come in, sir." He stood aside and I walked into the shop.

Mr Peters opened a door behind the counter and called up into the apartment above. "Mary, come down and mind the shop." A moment later a woman – his wife, I guessed – appeared with a baby on her hip. "This is a constable," said Mr Peters. "I'm to help him with his enquiries. We'll be in the back room." And he leaned forward and tickled the baby under the chin, making his wife smile.

Once we had settled in the tiny back room – the cutler perched on a high stool at a pristine workbench, and me sitting on an old upright chair alongside him – I took out my notebook. That morning I had sketched a dagger to match the description that Will Mason had given me when he told me about Nicholas Hodges: short, with a thin blade and a black handle. I showed my sketch to Mr Peters.

"The injuries in both cases would match a knife like this," I said. "Small, neat puncture wound, deep damage, lots of blood."

"A dagger," he confirmed. "Or, more precisely, a stiletto. First made in Italy in the fifteenth century. The name comes from the Latin *stilus* – the pointed writing instrument used on wax tablets in ancient times."

My fingers itched to write it in my vocabulary book, but I would do that later.

"I am trying to find out if such a knife – a stiletto – was bought here in Cambridge, and by whom," I said.

"I sell a few," said the cutler. "Mostly to men going to London, or on a long journey – for protection. Ladies too, sometimes, although they tend to favour the more decorative items."

"If my information is correct," I said, "this one would have been bought by a young man – very young. About fifteen years old. He was a sizar," I looked at Peters and he nodded in understanding, "but may well not have been wearing his gown. He was small, still a boy physically. With white blond curls."

Peters shook his head. "If he looked like a child and came in here without his gown, I would never have sold him such a thing."

"It may have been another sizar," I said. "Taller – growing out of his trousers by the minute. Thin in the face. Dark hair. One blue eye and one green."

The cutler pointed at me. "That I remember," he said. "The eyes."

"When was this?" I asked.

He thought for a moment. "This year – spring," he said. "After Easter."

"During term?" I asked.

He nodded.

"Did the sizar come in alone?" I asked.

"As far as I remember," he said. "He came into the shop on his own – if there was someone waiting for him outside, I didn't notice. But I did wonder if there was, because he bought two of them."

I looked up sharply from my notebook.

"Two of them?" I repeated. "Two daggers?"

"Two identical stilettos," said the cutler. "The cheapest I had, but still good quality. Not showy, I mean: just plain and practical. He said that he and a friend were going to the Continent. I wished him safe travels."

Chapter Forty-Two
EXCISED

The moment the *Fakenham Day* left the yard, I threw on my coat and walked as quickly as I could to St Clement's. It was much quieter than usual, with only a handful of undergraduates still in residence. George Chapman had brought his stool out of the porters' lodge and put it against a sunny wall, and with his hands folded over his belly he was snoring gently.

"George," I said urgently, shaking him by the shoulder. "George, have you seen Will Mason?"

He shaded his eyes with a hand and looked up at me, blinking.

"Mason? The sizar, you mean?" he asked.

"That's the one," I said. "Did he leave at the end of term, or is he staying on?"

"Staying on," said the porter, "but he left college yesterday. Said he was visiting friends. Not far from here – Bury, maybe?" He woke up properly and saw the look on my face. "Why? What's he done?"

"He attacked a gownsman," I said. "With a knife – tried to kill him."

Chapman jumped to his feet. "Like Mr Pears, you mean?"

"I'm afraid so," I said.

"Here?" said Chapman, looking about him. "Not in college – I'd know about that."

I shook my head. "In Newmarket. Mason followed him there and attacked him in an alleyway. He's lucky to be alive."

"Is he one of ours?" he asked.

"No," I said. "A fellow commoner from Sidney Sussex. He's recovering at home with his family now."

"And Mason?" asked the porter.

"Disappeared," I said grimly. "Officially it's a matter for the parish constables in Newmarket, but we should help if we can. I need to look into Mason's room again."

"O'course you do," said Chapman. He leaned into the lodge and grabbed his keys from their hook.

There was something eerie about the sizars' room. I am not a fanciful man, but I could feel an atmosphere in that room – an unhappiness, perhaps, or something unsettled. In that room, two young men had infected each other with their anger and their violence, with terrible consequences.

Nicholas Hodges's side of the room had been cleared. His trunk and few other possessions presumably had been sent home to his parents. What I saw on Will Mason's side of the room chilled me. His trunk was on the floor beside it, with a strap around it and a neat label on it. If he was staying in college during the vacation, why had he packed his belongings? And in the middle of his bed – which had been stripped, and the sheets and blanket carefully folded – was a letter. I picked it up. On the front it said "Constable Hardiman".

I walked unsteadily to one of the two chairs and sat heavily. I turned the letter over in my hands and took a deep breath before unfolding it.

The hand was small and precise, but at various points there were harsh, determined crossings out. I started to read.

Dear Constable Hardiman, it said. *I want to thank you for your kindness and I feel badly that I had to mislead you. But Nicholas and I had a mission to fulfil.*

As the Bible teaches us (Psalms), we must defend the poor and the fatherless, and deliver the poor and the needy from the hand of the wicked. Those who come to this University thanks to their ~~corrupt~~ *connections, having no academic worth at all, use their position and their* ~~influence~~ *wealth to oppress those who have that worth – they must be cut out like a tumour. They must be <u>excised</u> from the body of the University if it is to be healthy.*

Thanks to the brave actions of the Liberators, Pears and Harford have been excised. They were from the same evil mould: families recently come into wealth built on the sweat of others, buying their way into our University. Their minds were not open to the wonders of our age or to the possibilities of learning, but were closed and narrow and mean. They became <u>tyrants</u>, and as tyrants they had to fall.

Nicholas died a martyr's death, fleeing the injustices that see a tyrant mourned and his victims forgotten. I too must remain true to the Liberators, and seek for myself an honourable end rather than hanging from a noose commanded by these same <u>injustices</u>.

Please see that my belongings are returned to my parents, and tell them that I die willingly – <u>happily</u> – as a martyr, proof that the truly free man cannot be tyrannised by the worthless.

Yours respectfully, William Mason

I banged on the door of the Master's rooms and Francis Vaughan himself opened it.

"Mr Hardiman," he said in surprise. "I had not thought to see you in college, now that term has finished."

I waved Mason's letter. "We must act quickly, sir," I said. "William Mason plans to kill himself."

"Come in, come in," he said, holding out his hand. "Sit."

But I could not; I stood impatiently while he read the letter.

"Dear God," he said. "When did you find this?"

"Moments ago," I replied. "I have been working it out. I know Mason was in Newmarket yesterday at about noon. I'll explain later. The earliest he could have returned to Cambridge was early evening. The porter did not see him return, so we cannot be sure – perhaps yesterday evening, perhaps this morning. Either way, he packed up his room and wrote this letter. He has had plenty of time..." I did not want to finish that sentence.

"Indeed," said Vaughan grimly. "We must act quickly. We cannot search the whole of Cambridge, so let us use our brains. Method."

"He has a dagger," I said.

"He does, yes," said the Master. "And that would be an honourable death, in Roman terms. Falling on one's sword."

I shuddered – an image of a man run through with a sword, still trying to speak to me, blood bubbling from his mouth, rose in my mind. I pushed it away. "A dagger is too short for that, I said, "but he could cut his wrists with it."

"Like Seneca," said Vaughan. "And Mason would admire Seneca, with his devotion to virtue and justice. Now: location. Do you know of anywhere that was significant to Mason? Important to him?"

I shook my head. "I met him only a few times – here, in his room, in Trinity Street."

The Master looked again at the letter. "This may be something. He uses the word martyr twice. Do we have any monuments to martyrs here in Cambridge? Statues? Gravestones?"

"I cannot think of any," I said, running through a map of the town in my mind. "The only one I know is the church – St Edward King and Martyr."

We looked at each other.

Thanks to my regular duties I am used to running, but Francis Vaughan is not – and he is two decades my senior. Halfway along Bridge Street he stopped, bending over, one hand at his side and the other waving at me to continue. I raced on, ducking across the road, calling an apology over my shoulder to a rider who had had to pull his horse to a sharp halt for me, and turning into Trinity Street. People stopped to watch me as I galloped on, shouting "Make way, make way!" as I went. I passed Great St Mary's just as the bell tolled the hour, and a minute later I was all but skidding around the corner into St Edward's Passage, putting out a hand to stop myself crashing into the wall. The church was ahead of me, its squat shape dark against the evening sky. I ran to the church door and hauled it open with all my strength. My eyes took a moment to adjust to the dim lighting and then I saw him: a figure slumped on the stone floor in front of the altar. I sprinted up the aisle and threw myself onto my knees beside him.

As we had guessed, he had drawn the dagger, which lay beside him, across both wrists. There was a pool of blood around him, but as I leaned over him I saw a small flicker in one of his closed eyes.

None too gently, I slapped his cheek. "William," I said loudly. "William, open your eyes and look at me. You are not to fall asleep, do you hear me?" He groaned.

I looked around. Hanging from a hook on the wall was a surplice. I grabbed it and tried to tear it with my hands; it eventually gave way when I stood on it and pulled with both hands. I made two rough strips and tied one around each of Mason's wrists, winding round and round to halt the flow of blood. Then I fetched a kneeler from one of the pews and put it under his head. All the time I was talking to him – nonsense, about the weather and the church windows and anything that came into my head. The door to the church opened and in ran Francis Vaughan with another man. As they came closer, I recognised the surgeon Daniel Newsome.

"I came via Green Street," said the Master. "I thought Mr Newsome might be of some help."

The surgeon was already on his knees looking at Mason. He lifted the boy's arms in turn and inspected my makeshift bandages. "I'll leave these in place," he said, looking over his shoulder at us. "They seem to be working. Now, can you find a board or a door – something we can lie him on to carry him to my rooms."

Vaughan held up the decanter and I nodded.

"A large one, please," I said.

"Quite right too," he replied, pouring two generous drinks and bringing them over to me. He handed me one, clinked my glass with his, and drank deeply before sitting down heavily. "That poor boy."

"We found him in time," I said.

"Although he didn't thank us for it," said the Master, sighing.

"That was the mania," I said. "He is not in his right mind. Everything that has happened has..." I waved my free hand as I looked for the word, "distorted the way he sees things."

Vaughan smiled at me. "An excellent word. And just right in the circumstances." He took another sip. "Thank goodness we found him. Well done to you for thinking of that church. Martyr." He shook his head. "But he was closer to the truth than he realised."

"What do you mean, sir?" I asked.

"King Edward," he replied. "Back in the tenth century. They called him a martyr because medieval kings were sacrosanct, and murdering one was a mortal sin and made a saint of the victim. But history shows us that even by the bloody standards of the time, he was a very violent young man. He was about Mason's age when he died, if I recall."

We both sat in silence.

CONCLUSION

When I arrived at the Howards' house, the maid led me straight through and out into the garden. Mr Howard was sitting in a wicker chair reading a newspaper, while his wife was reclining on a chaise longue in the dappled shade of a tree, a piece of embroidery in her hands. He jumped to his feet and came towards me, his hand outstretched.

"Welcome, welcome," he said.

"We were so pleased to receive your note, Mr Hardiman," said Mrs Howard, smiling up at me.

"And I am pleased to see you looking so well," I replied.

"It is the warm weather," she said, "and being outside – it suits me to hear the birds and see the leaves. I pretend to be doing something useful," she waved the embroidery at me, "but in truth I am simply daydreaming."

"Lemonade?" asked Mr Howard, going over to a small table that had a tray, some glasses and a pitcher on it.

"That would be just right," I said, sitting down in a second wicker chair that the maid had carried out for me. "What a perfect spot this is, Mrs Howard."

Mr Howard handed me my drink and sat down.

"To your good health," I said, raising my glass.

"Oh, Mr Hardiman, I am too impatient for good manners," said Mrs Howard, and her husband smiled fondly at her. "Did you come to see us because you have news about your daughter?"

I laughed. "I should have known that you would guess," I said. "Yes, I have had a letter from Father Carrasco." I reached into my coat pocket and took out the letter. "As you know, my Spanish is basic and his English is the same, but we muddle through. And I think what he says is that the money arrived in good time. So you must pass on my thanks to your brother-in-law, Mrs Howard."

"Edmund is dull but very reliable," said Mrs Howard. "I knew he would see it through. Does Father Carrasco tell you how Lucia Maria has spent the money?"

"He does," I said. "He writes that los recién casados – I think that means newlyweds," at this word, Mrs Howard clapped her hands, "have spent some of it on land next to his family's holdings and are being sensible and saving some of it for when they start their own family."

"I hope your daughter also bought herself something pretty for her wedding day," said Mrs Howard.

"Talking of pretty things," I said, looking again at the letter, "Lucia Maria was delighted with the beautiful English handkerchief and asked Father Carrasco to thank the beautiful English lady who made it." I glanced at Mrs Howard and she was smiling broadly. "And in return, Lucia Maria has sent you this." I reached into my pocket again and handed the small, flat, linen package to Mrs Howard.

"What is it, Henny?" asked her husband, leaning forward.

"Give me a moment to open it, George," she said, carefully unfolding the cloth. Inside was a pressed flower, with five large pale pink petals and a striking pale pink and red striped heart to it. Mrs Howard smiled with delight. "An oleander flower, I believe," she said. "I have seen it in botanical drawings. What a beauty."

"Father Carrasco says that it is from Lucia Maria's wedding bouquet," I explained.

"Oh, Mr Hardiman," she said, holding out the flower on its linen bed, "then you should keep it."

I shook my head. "She sent it to you," I said. "And if I want to see it, I can always come here."

"I shall treasure it," she said, carefully wrapping it up again. "Please make sure that Lucia Maria knows how much I appreciate it. And you are always welcome here, Mr Hardiman – not least because I will want to hear regular news of your daughter from that nice Father Carrasco. After all, there will be your grandchildren before too long."

"Good heavens," I said. "I had not thought of that."

"And when that happens, we will have to find a way to send you to Spain," said Mrs Howard thoughtfully.

"Henrietta," said her husband, pretending at sternness. "Mr Hardiman is perfectly capable of looking after his own affairs. And he has responsibilities here in Cambridge – he can't just vanish off to Spain." But he smiled. "And talking of responsibilities, I hear that the poor Master of St Clement's has had a terrible term."

I folded up my letter and put it back into my pocket. "He has, yes," I agreed.

"And this Mason boy," asked Mr Howard. "The sizar. What has happened to him?"

I glanced at Mrs Howard.

"There's no need to worry, Mr Hardiman," she said. "My husband has told me the sad story. I'm tougher than I look, you know. I have had to be."

Her husband reached across and patted her hand. They both looked at me.

"He stayed in Mr Newsome's rooms for a few days," I said. "The college paid for a nurse to sit with him, in case he... tried again.

The physical injuries healed quickly – he's young and strong – but the ones in his mind will take longer." As I know only too well, I thought to myself but did not say aloud.

"But the doctor thinks he will heal?" asked Mrs Howard.

"He does, yes, with time," I replied. He spoke at length with Will, and his opinion was that the boy's motives were sensible but his response was not."

"Perhaps down to his immaturity," suggested Mr Howard. "We have all been impulsive as young men, have we not, Mr Hardiman?"

"We have," I agreed. "It seems that Nicholas Hodges was driven by revenge, after his brother's death, and Will, out of loyalty to his friend, fell in with his plans. But then Will experienced for himself the shabby treatment of the sizars by other – as he saw it – less worthy undergraduates, and became angry on his own account. And his anger led to violence. Thankfully, Mr Newsome and Mr Vaughan spoke on his behalf, about his youth and his promising future. And the magistrates in Newmarket agreed that he should be confined in a licensed madhouse until he is judged to be of sound mind and no further danger to himself or others. Mr Newsome kindly located a suitable establishment near Will's parents in Manchester and he has been sent there. We are told it is a progressive sort of place, intended for younger people."

"I am relieved to hear it," said Mr Howard. "One hears dreadful stories of cruelty and neglect."

"So much sadness," said Mrs Howard. "Three young men dead, one confined in a madhouse – all such a waste." She sighed and then seemed to straighten her shoulders. "But we must look to the future, gentlemen. There has been a wedding," she patted the linen package in her lap, "and soon we hope there will be a christening."

"A toast, my dear," said her husband, raising his glass. "To Lucia Maria, and the future."

"To Lucia Maria and the future," I said. And the thought of both filled me with more happiness than I had felt for some time.

GLOSSARY

Money

In the 1820s, nearly all money that Gregory would have encountered was in coin form. There were banknotes, but these were for large denominations and would not have been in common usage for people of his class and limited wealth.

The coins that Gregory would have handled are these (in ascending order of value):

- Farthing (a quarter of a penny)

- Halfpenny

- Penny

- Sixpence

- Shilling (twelve pence)

- Half crown (two shillings and sixpence)

- Crown (five shillings)

- Sovereign (a gold coin worth a pound, or 240 pennies)

You may also have heard of a guinea – this is one pound (i.e. a sovereign) and one shilling.

As for the actual spending value of these denominations, of course that changes as our modern currency values fluctuate. But at the time of writing – summer 2023 – here are some approximate exchange rates:

- A penny in Gregory's time would buy what would cost us about 30p today

- A shilling would buy about £3-worth of goods today

- A sovereign would buy about £60-worth of goods today.

So when Gregory buys a month's worth of opium for two shillings, he is paying about £6.

Argand lamp – a type of oil lamp, invented in 1780 by Frenchman Aimé Argand and popular as it gave off a light equivalent to about eight candles

Bank – banking a fire involves piling hot coals against the wall at the back of the fireplace before going to bed, covering them with ash and perhaps some kindling, so that the coals simmer gently overnight and enough to start a fire again the next morning

Bedmaker – a female servant employed in a college to perform housekeeping duties such as cleaning and doing laundry (sometimes called more informally a bedder)

Cast one's accounts – to vomit

Commons – formerly, an entitlement to cheap food taken in a college, but by Gregory's time used to refer to the food itself

Cutler – a tradesman who makes, repairs and sells items with a cutting edge, such as swords, knives and surgical instruments

Damper – lunch, or a snack before dinner, so called because it damps or allays the appetite

Dead men – empty glasses, tankards or bottles

Discommuning – if a Cambridge tradesman allowed undergraduates to run up debts or otherwise engaged in disreputable trading, the Vice-Chancellor had the authority to discommune him, which would forbid undergraduates from doing business with him (last imposed in 1956, and abolished in March 1971)

Dragsman – coach driver

Fellow commoner – a class of undergraduate at the University of Cambridge; from wealthy and sometimes titled and /or landed families, fellow commoners paid £5 a quarter for their place at the University, and were often academically weak – they could be excused from lectures and were permitted to graduate with an ordinary degree after only two years

Footpad – a robber who targets victims who are travelling by foot

Foreman of the jury – one who speaks for the rest of the company or group

Fudge – nonsense

Gownsman – undergraduate (frequently used in contrast to 'townsman')

Half-crown – a silver coin equivalent to two shillings and sixpence (and worth about £8 in today's money)

Hobnail – a country clodhopper, as the boots of country farmers and ploughmen were often stuck full of hobnails (short nails with thick heads) to repair them and make them long-lasting

Humbug – to deceive or tell a story, but in a jocular rather than a nasty way

In the suds – in trouble, in a disagreeable or difficult situation

Ostry – a room set aside for the ostler to live or rest in, often a loft above the stables

Outlander – a stranger, an outsider, a foreigner

Pea and thimble – a game where players bet on the location of a pea under one of three thimbles; of course, the game is rigged by sleight of hand and/or distraction

Petrean – an undergraduate or graduate of Peterhouse in Cambridge (formerly often known as St Peter's College)

Phaeton – a light four-wheeled carriage for two people, with open sides in front of the seat and front wheels smaller than the rear, and drawn by one or two horses

Pot Fair – an alternative name for Midsummer Fair, as it was known for the large number of stalls selling crockery and earthenware

Prinking – dressing up in fancy clothes, as for a ceremony or on a State occasion

Privy – toilet

Pudding-headed – stupid, with brains all muddled like a pudding

Ratafia – a sweet cordial flavoured with fruits and almonds

Receipt – recipe

Rustication – a punishment used by the University whereby an undergraduate is temporarily expelled from their college (the terms refers literally to being sent into the countryside)

Sampler – a piece of fabric that showcases a variety of embroidery stitches and motifs to demonstrate skill (or practice) in needlework

Scrub – a scruffy ragamuffin, a tatty person

Sharp – an habitual or professional gambler, often used pejoratively to suggest a cheat

Square toes – an old man, as they are fond of wearing comfortable shoes with room around the toes

Strings – the reins used to control a horse

Stump bed – a bed without posts (most of our modern beds would have been considered stump beds)

Suds – see *In the suds*

Surplice – a white tunic worn over other clothing by Christian clergy and choristers

Swell – a gentleman, a well-dressed (and therefore wealthy) man

Tanner – slang for sixpence (worth about £1.50 in today's money)

Whiddler – a talkative person, a tell-tale, not to be trusted with a secret

William Wickham – a British spymaster active in the early nineteenth century (when England was nervous about revolution), he advocated the use of undercover surveillance to unmask seditious conspiracies before they came to fruition

UNIVERSITY STRUCTURE

For readers who are not familiar with the organisational and command structure of Cambridge University in the 1820s, here is a very brief overview.

The ceremonial head of the university was the **Chancellor** – chosen for his ability to bring fortune and favour to the university. He did not reside in Cambridge or exercise day-to-day power, and so the head of the university for all practical purposes was in fact the **Vice-Chancellor**. He was one of the "heads of house" – heads of the colleges, who might be known as masters or principals – and was chosen by them from their own number every 4 November, to serve for a year. In the months of 1826 in which this book takes place, the Vice-Chancellor was the confusingly-named Joseph Proctor, who was Master of St Catharine's College and serving his second stint as Vice-Chancellor (his first had been twenty-five years earlier). The duties of the Vice-Chancellor included managing university finances and estates, deciding on prizes, holding authority in Cambridge city government, granting licences, deciding in matters of discipline, and opening Stourbridge Fair each September, as a prelude to the academic year.

Each college had its own command structure. At the top of the tree was the head of house, usually known as the **Master**. He had oversight of all college affairs – administering its property, seeing to the learning and good conduct of its members and presiding over meetings of college fellows – but he left most financial concerns to the **Bursar**. The Master received a good income and was provided with a gracious lodge in college grounds. He would also receive a dividend from the profits of college estates. Crucially, heads of houses were the only senior members of the university who were permitted to marry. In the 1820s, this small number of dignitaries and their wives formed Cambridge's upper class society of mixed-gender dinner parties and morning calls.

One of the fellows would serve as the college **Bursar**. It was often a thankless task, and finding a fellow willing to do it was sometimes tricky. The job of the bursar was to oversee college finances, with money coming in from leases and rents on college properties (buildings and extensive agricultural land), and money going out to maintain the college and its inhabitants. In the time period covered by the Gregory Hardiman books – 1825-1830 – college finances, and therefore the job of the bursar, were becoming more complicated. Bursars were expected not simply to take in college income and make payment for college expenses, but also to make sound investments to secure the future of the college. Many of them were not up to the task.

The teaching staff within a college were known as **fellows**. They had rooms assigned to them within the college and lived and dined within its walls. However, many fellows spent the majority of their time on their own research and writing, and delegated the actual teaching to **tutors**. The students were known as **undergraduates** or **gownsmen**. Some lived in college – often in a "set" composed of a bedroom and a sitting room – and some lived out in lodgings.

There were in fact five categories of undergraduate, each paying different fees and enjoying different rights and privileges. **Noblemen** (drawn from the upper echelons of society) paid £10 [about £600 today] a quarter for tuition, ate on high table, wore hats instead of the academic cap – and could ask to be given an MA (ordinary) after only six terms of residence, without any formal exercise or examination. **Fellow commoners** were a much larger group: sometimes titled and/or landed but always wealthy, they paid £5 a quarter – and again could do the six-term/MA thing. Most undergraduates were **scholars** or **pensioners**, who came for the most part from gentle and professional but not wealthy families: scholars had considerable financial help from their colleges, while pensioners paid their own fees and subsistence. Scholars and pensioners paid £2 10s a quarter for tuition. Finally, the **sizars** paid only 15s a quarter for tuition. In earlier times they acted as servants in college, but by Gregory's time they were living as rather impecunious undergraduates and performing more limited duties in college.

Afterword

Thank you for reading this book.

If you liked what you read, please would you leave a short review on the site where you purchased it, or recommend it to others?

Reviews and recommendations are not only the highest compliment you can pay to an author; they also help other readers to make more informed choices about purchasing books.

ACKNOWLEDGEMENTS

This book is part of a planned series of five, and as such I have had to do an enormous amount of research in order to get my cast of characters and my locations in place from the outset. And in doing so I have taken shameless advantage of the deep knowledge and boundless patience of a huge number of people. And here they are...

Richard Reynolds, crime fiction expert (and now proud part-owner of Cambridge's newest independent bookshop, Bodies in the Bookshop) – for suggesting a Cambridge series in the first place

Jon Harris, artist – for creating the beautiful map of Gregory Hardiman's Cambridge

Sian Owen and **Lisa Morgan** of the Department of Engineering in Cambridge, for scanning the beautiful map so that we can all see it

Tim Cox of the Cox Library – for his peerless knowledge of the history of horseracing (and gambling thereon) in Newmarket

Glenn Pearl, valuer and auctioneer at Lacy Scott & Knight LLP – for his worryingly detailed knowledge of nineteenth century daggers

Lucy Lewis (University Marshal), **Tim Milner** (Pro-Proctor for Ceremonial) and **Seb Falk** (Senior Proctor) – for their expert insight into the role of the university constable, past and present

Jacqueline Cox (Keeper of University Archives) – for helping me to untangle knotty bits of University history

Numerous experts on Quaker history, including **Marisa Johnson**, **Judith Roads**, **Selina Packard** and **Laurel Phillipson**

Alison from Caerphilly – for winning my competition to name a character, which means that Nicholas Hodges is her fault

Roy McCarthy – for being, as always, a simply sterling beta reader

I am extremely grateful to you all for knowing so much and then agreeing to share that knowledge and your time with me. Thank you.

And if despite this wealth of world-class assistance I have made errors, they are entirely my own.

REVIEWS

Praise for *Fatal Forgery*

"I loved the sense of place, with some surprising revelations about jail and courthouse conditions and operations, and an interesting change of setting at one point, which I won't reveal for fear of spoiling the plot. There was great attention to detail woven skilfully into the writing, so I felt I learned a lot about the era by osmosis, rather than having it thrust upon me. All in all, a remarkable debut novel." *Debbie Young, author and book blogger*

"From the start of this story I felt as if I had been transported back in time to Regency London. Walking in Sam's footsteps, I could hear the same cacophony of sound, shared the same sense of disbelief at Fauntleroy's modus operandi, and hung onto Constable Plank's coat tails as he entered the squalid house of correction at Coldbath Fields. I am reassured that this is not the last we shall see of Samuel Plank. His steadfastness is so congenial that to spend time in his company in future books is a treat worth savouring." *Jo at Jaffareadstoo*

Praise for *The Man in the Canary Waistcoat*

"Susan Grossey is an excellent storyteller. The descriptions of Regency London are vivid and create a real sense of time and place. Sam Plank, Martha and Wilson are great characters – well-drawn and totally individual in their creation. The dialogue is believable and the pace well fitted to this genre. The novel shows excellent research and writing ability – a recommended read." *Barbara Goldie, The Kindle Book Review*

"Regency police constable Sam Plank, so well established in the first book, continues to develop here, with an interesting back story emerging about his boyhood, which shapes his attitude to crime as an adult. This is not so much a whodunit as a whydunit, and Grossey skilfully unfolds a complex tale of financial crime and corruption. There are fascinating details about daily life in the criminal world woven into the story, leaving the reader much more knowledgeable without feeling that he's had a history lesson." *Debbie Young, author and book blogger*

Praise for *Worm in the Blossom*

"Ever since I was introduced to Constable Sam Plank and his intrepid wife Martha, I have followed his exploits with great interest. There is something so entirely dependable about Sam: to walk in his footsteps through nineteenth century London is rather like being in possession of a superior time travelling machine... The writing is, as ever, crisp and clear, no superfluous waffle, just good old-fashioned storytelling, with a tantalising beginning, an adventurous middle, and a wonderfully dramatic ending." *Jo at Jaffareadstoo*

"Susan Grossey not only paints a meticulous portrait of London in this era, she also makes the reader see it on its own terms, for example recognising which style of carriage is the equivalent to a 21st century sports-car, and what possessing one would say about its owner... In short, a very satisfying and agreeable read in an addictive series that would make a terrific Sunday evening television drama series." *Debbie Young, author and book blogger*

Praise for *Portraits of Pretence*

"There is no doubt that the author has created a plausible and comprehensive Regency world and with each successive novel I feel as if I am returning into the bosom of a well-loved family. Sam and Martha's thoughtful care and supervision of the ever-vulnerable Constable Wilson, and of course, Martha's marvellous ability, in moments of extreme worry, to be her husband's still small voice of calm is, as always, written with such thoughtful attention to detail." *Jo at Jaffareadstoo*

"Do you want to know what a puff guts is or a square toes or how you would feel if you were jug-bitten? Well, you'll find out in this beautifully researched and written Regency crime novel. And best of all you will be in the good company of Constable Sam Plank, his wife Martha and his assistant Constable Wilson. These books have immense charm and it comes from the tenderness of the depiction of Sam's marriage and his own decency." *Victoria Blake, author*

Praise for *Faith, Hope and Trickery*

"What I like about the delightful law enforcement characters in this series is their ordinariness. They are not superheroes, they do not crack the case in a matter of a quick fortnight, but weeks, months, pass with the crime in hand on-going with other, everyday things, happening in the background. This inclusion of reality easily takes the reader to trudge alongside Constable Plank as he threads his way through the London streets of the 1820s, his steady tread always on the trail of bringing the lawbreakers to justice." *Helen Hollick of Discovering Diamonds book reviews*

"The mystery at the heart of the novel is, as ever, beautifully explained and so meticulously detailed that nothing is ever left to chance and everything flows like the wheels of a well-oiled machine. There's an inherent dependability about Constable Plank which shines through in every novel and yet, I think that in *Faith,*

Hope and Trickery we see an altogether more vulnerable Sam which is centred on Martha's unusual susceptibility and on his unerring need to protect her." *Jo at Jaffareadstoo*

Praise for *Heir Apparent*

"*Heir Apparent* is possibly my favourite Sam Plank book yet, with great twists and turns to the plot and meticulous research. This author really gets the historical detail just right, but what stands out for me is the captivating character development the author has honed throughout the series, and I will own that for me the crime element is almost superfluous, as it is the characters who keep me coming back to these books." *Peggy-Dorothea Beydon, author*

"There's an authenticity to the characters, particularly Sam and his wife Martha, which not only makes these stories such a joy to read, but which also gives such an imagined insight into life in the capital in the early 1800s so that it really does feel as though you are moving in tandem with Plank, Martha and the intrepid Wilson as they go about their business, forever trying, and usually succeeding, to live their lives in the full glare of the criminal fraternity." *Jo at Jaffareadstoo*

Praise for *Notes of Change*

"I have followed this series from the start, and thoroughly enjoyed each and every one. Once again, the book immerses us in the streets of 1820s London, in the excellent company of constable Sam Plank and his wife Martha. This latest standalone case takes a number of well crafted turns, not least the reappearance of an old adversary in some unexpected circumstances, and all of which ties in nicely to the very apt title. A very worthy addition to the series and a very fitting finale." *Graham T, Amazon reviewer*

"This well-written and thoroughly researched series strikes a balance between historical correctness and feel-good fiction –

there's no hiding the harshness of life in Sam's era, but the warmth and depth of the central characters ensures they are comfort reads all the same." *Debbie, Amazon reviewer*

Praise for *Ostler*

"A first-rate historical crime novel, with a sympathetic hero, a good plot and convincing language and atmosphere. It's the first of a new series, and already I'm looking forward to the sequel." *Promoting Crime Fiction*

"Beautifully written by an author whose knowledge of Cambridge, and impeccable research, brings this nineteenth century world alive in such a way that place and people bound into life. The story wraps around you with ease and at each step of the mystery a little bit more is revealed, not just about Hardiman, who I am sure we will discover more about as the series progresses, but also about the intricacies of nineteenth century life in a bustling collegiate town." *Jo at Jaffareadstoo*

LEARN MORE ABOUT GREGORY'S TIMES

Every month I produce a free e-newsletter featuring some of the research I have done on Regency times – from food and celebrations, to money and policing. Like most authors of historical fiction, I do far more research than I can ever use in my books, and it's all fascinating!

If you'd like to receive my free e-newsletter each month, please sign up at www.susangrossey.com/insider-updates

And as a little thank-you, you will receive **a FREE complete e-book of *Fatal Forgery* (the first book in the Sam Plank Mysteries series)** – and the chance to take part in occasional giveaways and competitions. See you there!

Printed in Great Britain
by Amazon